PITCH QUEEN

Karin Gillespie

WHAT-IF PUBLISHING

Copyright © 2024 by Karin Gillespie

All rights reserved.

No portion of this book may be reproduced in any form without written permission from the publisher or author, except as permitted by U.S. copyright law.

This is a work of fiction. Names, characters, places, and incidents either are the product of the author's imagination or used fictitiously. Any resemblance to actual persons living or dead, businesses, companies, events or locales is coincidental.

CONTENTS

1. Chapter 1   1
2. Chapter 2   19
3. Chapter 3   34
4. Chapter 4   44
5. Chapter 5   52
6. Chapter 6   69
7. Chapter 7   74
8. Chapter 8   86
9. Chapter 9   104
10. Chapter 10   115
11. Chapter 11   124
12. Chapter 12   132
13. Chapter 13   146
14. Chapter 14   150
15. Chapter 15   156
16. Chapter 16   161

17.	Chapter 17	165
18.	Chapter 18	175
19.	Chapter 19	180
20.	Chapter 20	186
21.	Chapter 21	191
22.	Chapter 22	199
23.	Chapter 23	211
24.	Chapter 24	220
25.	Chapter 25	223
26.	Chapter 26	224
27.	Chapter 27	226
28.	Chapter 28	228
29.	Chapter 29	238
30.	Chapter 30	246
	Thanks!	255
	About the author	257
	Afterword	258

Chapter One

I'm in the business of seducing writers.

People's faces usually cloud in confusion when I say that.

"You're a literary agent," they say. "Aren't writers usually hounding you, hoping you'll help them to become the next Nicholas Sparks or Kristin Hannah?"

The answer is yes. Writers are always pursuing me. Hundreds per week send me letters, peddling their manuscripts, a constant whiff of desperation rising from my inbox.

But I'm only interested in one type of author: The kind who can command a six or seven-figure deal.

My current quarry is Quince Washington, a twenty-six-year-old Black woman with stunning good looks, which she unsuccessfully tamps down by shaving her head and wearing nerdy, Clark Kent-style glasses.

As an author, she's an editor's dream with beauty, diversity, and thousands of Instagram followers. Her book is also well-written but that's not what will attract the jaw-dropping advance. Instead, the most thrilling aspect about Quince's book is this: It's a dream to pitch.

Every time I think about my glorious pitch—the one that came to me immediately after reading Quince's query letter—my stomach goes quivery as if I'd swallowed a school of goldfish. I hadn't yet shared it with anyone for fear of jinxing it.

The pitch is so amazing that if Quince signs with me, her novel will go to auction, where at least a dozen editors will battle over it like cage fighters. I can already predict the glowing trade reviews and author endorsements: "Whip smart." "Sly social commentary." "A searing and darkly funny debut."

I daydream about Quince's sharp cheekbones and long neck highlighted on the cover of *Writer's Digest*. In the article, she'll almost certainly thank me, Claire Wyld, her literary agent.

"At least that's how I hope it goes," I said.

It was Monday morning, and I was discussing Quince with Rebecca, my colleague, who represented children's books. We were having our usual morning confab over caffeine—Red Bull for her, lavender latte for me. Rebecca was checking out Quince's Instagram.

"Not one bad photo of her," Rebecca said. "Deal with the devil, obviously."

"Or great filters." I peeked over Rebecca's shoulder as she scrolled through Quince's stunning feed. "Yesterday, I sent her a gift-wrapped box of Sharpies. The card said, 'You'll wear these out during your first book signing.'"

"Someone's in love." Rebecca thumped her ample chest in the rhythm of a heartbeat. She wore a ruffled pinafore dress that looked like a *Little House on the Prairie* cast-off.

"Too much?" I asked.

"Kidding me? Flattery is oxygen to writers." Rebecca reached into the bowl of Jelly Bellies she always kept on her desk; their pleasant rattle aroused the Pavlovian dog in me. "When does Quince give you the verdict?"

"Two p.m. today."

A lifetime away.

"Do you think she's talked to Morris?"

"Who knows? But my instincts say she'll sign with me."

Morris had been the number one dealmaker in debut novels for years. For the last six months, I'd been number two. If I signed Quince and sold her novel, the number one spot would be mine.

"Good luck," Rebecca said.

"Thanks." I plucked a red Jelly Belly from the bowl and bit into it. Not cinnamon or pomegranate, but my favorite, cherry. A positive omen.

I glanced at my watch. I was interviewing an applicant to become my new assistant, and she was late.

"I wonder where Amber is. She was supposed to be here by now."

"Her name is Bamber, and she called just before you came in, saying she'd be a little late"

I hadn't met Bamber yet, but her name didn't bode well. Bamber was a name for a wide-eyed, spindly legged creature, too skittish to be firm with my more troublesome clients, and that's what I needed most from her.

"Bamber? What kind of name is that?"

"I like it," Rebecca said. "Sounds like *Bambi,* one of my favorite kid movies. So unapologetic with its plot points."

"Because the mother dies?"

Rebecca slapped the side of her head. "What was I thinking? Pinch me hard if you want." She offered me her muscular arm, tattooed from wrist to shoulder with images from *Alice in Wonderland*, her favorite children's book.

"It's been over three years since my mom passed," I said. "The time for walking on eggshells is long over."

"Wrong. When you lose a parent and you're barely old enough to legally drink, you're entitled to endless egg walking."

"Thanks," I said, not wanting to linger on the subject. Per usual, my day was going to be breakneck busy, and I had no time to be maudlin. "Bamber is now officially three minutes late. Will I have to fire her before I hire her?"

The Ring buzzer sounded, and I went into the reception area and peered outside. Bamber was on the stoop with three coffees in a holder. Excellent. Three coffees almost made up for being three minutes late.

I allowed her entry, and she fluttered in, apologizing for her tardiness, saying she missed her subway stop. I didn't even want to ask how far away she lived from the agency. Murray Hill? Staten Island? Do or die, Bed Stuy?

Bamber wasn't the dewy ingenue I'd imagined. She was in her early thirties and had an angular frame, and frizzy brown hair. Her eyes matched the muddy color of her hair, and the tinted lenses of her glasses cast a yellow shade on her face that made her look jaundiced.

Her whole persona seemed to say, "Stick me in a back office, and I'll work quietly and efficiently. I'll even take my egg salad sandwich on gluten-free bread at my desk."

I relieved Bamber of two of the coffees, one of which was a lavender latte. "How did you know this is my favorite?"

"You tweeted about it three weeks ago."

Impressive or stalker-like? Time would tell.

"Welcome to Prestige Literary Agency," I said, crossing out of the reception area to the alcove that served as Rebecca's office. "This is Rebecca, the children's lit agent and keeper of the Jelly Bellies."

"Sorry. I didn't know what coffee you liked," Bamber said, handing her a cup.

Bamber's inquisitive gaze took in Rebecca and her contradictory appearance, pairing a frilly, childlike dress with lurid tattoos. Her eyes alighted on a prominent sign on my colleague's desk, which said, "Children's books are a bunny-eat-bunny business." After reading it, a smile tugged at Bamber's lips.

"Do you like kid books?" Rebecca asked.

"Oh yes," Bamber said. Her eyes were a pair of dry cups, thirsty for the smallest drop of approval.

"What's your favorite?" Rebecca smiled as if genuinely interested, but it was a trick question. My co-worker judged people by their taste in kid lit. She was scornful of obvious answers like *Charlotte's Web* or *Goodnight, Moon.*

And she also had a theory that certain choices indicated character defects. Once, while on a blind date at a Greek restaurant, she asked the guy what his favorite children's book was. When he said *The Giving Tree,* she left before the ouzo came.

"Any man who thinks someone should give and give until they turn into a stump is not a person I need in my life," she'd said.

Bamber answered Rebecca without hesitation. "*Donkey Business*. I bought it for my niece's birthday."

"Is that so?" Rebecca had sold *Donkey Business* a year ago for a tidy sum.

"Two copies because she's hard on books," Bamber said.

Rebecca pushed the bowl of Jelly Bellies in Bamber's direction. "Bless you, my child."

Well done, Bamber. I'd expected her to fail Rebecca's test. Most people did.

"Shall we?"

"It's so charming in here," Bamber said, glancing about the foyer.

"A lot of authors drop by the agency, so we wanted a welcoming space," I said.

Kippy, no last name necessary in the publishing world, was my boss, and she'd created a romantic office atmosphere, recalling the golden days of publishing before the advent of e-readers, AI, and Amazon.

The agency was housed in a cheery Victorian red brick building with green terra cotta shutters, and it crouched under the shade of a mature pin oak. In the Gilded Age, it used to be office space for one of the Vanderbilts, and I shared that bit of history with Bamber, who gobbled it up.

The foyer had a working fireplace, and its carved fleur-de-lis mantel always displayed a fresh flower arrangement—today it was pink peonies—flanked by the agency's most prominent books. I paused beside it so Bamber could ogle the familiar titles. A look of pure rapture crossed her face. It was like watching a shy preteen girl at a boy band concert.

Compared to the rest of the building, my office was starkly modern. I had a white chrome desk, a black mid-century office chair, and framed, abstract black-and-white prints on the wall.

Every morning, I dressed in what I called my "agent uniform"—a fitted, white button-down blouse and either a belted black pencil skirt or slacks. As a result, I looked perfectly at home in my monochromatic environment.

Rebecca once joked, "When I walk into your office, I'm convinced I've gone color blind."

Bamber sat in front of my desk, posture erect, hands folded neatly on her lap. Her gaze zeroed in on the Lucite bookshelf behind me, her eyes hungrily roving over the titles.

"The books are organized according to the size of the deal," I said. "Major deals, a half million and up, are on the top shelf. Significant deals above $250K line the middle shelf, and the bottom shelf is for good deals, between $100 and $250K."

"And what about books that sold for less than $100K?" Bamber asked, a note of caution in her voice.

"They're stored in the breakroom. A $50K book is bolstering a wobbly table leg."

I waited for a flicker of judgment or a wince, but Bamber's expression remained neutral. She paused before saying, "It's helpful to have a system."

I laughed. "I'm kidding about the table leg. I'm proud of every sale I've made, but mostly I represent novelists who command large sums."

"And you specialize in debut novelists."

"You did your research," I said.

Debut novelists were all about potential. I could spin enchanting fairy tales about them. Editors, like most everyone else, loved a Cinderella story and possibility of a very happy ending.

"Yes," Bamber said. "And the more research I did, the more I realized what a privilege it would be to work as your assistant."

I leaned forward. "So, why exactly would it be a privilege to work for me?"

In other words, please float more flattery in my direction.

Bamber gasped. Something behind me had caught her eye.

"What is it?"

"Nothing... I just couldn't help but notice... Is that a first edition?" Bamber pointed to a book behind me.

I knew what book she meant without even looking. It was a copy of *Galaxy,* first published in 1984.

"Yes, it's a first edition." I was annoyed by the detour in our conversation. "And I guess you already know that the author is my father."

"I so admire your dad. Book Riot recently chose *Galaxy* to be the best novel of the twentieth century."

Old news to me. Any time *Galaxy* got any recognition, I'd receive an email from Meredith, my stepmother, usually with an effusive subject line. The last one was: "My husband is an icon!"

"*Galaxy* is my favorite novel," Bamber said.

I was tempted to let out a prolonged and exaggerated yawn. *You and scores of other readers.*

Galaxy was almost forty years old, but it still sold close to a million copies a year—mostly to high school and college students who were required to read it but usually ended up loving it. That novel also launched my boss's career as a literary agent, and Kippy now repped dozens of award-winning novelists.

Did I need to show Bamber the door? I'd spent my entire life being known as the daughter of America's Most Beloved Novelist, and the last thing I wanted or needed was a giggly Peter Wyld fangirl swooning around the office. I loved my dad and his book, but I had my own life to lead.

"My father never drops by the agency," I said tersely. "If that's why you're interested in the job."

Bamber nibbled on a hangnail. "No! I mean... I love your dad's book, but I applied for this position because I want to work with you. I saw the job listing, and when I researched you, I was so impressed that you've accomplished so much at such a young age. I read the piece in *Mox* calling you the Pitch Queen."

That article came out three months ago, and yet anytime someone mentioned it, I still got lightheaded. Today was no exception, and because Bamber brought it up, I decided to give her another chance.

"Journalists love hype," I said.

"Not sure it's hype. Your sales record speaks for itself."

"Thank you. I'm proud of my authors." Gradually, Bamber was redeeming herself after the *Galaxy* faux pas.

"And it's a big day for one of your clients. I preordered *Schooled*, and I got a notice this morning that it was available on my Kindle."

Was that today? I'd been so swamped, the pub date had escaped me. I made a mental note to call Dani, the author, and congratulate her. Keeping track of pub dates was another task I could farm out to Bamber.

My phone buzzed. Wendy. That was the third time in a week. I frowned and let it go to voice mail.

"That was a call from a client who requires a steady diet of hand-holding," I said. "I need someone who will reassure needy clients but also put them off. Most understand how busy I am, but a few are persistent. The most persistent is a woman named Wendy Collins, and she—"

"You landed her a seven-figure deal. Your first of several. It was in that same *Mox* article"

"Yes and she keeps nagging me about feedback on her second book, and I've been putting off that difficult conversation."

"Why will the conversation be difficult?"

"Unfortunately, Wendy's first novel didn't sell well. So unless she writes *The Bible: A Sequel*, she probably isn't going to get another book deal."

"And you haven't told her that?" Bamber asked.

"Not in so many words." I scooted my chair closer to her and lowered my voice. "Here's an insider fact about authors: they can rarely handle the truth. Especially someone like Wendy, who is overly emotional. The solution is to soft-soap, distract, or when all else fails, ghost."

"I'll remember that."

"Being able to handle clients is vital. Kindness matters, but you also have to be firm. Do you think you can manage that?"

Bamber nodded vigorously. "One summer while I was in college, I worked for a mail order underwear company that sold panties and briefs that fell apart after one washing. I became an expert at placating unhappy customers."

I was warming up to Bamber. She seemed bright and eager, and she reminded me of myself when I started out as an assistant.

Take away my flat iron, my balayage highlights, my Tom Ford Traceless foundation stick, my Chloe pumps to add much needed height to my five-foot frame, and I was your basic Plain Jane. I even owned a similar plaid skirt to the one Bamber was wearing, one I wore almost constantly to my college classes at Scripps.

I glanced at her resume, which she'd sent via email. Bamber had also worked as a freelance copy editor for instruction booklets, which meant she had a high tolerance for tedium. Plenty of that around a literary agency, what with tracking royalty payments and proofreading contracts.

"As part of your duties, you'll also be dealing with my slush," I said. "Do you know what that is?"

A pained look crossed Bamber's face. "I'm sorry. I don't."

"Slush is the constant stream of unsolicited letters from wannabe writers. It's called slush because it's unmanageable and messy like melting snow. The good news is ninety-nine percent of slush can be ignored because I'm looking for very specific books. It might take a while for you to learn what will appeal to me. You can study my deals on Publishers Marketplace."

Bamber gave me a questioning look.

"Publishers Marketplace is a web site that lists most of the publishing deals." I brought up the site on my oversized computer screen. "Here's my latest deal." I zoomed in so Bamber could easily read it:

CAT SHAMING is about a millennial who's so fed up with dating she decides to become a premature cat lady, puzzling her friends and family until she becomes an Instagram sensation as the World's Youngest Cat Lady. To Flatiron Books in a major deal by Claire Wyld at Prestige Literary.

After reading it, Bamber gleefully applauded. "I can relate. I have three cats. And the title is genius!"

"Thought of it myself," I said proudly. "Not all authors are skilled at coming up with clever, sellable titles. So, I'm happy to lend a hand."

"Your clients are so lucky to have you."

Too bad they didn't always act that way, I thought.

"I'll commit all of your deals to memory," Bamber said, tapping her temple.

"Not necessary. It'll be helpful to know what I've sold in the past, but unlike most agents, my tastes are difficult to categorize because my greatest strength as an agent isn't recognizing what editors want. Anyone can do that. But there's a skill that's much more valuable."

"And what's that?" Bamber asked, wide-eyed with anticipation.

"Giving editors something they didn't know they wanted. And it all has to do with a killer pitch."

"Bravo!"

More clapping from Bamber, a trait that was swiftly endearing me to her.

My phone beeped. Another client I'd been avoiding. Time to get Bamber on board. "Can you start today?"

Bamber's breathing quickened. "Are you saying I'm hired?"

"Yes."

"Thank you, thank you." She waved her hand in front of her face as if trying to calm her excitement. "And yes, I can start today. Right this second."

"Is there anything you want to ask me?"

The question seemed to bounce around in her brain like a pinball. Finally, she said, "I'm curious about Queen Bea. How does she fit into your client list? She seems like the outlier."

I was so startled by her question that I paused before answering. "You know about my relationship with Bea?" Queen Bea was a nickname her fans had bestowed upon her.

Bamber nodded. "As I said, I've done my research."

A deep dive, I thought. Most people who knew me professionally weren't aware that I repped Bea, and I intended to keep it that way.

"I inherited Bea from my late mother who was also an agent."

In fact, it was one of my mom's last requests when she was near death in the hospital: *I love you, and please take care of Bea.* It was the last text I ever got from her.

"I'm so sorry about your mom." Bamber's eyes were cast downward, and she nervously jiggled her foot. Common reaction. Mentioning a death of a mother made everyone want to fall into a trap door in the floor.

"Bea's my client, but she's like family to me. That's why she doesn't fit in with the rest of my roster. Any more questions?"

"Not right now."

"Good. Let me show you where your desk and the copy machine are."

Once we left my office, a wiry woman with closely cropped silver hair burst through the back door, looking to the right and left like a stunned squirrel in the middle of a busy street. It took me a few seconds to recognize Nan Springer, one of the agency's top clients.

"Where's Kippy?" Nan's voice shook. "I've been trying to call her, but she's not picking up. I need to speak to her. Where is she?"

"Let me glance at her calendar," I said gently.

Kippy, my boss, usually didn't make an appearance until well after eleven. Today was her weekly appointment with her masseuse. But I wouldn't tell Nan that. Clients liked to imagine that every moment of every working day was spent furthering their careers. God forbid you tweet or post on Facebook while a client was waiting for you to read their latest manuscript.

"My editor called and said my novel debuted at number two on the *Times* list," Nan said. "There must be a mistake. Some strange young author who writes smutty books has seized the number one spot. Have you ever heard of anything so ludicrous? I always debut at number one. Surely, a retraction is in order. Didn't James Patterson get one from them once?"

"I'll call Kippy, Nan," I said.

The front door opened, and Kippy swept in like a cool breeze after a long humid afternoon. She wore a white linen dress, pearls around her neck, and a spritz of Opium. Her heavy blonde hair was done up in an artful chignon, channeling Grace Kelly.

"Nan. I just heard." Kippy's patrician features were arranged in a practiced expression of outrage. She linked her arms with Nan's. "A travesty. Come with me, and we'll sort this out."

The door of Kippy's office shut quietly. I could hear Nan's querulous voice contrasting with Kippy's composed alto.

"That was your boss?" Bamber said, awe in her voice. Who could blame her? Kippy traveled in her own personal cloud of charisma and style.

"It was," I said, proud to claim her.

Bamber said, "Who was the author?"

"Nan Springer. She writes magical realism novels."

"I've read her books." A confused look crossed Bamber's face. "But she looks nothing like her author photo."

"Another industry secret: authors never look like their jacket photos. Anyway, I'll introduce you to Kippy later when she's not so busy putting out literary fires."

"Can she really fix the *The New York Times* list?"

"No," I said. "But my boss is amazing at making her A-list clients feel like she can do anything. That's why Kippy is one of the most celebrated literary agents in the business."

"How long have you worked for her?"

"Seven years starting when I was eighteen. I was a literary agent assistant during the summers while I went to college. After I graduated, Kippy promoted me to agent. But enough about me. Let's get you settled, shall we?"

I led Bamber to the windowless annex office where she'd be working. She lowered herself into the decidedly non-ergonomic swivel chair, reverently touching the worn fabric arms as if they were part of a grand throne.

Before I left her to her new duties, I said, "I won't be here the rest of the morning. I'm off to run some errands, and then I have a business lunch."

"With an important editor?" Hopefulness shone in her muddy eyes.

"Not today. I'm actually having lunch with Queen Bea. She's in town to meet with her publisher's marketing team."

Bamber looked disappointed. My assistants were paid so little I always felt obligated to toss a little glamor their way to compensate. Fortunately, there was plenty of glamor to be had in our office.

"Right now, I'm courting a potential client named Quince whose book will likely create a bidding war. By the time it's over, she'll be at least a million dollars richer. The writer's giving me her decision today, and if she says yes, next week, I'll be lunching with several editors to stir up their appetites for her novel."

Bamber swayed in her chair as if my news was so thrilling it unbalanced her. "Another million-dollar deal? Quince must be an amazing writer to get so much money for her book."

I gave her a tight smile. "Well... not necessarily."

Bamber frowned. "What do you mean?"

"Here's another industry secret: good writing isn't as important as you'd imagine. Obviously, an author should be able to string a sentence together, but big deals in publishing depend on so much more than writing ability. For the most part, the hook or elevator pitch rules. Do you know what that is?"

"Yes!" Bamber said. "A description of a book that's so short you could pitch it during the time it takes to make an elevator trip." She said it quickly, as if she was answering a question for *Jeopardy's* Daily Double.

"A gold star for you. Screenwriters are masters at the elevator pitch. For instance, one of my favorites is for *Alien:* 'It's *Jaws* on a spaceship.'"

"Perfect."

"Isn't it? And today I have the ideal elevator pitch for Quince's novel."

"Can I hear it?"

I paused. I never shared pitches with anyone beforehand, not even the author. On the other hand, this would be a great learning experience for Bamber.

"Okay. But this is top secret information, understand?"

Bamber nodded vigorously.

"Picture a lunch with an important editor in a midtown restaurant."

"Michael's?" Bamber said breathlessly.

"Michael's is a little cliché. La Grenouille or Aquavit is more likely. Let's say we're at Aquavit, and we've just finished our arctic char, and we've run out of small talk."

"I hate small talk." Bamber's complexion blanched at the thought of it.

That was another thing we had in common, but, if you wanted to be "good at lunch," the small talk was crucial, and, over the years, I'd learned to master it.

"Now it's time for the sales spiel, which is called pre-seeding. I begin with the author, describing Quince's many credentials. I might even show an editor her Instagram feed because she's a very attractive author."

"Appearance matters?" Bamber smoothed her plaid skirt which was nubby from too many washings and sported a few white hairs that likely belonged to her cats. "Even for writers?"

I nodded. "Publishers love to play up the appearance of a young, attractive author. But the most important part is the pitch. I'll talk about the book, saying, 'It's about a brainy Black mother and daughter who move to an idyllic town in the South and discover that the townspeople's smiles mask an undercurrent of menace.'"

"Sounds really interesting."

"Doesn't it? But I don't want to merely interest the editor. I want her to leap across the table, jostle the coffee cups, and say, 'I need to read that book. Now!' So that's when I hit her with the zinger."

Bamber leaned forward, practically vibrating with anticipation. "Which is?"

"It's *Get Out* meets *Gilmore Girls*."

Bamber jerked back in her chair as if she'd gotten an electrical shock. "Wow. I mean, wow."

"Thank you." I glanced at my phone and squealed when I saw how late it was. "Gotta go. Text me with questions or ask Rebecca."

Before I left, I went into the break room to snag a biscotti, and Rebecca stomped in, wearing patent-leather Mary Janes. Her gait was like that of a baby elephant shaking the ground of the savanna.

"You hired Bamber?"

"Yes, and I think she's going to work out beautifully. Thank God. She has the perfect mixture of extreme deference and over-the-top admiration."

"Good, because you're going to need her even more after you get promoted. Speaking of which, will I have to curtsy in your presence after Kippy makes you partner?"

Kippy promised me that if I brokered one more big deal this year, she'd make me partner in the literary agency. At the age of twenty-five, I'd reach a level most of my peers only dreamed about.

"A deep bow from the waist will be sufficient."

Rebecca tried to bow and groaned at the effort. "I'll practice, Pitch Queen."

I washed my biscotti down with the dregs of my latte. "Might not happen, you know."

Rebecca punched my shoulder so hard it stung. "Yeah, it will."

"No client is ever a sure thing. And if Quince falls through, the promotion will be put off. Kippy gave me a number to hit by November 1, and if Quince goes with someone else, I won't make it. Not likely to find another seven-figure author in three months."

Rebecca crossed her fingers. "I got a good feeling about this."

"Keep those positive vibes coming."

Two o'clock couldn't come fast enough. Despite the delay of Quince's decision, I, too, felt like my dream of being number one dealmaker in debuts was going to materialize. Everything was falling almost effortlessly into place.

Chapter Two

Midtown used to intimidate me. So many sleek humans, swinging briefcases, jabbing phones, and powering down the sidewalks in the shadow of sparkling glass and chrome buildings.

There was a time when I minced along the sidewalk repeating "'Scuse me," awkwardly out of synch with everyone else. They were geese flying in formation, and I was the wild turkey, bumbling around in confusion.

But not anymore. Now I was one of them, a vital part of the churning river of people who were making the city spin. The Barnes and Noble on 55th carried novels that I'd sold. In Times Square, one of my client's books was lit up on the jumbotron. A month ago, *The New York Times* reviewed one of my titles. So, what if it was a pan? What mattered was the attention.

I was making my marks all over the Big Apple, which wasn't an easy feat. Every year, thousands of hopeful young people streamed into Manhattan, and the city shunned scores of them. But not me. New York didn't just welcome me. It let me sit on its lap for a hug and muss its hair.

The affection was mutual. Today, as I walked through the neighborhood of NoMad—so called because it was North of Madison

Square Park—I was heart-hitching, knee-buckling in love with my hometown.

In homage, I could have stood on the observation deck at the Empire State building, belting out, "New York State of Mind" or strutted into Tiffany's in a pearl choker, oversized sunglasses, and a little black dress.

I'd finished my errands and was on my way to lunch when my phone buzzed. It was Dani. *Damn.* I'd meant to call her first and congratulate her on her publication day, but I'd been so caught up with thoughts of Quince that I'd forgotten.

"I was just about to call you." I gave her my full wattage of energy. "Happy pub day!"

"Thank you. Hard to believe it's finally here. I know how busy you are, but I'm just calling to thank you for everything you've done for me. Every time I think of it, I practically burst into tears."

I wound my way through scaffolding covered in tattered fliers for a long-past Alicia Keys concert. "Me? Hey. You're the one who wrote a wonderful book that was a breeze to sell."

Pause.

"Maybe not that wonderful," Dani said. I could almost hear her swallowing back a lump in her throat.

"What do you mean? You have pre-publication praise so effusive your head must be the size of Alaska…Wait. You're not on Goodreads, are you?"

"Of course not… Okay. I lied. Maybe I took a little peek."

"You, of all people, should know better than that!" I was so loud and adamant, I startled a pigeon.

Dani wasn't the typical debut author. For five years, she'd been a senior editor at Dutton, and recently took a leave of absence to birth her debut novel as well as her debut baby. She was almost three months pregnant with her first child.

"I know," Dani said. "I always say to my authors: if you must read reviews, wait until your book's been out for a while and never on pub day. But I had to do something. I've been up since three a.m."

"Like a kid on Christmas day." I made my way around two tourists in cargo shorts and bucket hats, holding hands, taking up far too much sidewalk real estate.

"Exactly!" Another pause. "Only it's like waking up and there's no tree or presents. It feels so quiet."

Who said, "Some books come into the world with the fanfare of a stillborn"? Regardless, that wasn't the case with Dani's book.

"There's nothing quiet about your book," I said. "It's an Amazon editor pick. On the 'most anticipated lists' for *Time, Vogue,* and *Bustle.* Endorsements from at least ten mega-selling authors."

Also, those endorsements were over-the-top effusive. No mealy-mouthed comments like "an author to watch," which was code for saying, "but you can safely skip this first book."

"I know, I know," Dani said. "But who reads magazines anymore? And $14.99 for the ebook? What were they thinking? I'm at 371. Seems high."

"Are you looking at your Amazon ranking? Stop. Go out shopping or something."

"I can't. Too sick."

"I'm so sorry." Dani suffered from hyperemesis gravidarum—the same condition Kate Middleton had—which meant she got violently ill during the first trimester of her pregnancy.

"At least it's a fashionable malady," she'd once ruefully remarked.

Because of Dani's sickness, she had no author appearances on her schedule. But even if her pregnancy was trouble-free, book tours and launch parties weren't as common in the post-pandemic world. They were pricey and didn't move the needle much when it came to book sales.

"Didn't mean to be a whiner," Dani said.

"No worries. You're good."

"Not according to Cee-Cee Booked Up who says, 'If you were to look up the word slog in the dictionary, you'd see a picture of this novel.'"

"Step away from Goodreads!"

Normally, I avoided needy clients—that's what assistants were for—but Dani wasn't just any author. Before I sold her book, we had worked on several deals together and were now confidants.

Both of us had risen quickly in the publishing ranks at a young age. Dani's status as senior editor was especially impressive because editors were expected to push hundreds of boulders up the hill before they got any recognition. But, as a team, we brought several bestsellers into the world, and Dutton couldn't ignore that kind of star power.

"I didn't mean to make this conversation all about me, me, me," Dani said. "How are you doing?"

"Great. But I'm on my way to lunch so..."

"It's that time of day, isn't it?"

She sounded wistful, and I didn't blame her. Who wanted to spend time in a New York apartment the size of a boxcar, picking at a sad chicken fettuccini Lean Cuisine, watching the hosts on *The View* argue politics, when you could be tearing up the publishing world?

I was so caught up in my call with Dani that I almost passed by the restaurant on East Broadway where I was meeting Bea. Easy to do since the entrance to Accogliente Piatto was so unassuming. Just a black and white awning and a stenciled window with the name of the restaurant. You almost had to know it was there.

I went inside, and Bea was already seated. She wore a chartreuse suit and a chunky necklace made from seashells. Her glossy auburn hair was teased at the crown.

"Could it be any darker in this restaurant?" Bea said, a smile in her voice. "I feel like I'm dining in the bottom of a well."

"And yet somehow, you manage to light it up."

Bea let out her wonderful, full-bodied laugh. "You're such a flatterer, and I adore that about you. And if there's a hair in the minestrone, at least I won't see it." She flapped a red-and-white checked napkin on her lap. "But we both know why you take me to these out-of-the-way-places when I visit."

"So your fans won't mob you," I said smoothly.

Bea pulled out a compact and glossed her lips until they looked like candied orange slices. "New Yorkers are too aloof to mob an author, and besides, they don't read my novels."

"The tourists do, and this city is crawling with them."

"That's not why you chose this restaurant, Claire Louise, and we both damn well know it."

Not only was Bea dragging out my middle name, but her tone seemed serious. Heat crawled up my neck. Was I about to get reprimanded?

"You take me to obscure restaurants," Bea said. "You never mention me on your website or in interviews. It's almost as if you're embarrassed to have me as a client."

"Bea. That's not true. I—"

"And it's high time I tell you how I feel about it."

I made a production of spreading my napkin over my lap so she wouldn't sense how distressed I was. She'd never talked to me like this before. Was she going to can me?

"I'm fine with it," Bea said.

"What?"

"Got ya, didn't I." Bea laughed again.

"It's just that… Well, you've never mentioned those issues before."

"Because they *don't* bother me." Her tone was gentle. "I know I don't fit into your glamorous roster with my down-home humor and my lazy, Lowcountry settings."

"I love, love your novels!" I was so animated I knocked over the saltshaker.

"You might. If you've read them, but I suspect you haven't, which, by the way, also doesn't bother me. I'm not everyone's cuppa. No author is. And you don't need to read my books to sell them. Not with my sales record."

"Which is sensational." I righted the saltshaker and centered the vase filled with cheap red alstroemerias. "And you must know how grateful I am to have you as my client."

"You don't have to pretend with me, sweetheart. You and I are family. Not by blood, but family all the same. As you well know, your mother meant the moon to me."

That was the third time my mom came up today, and as always, I experienced an unpleasant hollowness in my chest. With the first two mentions, I had deftly changed the subject and the hollowness had gone away, but I couldn't deflect as easily with Bea.

"My mom was crazy about you too," I said. "She used to call you her big sister by another mother."

"Glenda was a treasure." Bea smiled, showing off her enviable dimples. She was one of those rare women over fifty who could still be described as cute. "And speaking of Glenda, there's something serious we need to discuss."

I didn't like the sound of that. Before Bea could explain, our waiter asked to take our orders, which ended up being a drawn-out process.

Bea had to retrieve her half-moon reading glasses—peepers she called them—and dicker over her choice of entrée: lasagna or spaghetti. She chose the latter, and I ordered bigoli.

"Doesn't that say it all?" Bea said after the waiter left. "I'm country-mouse spaghetti; you're big city bigoli. And what, in the name of macaroni, is bigoli?"

"Pasta made from buckwheat flour and duck fat. It's delish. Now back to our discussion."

"I got a letter about your mom's cottage from the Gull Island Historical Society."

"And?"

"They say you won't be able to rent the cottage as an Airbnb anymore."

"What?" A huge setback. An Airbnb was far more lucrative than renting the cottage out by the month. "Why? There are countless cottages on the island that are Airbnbs."

"The letter says the cottage is located in a designated historical area. You can appeal, but you must do it in person by August twelfth."

"In person? That's ridiculous. I'll call. Do you have the number?" I picked up my iPhone so I could enter it in.

"The letter said no exceptions."

"I can get around that." As a literary agent, I knew a thing or two about persuasion.

Bea pushed the envelope with the letter across the table. "Maybe you can, Claire, but honestly, isn't it time to put your mama to rest?"

I winced. "I know. I know. But in my defense, there was all that time during COVID when it was challenging to travel."

"Long over. Every plane is so packed they've got people spilling onto the wing."

"And I've been busy at work."

It was the song everyone in publishing was always singing. Dani liked to imitate Marlon Brando in *The Godfather,* saying "This is the life we have chosen." A book life meant that your career took precedence over most everything else.

"Come to Georgia," Bea said. "It's been over three years since Glenda passed, and you haven't been there yet."

It'd be tricky to get away from the office, especially now. Getting ready for Quince's deal would take time, particularly in August when so many editors kept loose summer hours, and nobody worked on Fridays.

"I'm sorry, Bea. I know it's an imposition to deal with the property management company from time to time. And I feel terrible about that but—"

"It is *not* an imposition. That's not why you need to come. It's time to deal with your mama's remains and get your closure."

Bea was talking about my mother's ashes, which were currently residing in my apartment's never-used oven in a cardboard box. Bea had arranged for the cremation in Savannah and had sent them to me afterward.

"You're right. I need to come down there, but I'm still growing my influence. I've only been a full-fledged agent for four years."

"You can afford to take time off. You've made a splash as big as a sumo wrestler in a kiddy pool."

"Vivid metaphor. Also, an extreme exaggeration."

"I don't think so... Pitch Queen."

I glanced away, embarrassed. The nickname sounded a little cheesy and self-important coming out of Bea's mouth.

"Don't believe everything you hear," I said.

"August is the least busy time in publishing, so it's an ideal time to come."

"Not this August. I'm anticipating a huge deal this month, maybe the biggest of my career."

Bea's phone buzzed, and she squinted at the screen. "Oh, my heavens. I need to speak with my plumber. You mind?"

"Of course not." I was grateful for the change in subject.

Bea left the table to have her conversation, and I checked my own messages. When I looked up, I spotted Morris, the last person I expected to see in an off-the-radar restaurant like this one. My rival was more likely to swan around in Manhattan's be-seen haunts like Bar Pitti or Morandi's. What was he doing in this decidedly unstylish restaurant?

My question was answered when I saw Morris's lunch date. Quince was on his heels, her beauty evident even in the gloom of the restaurant. She glanced about nervously as if afraid of being seen by someone she knew.

I felt a chirp of alarm in my chest, like a smoke detector before it starts squealing. I'd chosen this restaurant so as not to be seen with Bea, and Quince was hiding out so as not to run into me while she was with Morris. What were the odds? It was as if I'd found myself in a Moliere farce.

The strong citrus stench of Morris's cologne arrived before he did. His three-piece suit was made of such shimmering, flashy fabric it seemed to glow in the dark. When he spotted me, his mouth curved into a smile so wide, his bridgework was on display.

"Look who's here, sitting in the shadows," he said. "Claire Wyld. Quince and I were just talking about you."

"What a surprise." My voice was calm, and my expression was placid even though I wanted to leap at Morris's throat.

In her Instagram posts, Quince usually wore a look of cool disdain, like a model in a Banana Republic ad. But now, her eyes were wide, and her pinky finger was toying with the side of her mouth.

"It *is* a surprise," Quince said. "What I mean is, it's a last-minute thing. I have a friend who is a friend of Morris's and he asked me to lunch and... well..." She swallowed. "Morris is a hard man to turn down."

"Nothing wrong with a little lunch. Everyone's gotta eat." That was my way of saying all was well, and I forgave her this clandestine meal with my competition. "But I'm looking forward to our talk later."

"Me too," Quince said. There was a pleading look in her eyes which reassured me I hadn't lost her yet. "Morris, we should probably go ahead and sit because I definitely have an appointment with Claire at 2 p.m."

I glared at Morris. "A very important appointment."

"Maybe that appointment won't be necessary after our lunch is over," Morris said but his voice lacked his usual certainty.

"I doubt that," Quince said. "In fact, I very much regret being here. The truth is, Morris, I've talked to Claire extensively, and although I agreed to this meeting, I've already decided—"

"Lordy. Is it hot in here or is it just me?" Bea had returned to the table and was fanning herself with a paper towel. "Hi y'all. I'm Bea."

"I've enjoyed our chat," I said quickly. "Quince. Can't wait to discuss your future later and—"

"Bea?" Morris's craggy face split into a grin. "Queen Bea, the beach book writer?"

"One in the same." Bea squinted at Morris. "Have we met?"

"I've not had the pleasure," Morris said. "But I'm familiar with your work, and who isn't? You're a household name. What's your relationship to Claire?"

"She's my literary agent," Bea said.

"That so?" Morris clapped his hands together. "I had no idea. The Pitch Queen reps Queen Bea. But I'm not surprised. Claire's always been in step with the literary tastes of the masses."

"The masses?" Quince said, a puzzled look on her face. Recently, Quince wrote an essay for *Literary Hub* criticizing the quality of commercial novels. (Ironic, because the concept of her manuscript, despite its literary pretensions, was wonderfully commercial.)

While I was in the process of wooing her, I praised her essay, implying that I agreed with her opinions even though I didn't.

"Not that there's anything wrong with popular fiction," Morris said with a chuckle. "Literature is literature, right? Claire likes the fluffy, beachy stuff, I prefer weightier books that win prizes."

That was a lie. Morris would sell an adult coloring book if he thought it would cause a bidding war.

"As literary agents, we all specialize," Morris continued. "And that's the best way to serve clients."

"Excuse me, Quince," I said. "Morris is misleading you."

"Am I now?" Morris folded his arms in front of his chest, and Bea gave me an expectant look.

"The fact is, I don't like beach books," I said.

Quince smiled, as if to say, *I knew you had an explanation.*

"Like is too mild of a word for how I feel about beach books," I said. "I adore them! If beach books were black-and-white cookies, I'd stuff my face with them at every meal and chase down the crumbs. People consistently underestimate them, and that annoys me. Bea's latest book, for instance, has countless evocative descriptions of the shoreline. Faulkner himself couldn't evoke the elegant flight of egrets any better than Bea."

Morris lifted his chin and fingered the fat knot of his tie in a triumphant gesture, and Quince's chiseled features turned to stone.

"We'll let you two ladies have your lunch," he said, hustling Quince away.

Quickly, I texted Quince: *I'll explain during our meeting.*

Was I too late? If so, *goodbye number one dealmaker spot, goodbye seven-figure deal, goodbye partnership.* But as valuable as Quince was to me, she wasn't family and Bea was. I didn't share DNA with Bea, but she was my mom's best friend and had been incredibly kind to me after her death.

"Who was that shady fellow?" Bea said.

"Morris," I said. "We're always competing for clients."

"And Quince is—?"

"Just a writer I know… Listen, I hear they have a to-die-for tiramisu here. We should probably treat ourselves."

Bea was shaking her head. "Evocative descriptions of shoreline? Elegant flights of egrets?"

"I was caught off guard. And I didn't appreciate Morris calling your books fluffy."

Even though it was probably an accurate description. Not that I knew because Bea was right. I hadn't read her novels. One day I'd get around to them.

Bea smiled. "For your information, my newest novel is egret-free. Another reason you need to visit me on the island. It'll give you time to finally relax and read a beach book or two."

My phone beeped with a text. It was from Quince.

You said you hated commercial fiction. Snow job? Let's put off our meeting so I can have a think about this.

"What was that?" Bea said.

"Nothing."

That was a lie. It was everything. Quince held my entire career in her hands. But I didn't want Bea to worry. "I'm putting my phone on silent. Now where were we?"

"We were talking about you coming to Gull Island."

The waiter appeared with our meals, and I was grateful for the interruption. Yes, I knew I was shamefully overdue dealing with my mother's ashes and personal effects, but I had a resistance toward completing both tasks.

My mother hadn't raised me, and we hadn't been close because, as a child, my stepmother was determined to keep her away from me. Even as an adult, I only saw my mom a couple of times a year and, because of that, it was easy to imagine she was still alive and well and living in coastal Georgia, contentedly sipping mint juleps, white zinfandel, or whatever they drank in her neck of the woods.

If I went to her cottage, I could no longer fool myself, and I'd have to deal with the complicated feelings I'd been stuffing away ever since she died. I was regretful that I hadn't made more efforts to get close to her. I thought we'd have more time.

"Parmesan cheese?" the waiter asked.

"Please!" Bea said.

"Tell me when," the waiter said.

The waiter grinded until Bea's spaghetti looked as if it had been through a blizzard, but she still didn't stop him.

"Are you ever going to say when?" I asked.

"I'll say it when you agree to come to Gull Island."

The waiter's eyes darted as if he'd realized he'd become an unwilling hostage in our discussion, but he kept delivering the cheese. It was maddening, and I had to make it stop.

"Okay. I'll come."

Might as well. Quince was likely lost to me, and I'd been putting off a visit to Gull Island for far too long. Bea had been so patient with me. Plus, I needed to appeal that ridiculous Airbnb ruling.

"Wonderful." Bea glanced at the waiter and said, "That's enough."

The waiter stopped grinding cheese and sprinted away.

"When can I expect you?" Bea asked.

"In a couple of days. As soon as I can make arrangements."

"Wonderful. I know you're not jumping up and down, but we both know you need this closure. And you can relax for a while. Gull Island is a laid-back place. Some people call it Dull Island and that's meant to be a compliment."

As if that was a selling point to a person who loved the relentless rhythm of a city that didn't sleep or even cat nap.

"Fair warning," I said, narrowing my eyes. "The sound of the surf and the caw of the pelicans won't wear down my big-city edges. Just in case that's your plan."

"Sugar, pelicans don't caw. They grunt."

"And what about this plumber you were talking to. Will there be a set-up? Hoping he'll unclog my emotions? Lay a little pipe?"

I was at that age where everyone I knew thought I needed to pair up, pronto.

Bea shrieked with laughter. "What an active imagination you have."

"I know how beach plots work."

"Not mine. They're not quite that cliché. As for my plumber, are you interested in dating a fifty-year-old woman named Vera?"

"So, it's not a plumber you have in mind for me. Maybe it's a handyman or a lifeguard."

"Claire."

"Surfer?"

"There's no agenda." Bea's tone was suddenly serious. "You've been putting this off too long."

It was true. Even without the Airbnb issue, it was past time for me to go. But I still dreaded the trip. In Manhattan, I knew exactly who I was and what I was supposed to do. In Georgia, I'd have to confront my failings as a daughter. Not looking forward.

Chapter Three

Help! My Amazon numbers are going in the wrong direction.

It was a text from Dani.

My plane had just landed at Savannah/Hilton Head International Airport and, while the pilot traveled to the gate, I was finally able to use my phone. That text was only one of several I'd gotten from Dani, who obviously was ignoring my advice about staying off the internet.

My book advance was too large. I'll never earn out. Why didn't Good Morning America pick my book? What's wrong with Jenna? Doesn't she remember the tampon I lent her at BEA five years ago? I'm a loser. In a week, my books will be at the dollar store, marked down fifty percent. In two weeks, they'll be in a landfill, mingling with dirty diapers.

Just as I was about to send her a reassuring text, another one came in.

Ignore all these texts. I was hangry. Just devoured an everything bagel with a schmear and feel a lot better. Love you and thanks for all you've done for me.

I texted: *Wait until Wednesday. Fingers crossed for good news!*

Wednesday afternoon was when we'd find out if Dani had made *The New York Times* list. I was almost one-hundred percent certain she would. Hopefully, that would placate her.

While it was true most authors got a little weird and needy after publication, I hadn't expected that from a seasoned professional like Dani. Was it hormones from her pregnancy?

The plane finally stopped, and I joined the slow, shuffling line to disembark. This would be my first trip to the South, and all I knew about the area was that the natives loved grits and barbecue, sweated buckets in the summer heat, and still debated the Civil War.

I'd also seen *Sweet Home Alabama*, *Fried Green Tomatoes*, and *Forest Gump*, but suspected that Hollywood's version of the South probably had as much precision as a fat crayon in a preschooler's fist. Or maybe not. There was usually a sliver of truth in stereotypes.

Bea had insisted on picking me up at the airport, even though I told her I'd be happy to take a cab or a shuttle. "New Yorkers never pick up anyone at the airport," I said.

"Well, here in Georgia, we insist," she'd said.

Once I saw the inside of Savannah/Hilton Head International, I understood why no one minded a trip to the airport. It was a mellow place, even charming. Inside there was a clock tower and old-fashioned gas streetlights, making it look like a set for *Our Town*. The crowds were light, and people were actually strolling instead of racing about with grim looks on their faces, intent on getting a good spot in the taxi line.

I went outside to the passenger pickup area, and Bea was waiting for me behind the wheel of a red, convertible mini-Cooper. She wore a sundress splashed with pink flamingos, a floppy hat, and a pair of oversized, white-framed sunglasses.

You're not in NoMad anymore.

I hadn't checked my mother's ashes, fearing the airline would lose them. I'd stashed them in the overhead compartment, and now that I was in Bea's car, the box containing her ashes was on my lap.

"I can put that in the trunk for you," Bea offered.

"It's fine." Knowing that I'd be scattering the ashes soon, I'd gotten oddly attached to them. They were heavy, but it was a comforting heft, like a weighted blanket.

"Oh. Are those—?"

"Yes." Bea had sent the ashes to me a few days after my mom's cremation.

"Glenda's last trip to her beloved island," Bea said wistfully. She lovingly brushed her hand over the top of the box. "Hungry? I thought we might go out to lunch before we went to the cottage."

"Great, I'm starving." Anything to delay going to my mom's house.

"You're a bit overdressed for where we're eating."

"I know. I'll have to go shopping."

While I was packing for the trip, I stared at my closet for a long time, almost as if I expected a hot-pink sundress to reveal itself amongst all the monochromes, but alas, no such luck. All I owned were high-end work clothes and skid row, ratty sweats. There was nothing in between.

That's because I was either working or recovering from work by vegging out in my apartment, eating cold sesame noodles, and streaming whatever was in the top ten on Netflix.

"There are a couple of shops on the island. We'll get you fixed up."

The closer we got to Gull Island, the more signs I saw of the ocean. Sea gulls soared, marshland spread out for miles, and palmetto trees swayed in the breeze. Some people got excited about harbingers of the coast. Me, not so much.

My dad, my stepmom, and I used to go to The Hamptons every year when I was a child, but I'd been a bookish kid who preferred to curl up on a window seat reading instead of romping on the shore, playing tennis, or swimming.

Also, the beach had always seemed too much to me: too windy, too sandy, too bright, and too loud. I didn't like bathing suits because they showed the world how pale and thin I was, and I disliked rubbing greasy lotion all over my skin.

Now that I was an adult, I doubted I'd like the beach any better, but my mom had obviously adored it. Five years ago, after her own ailing mother died, she'd left Staten Island to relocate to Gull Island. I winced, thinking about how many times she'd invited me, and how many times I begged off due to work obligations.

We crossed a suspension bridge that overlooked blue water where tethered boats bobbed in the docks. Once we cleared the bridge, a sign said, "Caution: Book Worm Crossing" and shortly after we entered Gull Island city limits, another sign said, "The beach where readers rule."

"What's with all the reading signs?" I asked.

"A couple of years ago, the city fathers decided to brand the island as a haven for book lovers. All the public art has to do with books, and the streets have been renamed to reflect the theme. There's a Little Library on almost every corner, and many of the businesses have also gotten into the spirit."

We arrived at a modest seafood place called The Clam Shelf which was lined with bookshelves. One wall had a display of pictures of people with books. The display was entitled, "Caught Reading." Another wall was covered with book recommendations, and a felt tip pen was provided so that patrons could add to the list.

I marched up to it and immediately added Dani's book. No need to add Bea's books because they were already listed.

Our waitress, who wore a pink uniform and matching hat without a hint of irony, knew who Bea was and made a fuss over her, saying how much she loved her books.

"How thrilling to be with a VIP," I said to Bea.

"Please." Bea blew the wrapper of her straw in my direction as if to trivialize my comment.

The menu was basically fried everything—even the dill pickles were fried, and sandwiches were called sammiches. Hate to say it, but expectations were low, low, low.

You're not here for the cuisine.

Bea looked up from her menu and said, "Sorry to tell you this, but they don't offer the official food of publishing."

"And what's that? Crow?"

Bea laughed. "Arctic char."

"How will I ever survive?" I said with mock horror. It was true, I'd probably eaten a boatload of arctic char at lunch over the last few years.

"Try the shrimp po' boy. It's decent."

Not long after we ordered, the waitress, who was snapping gum, once again, without irony—delivered our food. I was tempted to take a picture of her and send it to Rebecca saying, "The stereotypes are real!" But that would be snarky, and besides, a text from Quince distracted me.

Decided to go with Morris. I need an agent I can trust.

Even though I'd expected the text my heart dropped.

"Then Morris is the last person you should sign with," I whispered.

"What's that?" Bea said.

I couldn't hide my disappointment, so I told Bea about losing Quince and how the deal was tied up with my possible promotion.

"I'm sorry," Bea said. "How big of an advance do you think she will get?"

"With me it would have been seven figures."

But with Morris it would likely be less. He wasn't privy to my ingenious pitch.

"Seven?" Bea waved a napkin in front of her face as if she were having another one of her flashes. "From a spanking-new author?"

"Happens all the time."

"Name some of these million-dollar babies."

"Dani Cline was my biggest deal ever. Her book just came out a couple of days ago."

"Why, pray tell, did she get so much money?"

I removed the pink, rubbery tomato from my sandwich. "To begin with, she's a senior editor for Dutton, and she's worked on major blockbusters."

"Bully for her, but that doesn't explain why her publisher is throwing money at her. Do you think the average reader cares about her editing background?"

"They do when they read the back cover of the book and bestselling authors are singing her praises."

"Agreed that some people are impressed by endorsements, but I think seasoned readers know that such praise is mostly about who-you-know."

"Do they really?" I had my doubts about that.

"Readers are savvier than you might imagine. What is Dani's book about?"

"I pitched it as *The Secret History* meets *Mean Girls*." It was a pitch I was particularly proud of.

"Oh my. *The Secret History* is a high bar."

"The novel deserves it," I said. I had to talk Dani into using it because she thought it was too much.

Bea looked doubtful. "Expectations are gonna be sky high. So many people think *The Secret History* is sacred."

In my opinion, no novel was sacred when it came to pitches. Well, maybe one novel. I'd never compared a book to my father's novel, *Galaxy*. Even for me that was a little egregious.

"You can judge for yourself," I said. "I'll get you a copy of Dani's novel asap."

"Looking forward. And speaking of readers, later tonight there's a meeting of the Beach Time Book Club. Would you like to come? Your mother was a member, and the ladies will be thrilled to meet you."

"My mom belonged to a book club?" I pushed aside my plate. Quince's news had ruined my appetite.

Bea squeezed lemon into her ice water. "Why are you surprised?"

"She was so shy." Or as my stepmother would say, "Such a field mouse."

"Your mother wasn't shy; she only talked when she had something worthwhile to say."

I winced. More evidence that I didn't know my mom as well as I should have.

"Have you ever attended a book club meeting?" Bea asked.

"No, but I'm sure it'll be a novel experience. Excuse the pun."

Bea laughed. "I love a pun but there's no excuse for that one."

"Agreed, and I'll be glad to come to the meeting. How often does the book club get together?"

"Monthly during most of the year, but in the summer months it's weekly. It's a part of the town's 'Twelve Books Every Summer' challenge." Bea pointed to a flyer that was hanging on the bulletin board advertising the program.

"What are you discussing tonight?"

"*The Missing Fiancé.* Have you heard of it?"

"*Gone Girl* reversed. Sold at auction to Doubleday for high six figures. If the author would have signed with me, it'd have been seven figures."

Bea smiled. "So, you've read *The Missing Fiancé*?"

"No. I don't read my competitors' books. What's the point?"

"For pleasure?"

"Hard for me to lose myself in books anymore. I know what goes into the sausage."

Authors' tears, authors' neuroses, authors' egos.

Bea frowned. "A shame. Your mother used to say you always had your nose in a book."

That was true. No kid was more impatient to unlock the mysteries of reading than I. Starting at age three, I devoured tedious early readers, impatient to tackle more tempting chapter books. When I finally got proficient enough, I'd take home armfuls of books from the library.

My stepmother belonged to the Book of the Month Club, and, starting at the age of eight, I read every single title that came to the house. Adult books from my childhood included *Water for Elephants*, *A Thousand Splendid Suns*, The *Twilight* series and even *The Road*. (The cannibalism parts gave me nightmares.)

At first, I'd put a *Harry Potter* jacket over the more mature titles, but, after a while, it became clear that no one in the household ever cared what I was reading.

My addiction to reading continued right up until the time I found success as a literary agent. But at some point, I was like a baker who balks at the idea of eating any more croissants. Of course, I had to read. It was my job. But I often found my mind drifting, and frequently I'd put down manuscripts in favor of literary gossip on Twitter.

Bea broke off a piece of her hush puppy. "Well, your mom loved reading and adored our book club. Speaking of which, I'm sure the members would like to attend any memorial service you plan."

I winced. "Uh… I wasn't planning on a formal service."

"I'll help you. Glenda's life deserves to be honored and celebrated."

"Of course it does," I said quickly.

"Wonderful. Also, it'd be lovely if you wrote a eulogy."

"Me? Why not you? Writing is your strength, and you knew her so well."

"I did. But you're her daughter, and writing a eulogy is a healing exercise. It forces you to truly examine what the person meant to you. Let me be frank with you."

I winced, wary about what was coming.

"You've been skimming over your mom's death instead of confronting it."

A eulogy and a memorial service made it all too real. If my mom was truly dead, it meant I'd never get a chance to be closer to her and be a more attentive daughter. It was magical thinking of the worst kind. Joan Didion knew what she was talking about.

"I'll write the eulogy and you're right," I said quietly.

Someone put money in the jukebox, and "He Stopped Loving Her Today" played, which was the world's saddest country song.

Suddenly I felt exhausted, thinking about the days ahead of me. I didn't want to be in this sleepy, sticky beach town, eating fried everything and listening to impossibly maudlin country songs. I didn't want to go to my mom's cottage and sort through her belongings. I didn't want to write a eulogy and experience the emotions that weighty task would unearth.

Even though I'd only been in Gull Island for an hour, I already longed to be back in the city, preparing for Quince's submission, my mind preoccupied with the pitch. But, of course, that wasn't an option since she'd dumped me.

No wonder I'd put off this trip for so long. It had been over three years since my mom's death, but I still wasn't ready to deal with it.

Chapter Four

On the way to my mom's house, Bea and I passed dozens of beach houses, all painted in bright, Easter egg colors: lemon-meringue yellow, not-so-bashful pink, punch-you-in-the-face purple. They also had impossibly cutesy names like *After Dune Delight*, *Once Upon a Tide* and *Cast a Waves*.

Most were bordered with white picket fences and had porches littered with boogie boards, beach towels, and sand toys. It was exactly the sort of place that would attract my mom, who was an unapologetic fan of kitsch.

"Does my mom's cottage have a name?" If she'd mentioned it while she was alive, I didn't remember.

"Yes," Bea said. "It's called Off the Beaten Path."

"Why?"

Bea turned down an overgrown cul-de-sac, and at the very end was a single, lonely looking cottage.

"That's why," she said, pointing at it.

The cottage had porthole windows, a widow's walk, and a house number fashioned from old rope. A gang plank flanked with pilings led to a porch with two bright yellow Adirondack chairs. It was almost a caricature of a beach cottage.

As we approached, glass crunched beneath our feet.

"Broken beer bottle," Bea said. "A souvenir from the last Airbnb guests. Sorry, I haven't been here in a while to check."

"That's not your job. The management company should have noticed that."

Bea let me inside with her key. I'd paid the management company to stage it as an Airbnb, and they'd done a decent job. Lots of bland, beachy décor. A starfish print here. A mirror with a shell-frame there. A faux weathered sign that said, "Gather."

Nothing in the front room had any connection with my mom, which was honestly a relief.

"All of her personal things, including her book collection, are in the attic, which is off-limits to guests," Bea said.

We went upstairs, and the attic felt close and hot in the summer heat. Bea turned on a window air-conditioning unit which coughed a few times before humming to life.

Near the window was a sidebar covered with photographs of me at various stages in my life. Me with braces. Me reading on the window seat in her Staten Island apartment. Me toddling around with spoons in my chubby fists.

"Glenda had these displayed in her office so she could look at them while she worked," Bea said.

Growing up, my mom was continually taking photographs of me, as if trying to preserve our rare moments together. My stepmother was always creating distance between the two of us—sending me far away to boarding school. My mother didn't have the means to fight her.

There were signs of my mom everywhere in the attic. The books she loved. Her collection of piggy banks. Daisy-patterned metal kitchen canisters passed down from my grandmother. Gingham throw pillows.

I spied her familiar canvas crossbody purse on a rocking chair; my mom carried it for years. When I questioned her about getting another one, she claimed she was too attached to it, and that she loved all the compartments. No doubt it had been with her in the hospital when she died.

I sneezed. The air conditioner had stirred up dust. Suddenly, I felt as if I couldn't breathe. The attic room was like a mausoleum.

"Let's go downstairs," I said. "A little stuffy in here."

After we were back on the ground floor, Bea gave me a pat on the arm. "I'll let you get settled in."

"You're leaving?" I said.

She patted her helmet of auburn hair. "Beauty appointment."

"You're already beautiful."

"Claire, it's gonna be okay. I'll check on you later today."

The little girl in me wanted to encircle her waist and shout, *don't leave me*. I didn't feel remotely ready to be alone in my mother's cottage.

Once Bea left, I had the urge to flee, but where would I go? Best to distract myself with work. What I really wanted to do was find a new fabulous author to replace Quince. It was a long shot but it wouldn't hurt to try.

To help me in my search for new voices or intriguing stories, I regularly checked a database of newspapers, online magazines, and writing sites like Wattpad and Substack.

Since I lacked outdoor space in the city, I decided to take advantage of the cottage's porch. I was used to working in a bustling office with phones ringing and honks and sirens outside the window, occasionally a jackhammer rat-tat-tatting in the street or sidewalk below.

At my mom's cottage, all I heard was the swish of the ceiling fan blades, the titter of birds, and the tinkle of wind chimes. The latter was likely supposed to be soothing but felt more jarring than jackhammers.

The location of my mom's cottage added to the quiet. Mature bamboo trees surrounded three sides of the home, providing a natural privacy fence, but it seemed unnecessary since "Off the Beaten Path" was already isolated.

A wasp buzzed by, and I glanced up, looking for a nest. I didn't see one, but I noticed that the porch ceiling's blue paint was faded and flaky. It didn't match the rest of the cottage, which was painted white. Why the different colors?

I put in a couple of hours of work on the porch, wishing my phone would beep and Bamber would text: *You won't believe what I found in the slush pile.*

No such luck. Eventually my phone came to life, but I knew it wasn't Bamber. The ring tone was Katy Perry's "Roar." It was the song I'd assigned to my stepmother.

"Claire," Meredith said. "Doing well. I hope?"

It sounded like an innocent question, but interactions with my stepmom were always loaded with landmines and booby traps.

"I am, thank you."

"Dating anyone?"

"Not at the moment." That was always my answer; my career didn't allow time for romantic relationships.

"*The Times* published an article on dating apps. There's one called Jungle which encourages group dating, in case you feel intimidated dating one-on-one."

"Thanks, but I don't—"

"Or Coffee meets Bagel, which is for people who are looking for serious relationships."

"Which I'm not. At least not right now."

"Fine. But if you use Tapdat, please be sexually responsible."

"Meredith. I'm not interested in guys right now."

Long pause. "What do you mean, you're not interested in guys?"

She'd always been weirdly paranoid about my sexuality as if I was consistently tripping her gay-dar.

"I misspoke. I meant I'm not interested in dating."

"But if you were interested—?"

"Males," I said. "The hairier, the better. A human version of Bigfoot."

Another long pause. My humor always seemed to go over Meredith's head.

"I'll forward the article. Speaking of work, did you get that promotion you mentioned last time?"

"Not yet, there was a setback."

Meredith sighed. "Still an assistant then?"

Deep prana breath.

Dealing with Meredith was like trying to maintain the handstand scorpion pose in yoga.

"As I've told you before, I haven't been a literary assistant for years. I was a junior agent for a while, which is different from an assistant. You continually mix that up. Then I was promoted to agent and—"

"Kippy is your father's agent, and it's so important you don't embarrass him by disappointing her." Meredith, like most people, was in awe of the ever-so-glamorous Kippy.

"Meredith, I'm not disappointing Kippy. In fact, it's the opposite, I'm— "

"You can tell me your excuses later. Your father's angling to get on the line."

"Claire? Are you there? Claire?"

On the phone my father always sounded like a séance participant who didn't expect any ghosts to answer.

"I'm here, Dad. How is Montenegro?"

"It suits me," my dad said. "I found a café to read in, but poor Meredith isn't happy. She calls it the Dollywood of Eastern Europe. Lots of people from cruise ships. She doesn't like people from cruise ships."

"I know." There was a lot of stuff that Meredith didn't like, and she was vocal about them.

Meredith mumbled something in the background.

"Meredith says it rains too much here. And the art galleries disappoint."

Meredith was a serious art collector, but oddly none of it was displayed in her home. She was too worried about theft or damage, so she kept her art in a concierge storage unit in Long Island.

Occasionally, she and my dad made pilgrimages to view her collection, taking along a bottle of Bordeaux, a charcuterie board, and a pair of lawn chairs.

My dad lowered his voice. "There's a forest here called Black Pine Forest that's packed with bears and wolves."

"As any proper forest should be. And what book are you reading?" My father always read books that had a connection to the place he was visiting.

"*An Illustrated History of Slavic Misery.*"

"Uplifting."

"It's a love letter to murderous Montenegro and other Slavic warlords, but it's surprisingly funny."

"So glad you're enjoying yourself."

"I'm easily amused."

More mumbles from Meredith in the background.

"We'll be in Manhattan in two days, and Meredith thought you might want to have dinner."

"Tell her to make a reservation at I Sodi," Meredith said loudly in the background.

I Sodi, a Tuscan-style Italian restaurant on Bleecker, was almost impossible to get into and certainly not in two days.

Meredith religiously read a New York magazine called *Culture* that listed all the hot eateries, and she always wanted to try the recommendations when she came into the city from Short Hills, New Jersey where they lived. Once I had to stand in line an hour at the Lafayette Bakery to secure her a crème filled croissant called the Supreme.

"I'd love to have dinner with you, but I can't. I'm in Georgia."

"If you have trouble getting a good table, tell them who your father is," Meredith said, directly into the phone.

"We were in Georgia last year," my dad said. "Be sure to try the Khinkali dumplings."

"But avoid the chacha," Meredith said. "Eighty percent alcohol. One shot did your father in."

"Not Soviet Georgia," I said. "Deep South Georgia. I need to deal with... uh... Glenda's cottage and her personal effects."

I didn't refer to Glenda as my mom in the presence of my dad or Meredith. If I happened to slip up, Meredith would bristle and say, "You have lived in my household all your life. If anyone is your mother, it's yours truly."

"Oh," my father said. "You haven't already dealt with Glenda's things?"

I couldn't see my dad, but I knew at this moment his pale skin was flushed, and he was likely toying with the collar of whatever stylish shirt Meredith had foisted upon him. Any mention of Glenda always made him ill-at-ease.

"No," I said. "There hasn't been time."

"Will that woman ever leave us alone?" That was Meredith, practically shouting.

"I should go," my father said and, just like that, he'd severed the connection.

I stared at the phone, shaking my head. For as long as I could remember, Meredith was feverishly jealous of my mom. I thought it would end with her death, but it hadn't.

Her jealousy had to do with my mom's influence on my dad's novel, *Galaxy*. Glenda had been working for Kippy as a literary assistant, and she fished my dad's manuscript out of the slush. She knew it wasn't ready for Kippy's eyes, but she saw promise in it, so she called my dad and offered to work on it with him to get it in salable shape.

It took almost a year, and when it was sold, in a weak moment, they shared a bottle of champagne and ended up sleeping together. Six months later, my mom called to tell him she was pregnant.

By that time, my dad had met and married Meredith, whose father made a fortune from Pop and Stop convenience stores.

When I was born, my dad and Meredith sought custody. My mom didn't fight him. She was a nineteen-year-old, single literary assistant from a religious Baptist family who were horrified by her pregnancy, and my dad was married to a multi-millionaire who was unable to have children of her own.

After the call from my dad, I continued to work on the porch, but it started to pour, and the wind blew the rain sideways, dampening my computer keyboard.

Time to go inside. It was the last thing I wanted to do.

Chapter Five

I wasn't used to the isolation and silence of my mom's cottage, and once I'd finally crawled into bed, I feared I'd be up all night. In New York, my upstairs neighbor was addicted to Zumba, and I heard her athletic shoes pound the floor day and night. There was also a jazz club a block away, and the *wah-wah* of a trombone would reach my ears every time someone entered or exited.

Now I could only hear my thoughts, blaring their usual bad news—everything from career concerns to worries about an odd twinge in my tooth. (Cavity? Abscess? Trench mouth?)

Finally, after an hour of twisting in my sheets, I went into the stuffy kitchen and opened all the windows, straining to hear any sound at all but the cottage was still quiet as a tomb.

I asked Alexa to play John Coltrane as loud as possible. When I closed my bedroom door, I imagined I was in New York with jazz music drifting down the street. That did the trick because the next time I opened my eyes, sunlight was streaming into the bedroom.

A glance at my phone said it was nine a.m. Wow. So late. On weekdays, I was usually up with the sanitation workers. I clumsily dropped my phone, and it fell under the bed. While I was looking for it, I found an empty beer bottle.

So much for the maids doing a thorough cleaning job. I picked up the bottle, planning to dispose of it, and flung open the plantation shutters.

Outside my window was a white-haired man wearing a bow tie. He'd parted the thick bamboo in the back yard and was peering at me through his binoculars.

I slammed the shutters, but not before the senior citizen got an eyeful. The only thing I was wearing was a thong and a retinol moisturizer. Was he a peeping Tom? He seemed a little too geriatric for that, but then again, there must be a reason for the phrase "dirty old man."

I opened my bedroom door, and John Coltrane nearly busted my eardrums. I'd left it on last night for background noise, and this morning it sounded loud and jarring. Quickly, I ordered Alexa to turn it off.

It felt as if half the day was gone, and there was so much to do: shopping, sorting through my mom's things, work chores, and more. But first, coffee.

I'd seen a coffee maker on the kitchen counter, but I required dairy with my daily cup. In fact, my tastebuds were set for my usual lavender latte.

I googled "coffee near me." What came up was Plain Jane Java. A Google review said, "Plain Jane isn't just a name. It's a way of doing business. All they have is plain old coffee." I frowned. I was a big fan of coffee that doubled as dessert, but it looked as if it was Plain Jane or nothing. At least they'd have sugar and cream.

I padded into the guest bathroom, and the mirror above the sink gave me bad news. My hair needed a flat iron, my face begged for bronzer, and my dry lips cried out for Bobbie Brown's City Dawn Muted Coral. But I was in no mood to spend an hour grooming myself before my jolt of caffeine.

"Natural it is," I said to my uninspiring reflection. "It's not like you're going to run into anyone you know."

I wrangled my frizzy hair into a ponytail holder and put on a sleeveless black dress and a pair of ballet flats. Town was only a few blocks away, and I went on foot.

It was already hot outside, and the sun zeroed in on my scalp. I could feel the heat of the pavement through the thin leather of my shoes. By the time I got to the coffee shop, even the spaces between my fingers were sweaty.

I ordered my boring coffee at Plain Jane and sat in a back room that was empty of people. As I sipped, I checked my email. Bamber hadn't forwarded anything to me, so I texted her.

Nothing going on?

Very quiet. A couple of clients have emailed. But other than that, nothing. I'm so sorry.

I could imagine Bamber wringing her hands as if it were all her fault.

I almost forgot. Wendy called. But I handled her, Bamber texted again.

Thanks!

As always, my heart dropped whenever I thought of Wendy. She was one of my first clients, and I'd discovered her on Twitter. Someone had shared a blog post she'd written about her sexy escapades delivering pizza.

I followed the link and discovered over a dozen raw and hilarious posts. I contacted her about writing a novel featuring her pizza delivery life, and nine months later, I sold it at auction, all because of my pitch:

FOODIE CALL when an agoraphobic man falls in love with his sexy pizza delivery person, and the pair struggle to reconcile his homebody tendencies with her adventurous spirit.

Expectations were high for Wendy's book. Her editor arranged for her to fly to New York to meet with members of the publishing team and key buyers. Everyone was charmed with her youth, good looks, and smart-ass humor. At lunch, the publisher asked Wendy if she was ready to be a superstar.

But, despite all the advance buzz, hardly anyone read Wendy's novel. Readers who usually bought into the hype machine gave *Foodie Call* a pass. In less than a month, Wendy went from being the toast of the literary world to an untouchable, and she couldn't accept it.

My phone beeped with a text. *Why are you passing me off to your minion? She can't help me!!!!!*

Usually, I was far too busy to deal with Wendy and her drama, but that wasn't the case today. I reluctantly called her.

"Claire. Oh my God. You finally called me. I can't believe it. Thank you. Thank you."

Already, I regretted my decision.

"Of course, I called," I said briskly. "I'm your agent. I've just been underwater. That's why it's taken me a while to get back to you."

"Two months and three days. Not that I'm counting. I've left messages, and I hope you don't think I'm being pesky."

I almost laughed out loud. She was incredibly pesky. Worse than potential spam callers.

"Did you have a chance to read my newest manuscript?"

"I did."

In truth, I'd only read the first chapter, but that was enough. I didn't have to eat an entire loaf of brioche to know it was moldy.

"And?"

I took a big gulp of my Plain Jane coffee. "Wendy, I'm so sorry but I don't see this as your next novel."

"What do you mean? What's wrong with it?"

Everything was wrong. *Foodie Call* fetched a large advance because of its cute pitch and charismatic author. But, unfortunately, those two things couldn't overcome the novel's many negatives: a messy narrative, convoluted prose, and unlikeable characters.

Early unsympathetic readers skewered it on Goodreads, and it never took off. Wendy's latest novel had the same flaws as *Foodie Call* minus the great hook. It was a women's fiction novel about a fraught relationship between a mother and daughter. *Yawn*. Nothing juicy about that, and it was impossible to pitch well.

"It's much quieter than your last novel," I said. "Quiet" was publisher speak for "nothing happens."

"What did my editor say?"

"She wasn't enthusiastic."

That was an understatement. Emma called me and said, "You gotta be joking, right? That prima donna's not getting another nickel from us. I almost got fired over her book."

Emma wasn't the first editor who'd told me they feared for their jobs after buying my clients' underperforming books. I used to worry I'd get a bad name among editors, but Kippy reassured me, saying, "Privately, they might resent you, but they'll still want to work with you. You broker the big deals. Everyone knows that success breeds success. Also, publishing is a business that is always looking forward, rarely backwards."

And failure breeds failure, I thought, wishing I had better news for Wendy.

"Emma's not returning my calls," Wendy said.

"I told you not to call Emma. Let me deal with your editor."

"I assumed it'd be okay. I thought she cared about me."

Emma once told me that Wendy was the most high-maintenance author she'd ever worked with. She treated Emma like a therapist/girl

Friday, calling her for love advice or asking her to make restaurant reservations.

Wendy also made over-the-top demands like expecting the publisher to pay for a bikini wax. Initially, Emma was a good sport, thinking *Foodie Call* was going to be a mega-seller, but now that the book had failed, she never wanted to speak to Wendy again.

"It's best if I deal with Emma," I said.

"If Emma would read the entire novel instead of just hearing the concept, I know she'd pee her La Perla panties with excitement."

Ick, I thought. "No, she wouldn't."

"Why not? I was reading about another mother/daughter novel that sold for big bucks from a writer named Anna Kay."

I hated it when authors compared themselves with other authors. Most of the time it was like comparing a Chips Ahoy cookie to a Pain Au Chocolat croissant from Domnique Ansel's bakery.

"Anna Kay is the daughter of an Oscar-winning actress who committed suicide three years ago."

"So?"

"You aren't her. And if you want to another contract from Emma, you're going to have to write something ground-breaking, and this novel doesn't qualify."

"How about another publisher? I'll use a pen name. I've already thought of one: Anatasia Ferrari."

Oh, brother.

"Too bougie?"

"You're not hearing me, Wendy. A pen name won't help with this novel. It doesn't have the pizazz of *Foodie Call*."

Wendy started to cry. "But people didn't buy *Foodie Call*, and I don't understand why. You loved it, and the whole publishing team said it was a winner. Did I determine the size of my advance or design the cover or decide how it was going to be marketed? No! I had zero say in those decisions. Yet, I'm the only one who's being blamed and punished for the failure of the book. How fair is that?"

I had to admit that Wendy was making some valid points. Unfortunately, I wasn't the one who came up with this system. I was just a player.

"I feel like I'm washed up at the age of twenty-one," Wendy said.

"Listen. I feel terrible for you but—"

"You know who's truly to blame for this?"

"Who?"

"Look in the mirror, Claire. You were supposed to be my advocate, and you failed miserably. You didn't point out the flaws in *Foodie Call*. You offered no guidance on my second book. This is all your fault!"

I was momentarily shocked. Wendy often railed at the state of publishing, but she'd never directed her anger at me like that before.

"Are you there?" Wendy said.

"You blame me for the failure of your novel?"

Wendy sniffed a couple of times and said, "Yes. You did this to me." But now she didn't sound quite so sure of herself.

It took me a sec, but I recovered my chill. "Here's what I *did* to you: I made your publication dream come true; I came up with the pitch for your novel and landed you a seven-figure advance, a book tour, and ten minutes of fame. Is it my fault that the public didn't embrace your book?"

"Why are you yelling at me?" All the bravado had left her voice, and she was back to being weepy Wendy.

"I'm not yelling. I'm being honest." A rarity for me, but when it came to Wendy, I didn't have a choice. "It's obvious you're not happy with me, and it seems like we're at an impasse. So maybe it's time you found a new agent."

"Wait. You're firing me?"

Was I? I'd never let a client go before, but honestly, I was so over Wendy.

"Let's call it a parting of the ways."

"As if a euphemism is going to make me feel better."

"Wendy, I'm sorry but—"

"You can't leave me, Claire. Not like this. Please don't. You're my only connection to the publishing world. I'll be lost without you."

"Wendy, there are hundreds of agents out there. You deserve someone who's enthusiastic about your work."

"You used to turn cartwheels over my work. You discovered me. What happened? Don't see dollar signs anymore?"

"Wendy. I'm sorry. I need to go."

My coffee had gone cold, and the sky outside the window had turned a dark gray. Thunder mumbled a warning. I stared at my phone, feeling bad about the ugly turn the call had taken and stung by Wendy's remarks about money.

My job compensation was amazing, but Wendy was wrong. I didn't put in eighty hours a week for a big paycheck.

The real reason I lived and breathed work was because I adored making deals. There was so much excitement before a book was sold. The client was thrilled with me; I was thrilled with them! The editor was giddy. Everyone adored me.

If only it could stay that way.

I sent Bamber a text saying Wendy Collins was no longer a client.

Do you want to talk about it?

I almost texted back, *no*. But I was in the mood to vent, so why not? I called her, and Bamber said, "So how is Gull Island?"

"All play and no work makes Claire a dull gull."

Bamber laughed at my lame-o joke, an excellent quality in an assistant because sadly, I had plenty more where that came from.

Now that we were done with the preliminaries, I launched into my Wendy tale.

"Wendy deserved to be fired," Bamber said, after I was done. Her indignation was exactly what I needed to feel better. "Publishing is supposed to be a civilized business, and Wendy is crass. She used the F-word with me more than once."

That made me feel even better about my decision. How dare Wendy abuse my unfailingly polite and somewhat prim assistant?

I chatted with Bamber for several minutes and was reluctant to end my phone call, even though I was out of coffee. My assistant was such a sympathetic listener. I found myself talking about some of the other writers I was having trouble with.

There was Kaylor who'd written a bestselling novel that was *Twilight* fanfic, and now had no idea how to write the second novel in her contract. Or Gisela, a former Goodreads darling, who'd written a follow-up novel that even her biggest fans hated. She called at least once a week to kvetch about bad reviews and to explain to me why they were unfair.

"Who knew writers could be such divas?" Bamber huffed after I finished my tales of woe.

"To be fair, I found Kaylor on Wattpad, so I knew she was a fanfic writer. Not a huge surprise that she'd have trouble with the second book. And Gisela's debut novel was so popular that the publisher rushed out her sophomore book. Her editor hoped her foaming-at-the-mouth fans wouldn't notice its shortcomings, but they must have gotten their rabies shots because they did."

"Still. Aren't these people supposed to be professionals?"

Not really, I thought. They were all inexperienced authors, and many had a weak knowledge of everything from storytelling craft to comma splices. That was the downside of repping newbie writers.

"Don't you worry," Bamber said. "I'll handle them all with aplomb."

Gotta love a gal who casually uses the word aplomb. "Thank you," I said gratefully.

We talked a bit more, and I finally ended the call, feeling warm and fuzzy about Bamber. She'd ended up being a great hire.

I was about to leave the coffee shop when my phone buzzed. Incoming text from Dani.

I'm crying!!!!

I sighed at her drama. Dani had been a friend before she'd become my client, so I couldn't slough her off on Bamber, but who knew an editor could be so high maintenance?

I texted: *Why are you crying?*

You haven't heard? My book is a Charmi pick.

Get out of town!

Can you believe it?

It used to be that being a Reese or Jenna pick was the best thing that could happen to a book, but in recent months, Charmi, a TikTok influencer with over a hundred million followers was trumping them both.

Thrilled for you, Dani and so well-deserved, I typed.

Dani texted back: *I can't stop bawling. It's so crazy. I thought the book was dying on the vine, but now this. Have I told you lately how amazing you are?*

Me: *I can always hear it again.*

XOXOXO

Nothing like a happy, grateful client, I thought. Next to wowing editors with my pitches, the second-best part of my job was getting good news. Publishing was a business of soaring highs and snake-belly lows, so keeping clients happy could be tricky.

Today hadn't started out well, but it was looking better by the moment. Since I was on a roll, I decided I might as well swing by the historical society and see if I could appeal the silly Airbnb ruling.

I googled the address and left the coffee shop.

As Bea had mentioned, the public art on the streets of Gull Island was all reading related. There was an iron sculpture of an open book on a pedestal, stone children statues engrossed in stories, and a bronze archway made of books that led to a small park. Book flags flew on every corner.

Google directions led me to the historical society housed in what looked to be a used bookstore. How many bookstores could one small island support?

A dirty window revealed a collection of old volumes stacked in precarious piles. There was no signage out front, just a note on the door that said, "By appointment only," but there was no number to call, and Google didn't provide one either. I tried the door, and it was unlocked, so I decided to pop in.

The first floor of the two-story building was a labyrinth of shelves stuffed with old volumes. Dust motes danced in a ribbon of light, and the store emitted a sweet, earthy old book smell that begged to be bottled.

I hesitated to venture into the stacks, fearing I'd never find my way out. Also, as far as I could see, there was no one manning the place. I couldn't imagine anyone wanting to browse in this messy, disorganized store, appointment or not.

Out of nowhere, a book came tumbling down from the heavens, and nearly beaned me.

"Rubbish!" said a male voice.

Not the most welcoming of places. "Hello?" I called out.

"Who's there?" The voice drifted down from the second floor, which was an open loft. I squinted into the gloom and spied an unmade cot and a rusty looking vintage stove, but I didn't see anyone.

"My name is Claire Wyld. I got a letter from the historical society saying I wasn't allowed to run an Airbnb in my cottage. I'm here to appeal that."

"What's the address?"

"One Charles Dickens Way."

"Appeal denied."

"Wait. What kind of appeal is that?"

"Your cottage is in a designated historical district that doesn't allow short-term rentals. End of story."

"I came all the way from New York City. If there was no chance of an appeal succeeding, why even mention it in the letter?"

"The decision is final."

I glanced up, scanning the loft, and I finally spotted an old guy sitting at a desk, his nose buried in a book. All be damned if it wasn't the same old man who'd seen me almost completely naked. I recognized the bowtie and abundant white hair.

"That's extremely unfair."

The wheels of his office chair rolled back and forth over the wooden flooring. "Forgive the impertinence, but how old are you?"

"Twenty-five."

"And you're just now learning that life isn't fair?" His voice was world-weary. "What a charmed existence you must lead."

"Why don't you come down here, and we can talk this out face-to-face."

"I think not. I encountered one of your rowdy and brazen guests this morning. Your days of hosting drunken naked parties with loud music that last until dawn are over."

So, he had seen me with his binoculars. Just didn't recognize me.

"That wasn't a guest. That was me. And yes, I had a beer bottle in my hand, but it wasn't mine, and yes, I sleep in the buff, but many people do and that doesn't make them brazen. And yes, I forgot to turn off the music last night. I was just so tired that—"

"My ruling stands. Good day, miss."

"Thanks for all your help." My voice was thick with sarcasm. On the other hand, at least he'd forced me into a decision. I'd have to sell the cottage instead of renting it out. But that meant I needed to get it ready to put on the market. I'd have to face a lot more work and a longer stay on Gull Island.

After leaving the so-called historical society, I traveled two blocks to visit Irene's Bookstore, an airy, cheerful place. So different from the old man's shop.

My intention was to take a photo of Dani's books and send it to her with the caption, "Seen in the wild."But when I asked the woman behind the counter about the title, she said, "Sorry. We don't have it in stock, but I'll be happy to order it for you."

"Not in stock? But it's a big book. On *Bustle's* most anticipated list."

"What's a bustle, sugar?" She was a sixty-something woman with platinum blonde hair worn in a top knot. Feather earrings dangled from her lobes, and she wore zebra print leggings.

"It's also a Charmi pick. She's huge on TikTok."

"TikTok? My goodness. Isn't that how the Chinese spy on us?"

"Never mind. I just assumed you'd have this book. It's probably going to be a bestseller."

"Sorry to disappoint, but I have limited space here and only order books I can sell to my customers. I've owned this store for over thirty years, and I know their tastes. But it's possible I accidentally overlooked this title. What's it about?"

"It's *The Secret History* meets *Mean Girls*."

She scratched her cheek with a pencil. "I don't get it."

Obviously, she didn't speak pitch. "Never mind. Thanks for your help."

"I can recommend something else. Have you read Queen Bea? Everyone is gaga over her latest."

"Maybe another time."

I'd just have to text Bamber and ask her to overnight a copy of Dani's book to me. Once it arrived, I'd take a selfie with the book outside the store and say, *Only one left! Owner says they're selling like cronuts.*

"If you haven't read a Queen Bea book, you're missing out," said the woman, whom I presumed was Irene. "I have some of her books in trade paperback if you don't want to commit to a hardcover."

"I'll think about it. By the way, I don't suppose you have any extra boxes lying about?"

"Plenty. They're out back. Help yourself."

Outside, the air was still and thick. My lined black dress felt as stuffy as a full-length mink coat. Sometime today, I needed to shop for summer clothes.

I carried a collection of boxes back to the cottage, intent on dealing with some of my mother's possessions. But when I went up to the attic, I found myself looking at her things with my hands behind my back as if I were in a museum of precious artifacts that couldn't be touched.

In a basket, there was a half-used jar of Oil of Olay, a straw hat with a black ribbon, an unopened tin of Altoids, and a grocery list that included freezer bags, TP, olive oil, and Hershey's kisses. (Just like me, she was a fan of sweets.)

I couldn't bring myself to place anything into a box. Writers talked about writing blocks. Well, I had a packing block.

Instead of packing, I went downtown to do some shopping. A place called the Shore Thing sold clothing, but if you were looking for coastal chic, you were out of luck. Mostly they had cheap novelty attire.

"When in Rome," I said to myself.

I went all in, buying t-shirts with fun logos like "Drink in my hand, toes in the sand" and "Eat, Beach, Sleep, Repeat." I also got a sun hat, several pairs of flipflops, and a huge bottle of powerful sunscreen to protect my pasty New York skin.

"Somebody's ready for a day at the beach," said the clerk when I paid for my clothes.

Not really. I just wanted to be cool and comfortable. But to be friendly I said, "Thinking about swinging by today."

"What are you going to read?"

Nosy question, but maybe that was the Southern way. "A magazine? Maybe *Vogue*."

She shook her head. "You might not know this, but every Wednesday is Bring a Book to the Beach Day. You'll look out of place if you don't have one."

"Thanks for the intel."

Maybe I'd go to the beach after all. It'd be fun to see if anyone was reading Dani's book.

I returned to the cottage, changed into my new duds and explored the shed out back. My mom had obviously been a professional beachcomber because she had all the essential gear: a red umbrella, colorful beach towels big enough to accommodate a sunbathing hippo, a Yeti cooler, drink koozies, and a wagon to carry it all. I grabbed a Mary Kay Andrews novel from her shelf in the attic, so I'd fit in with everyone else.

To get to the beach, I had to travel down a sandy path lined with seagrass. The closer I got to the ocean, the cooler the air felt, and the sound of the surf grew louder and louder.

It had been ages since I'd seen any body of water except the East River and Hudson River. I crested a hill and there it was: the Atlantic Ocean in all its roiling, crashing, frothy glory. Boats, far out to sea, dotted the horizon. The panoramic vastness of it all was momentarily dizzying.

But after a second, the spell wore off and I said, "Meh." I'd take a skyscraper view any day of the week.

On the beach were hundreds of people, and, as promised, all were reading books. I dragged my wagon around and surreptitiously glanced at the covers. Plenty of Bea books but a good selection of others, everything from James Patterson to Elin Hilderbrand.

I also spotted some books by high-brow authors like Jennifer Eagan and Colin Whitehead, but no Dani. I wanted to shout, *What's wrong with you people? Get with the zeitgeist.*

The print run for Dani's book was announced at a hundred thousand copies, which was always an exaggeration. The publisher had probably only printed a third of that.

Still, you'd think at least one copy would make it to the beach, but if it was out there, I didn't see it. Never mind. I'd be sure and tell Dani I'd spotted plenty of her books, and once Bamber sent me a copy, maybe I'd even ask a few people to pose with it.

Since I was already at the beach, I decided to stay a while. I felt very purposeful, drilling the umbrella into the ground, unfolding the chair, spreading sunscreen on every inch of my exposed skin, but when it came to sitting down and reading, I failed miserably.

The novel was engaging, but I kept reading the same paragraph over and over because my mind was worrying about packing, finding the next hot author (damn you, Quince!), and writing that problematic eulogy.

Trying to distill someone's life into a eulogy was similar to summarizing an entire novel in order to sell it. But my mom's life was impossible to boil down to an elevator pitch.

A kind-hearted literary agent moves to the coast and dies. "Beaches" meets "Book Lovers."

Too sad.

A young woman gives up custody of her daughter to her author lover and his ridiculously wealthy wife. The young woman thought her daughter would have a better life with them but instead, the stepmother treats the stepdaughter like she's a dolt who can't attract a man and might be gay.

That was my life story, not my mother's and there was nothing hooky about that tale.

A mother rescues her daughter from the brink of darkness.

Maybe.

But then I'd have to talk about my unfortunate past to everyone who came to the memorial service. I doubted even Bea knew about that horrific time in my past.

Chapter Six

I experienced the worst summer of my life when I was working with Kippy as a junior agent, and I was barely paying my bills. Meredith sent me a check each month, which I never cashed because I was determined to prove to her that I was far more competent than she imagined.

I'd started out in a modest but clean apartment on Delancey Street which I shared with an assistant publicist at Penguin. But after three months, I couldn't keep up with my share of the rent payments. I moved to a room in a defunct theater in the Bowery with no windows and a communal bath with a shower so dirty and mildewy I always wore socks when I got in it.

Also, because my funds were so low, I barely ate. Mostly eggs, corn tortillas, Saltines, peanut butter, and bananas. I knew I was losing weight, but the only mirror in the bathroom was too high for me to see myself. I also wore oversized sweaters to disguise my weight loss, even though it was sweltering out. Not that I felt the heat. I was continually shivering no matter what I wore.

By that time, my mom had moved to Gull Island. We talked once a week, and she kept wanting me to visit her, offering to send a ticket. But I knew she'd find my appearance alarming, so I always said I was too busy.

Meredith and my dad were on a year-long, around-the-world cruise, so they had no inkling of my troubles.

One evening, my mom appeared at my door—my old roommate had told her where I lived. She took one look at me and said, "Something is terribly wrong. You're seeing a doctor tomorrow."

The next day I was diagnosed with depression, complicated with a mild eating disorder. The doctor recommended immediate treatment. Knowing how important my job was to me, my mom found a tele-program that I could do while I was working.

On weekends, I went to a nearby treatment facility for in-person therapy. My mom paid for all of it and found me a different apartment, saying I lived in a firetrap. Meredith and my father knew nothing about any of this, thank God.

During therapy, I rethought my goals as a literary agent. Initially, my plan had been to discover the next *Galaxy*, but focusing on literary authors wasn't panning out. Instead, I decided to specialize in debut authors.

It made sense. New authors weren't jaded or know-it-alls yet. Many were extremely grateful to be given a seat at the publishing table, and editors loved them because they were like ski slopes after a snowfall, pristine and full of promise.

Once I focused on debut novelists, my career took off in a spectacular way.

Had it not been for my mom rescuing me, who knows where I'd be now? No question it would make a wonderful eulogy story, but did I really want to share that pathetic tale with people I barely knew? Mostly, I wanted to put that time behind me. Also, I hadn't been as grateful as I should have been. Once my career started taking off, I became an inattentive daughter.

Now, as I stared at the ocean, it occurred to me that this was the first time in a while that I'd attempted to relax. My life in New York had only two speeds: one hundred and zero. Sometimes after a jam-packed eighty-hour work week, I'd spend my Saturdays under the covers, an exhausted bag of bones, emerging only for bathroom visits and bowls of Breyers mint chocolate chip ice cream.

As a result, I was out of practice when it came to relaxation, and the beach with its relentless wind and sun was making me cranky. *Time to get moving.* I gathered the beach gear and packed up.

Back at the cottage, an envelope was stuck in the door. It was from the historical society, giving me official notice that my short-term rental permission had been denied, and that I'd face a hefty fine if I violated the rule. *Fine.* I'd already made my mind up to sell the cottage.

After putting away the beach gear, I toured the cottage with the eyes of a potential buyer. Paint looked new. Kitchen and bathrooms were updated. Hardwood floors were scratch-free. All appliances worked.

Next, I stepped outside and strolled the perimeter of the grounds. The lot was punctuated with appealing tropical plantings like palmetto trees, bright pink bougainvillea, angel trumpets, and lemon trees.

In the back yard, an opening in the bamboo revealed a path that led to an impressive, gilded gate that was overgrown with a tangle of bushes. It was tempting to peek at what was behind the gate, but there were so many "no trespassing" signs, I didn't dare.

I found several beer bottles outside, which made me wonder how wild the Airbnb guests had gotten, but at least there wasn't any discernable damage to the cottage or grounds. To sell, I'd need to pack up my mom's things and paint the flaky blue ceiling. Next time I saw Bea, I'd ask her if she knew any painters.

I dreaded it, but it was time to tackle my mom's extensive book collection. Most could go to Goodwill, but maybe I'd keep one or two for sentimental value. I went up to the attic and started sorting through them.

These days, most of my client reading was done on a Kindle, so I'd forgotten what a tactile pleasure it was to feel the heft of books in my hand and to admire the dust jacket. I got lost in the task, spending far too much time reading the acknowledgements, searching for names of agent colleagues, and sometimes I paused to read the first page to see if it sucked me in.

Of course, my mom had a copy of my favorite book, *The Secret History* by Donna Tartt. It had a tantalizing first line: "The snow in the mountains was melting and Bunny had been dead for several weeks before we came to understand the gravity of our situation."

I picked up *The Book Thief*, a novel I'd heard so much about, but hadn't read. The first line was: "Here Is a Small Fact: You Are Going to Die."

I slammed it shut. It was an extremely compelling first line, but considering I was going through my deceased mother's book collection, I didn't want to read further. I put it on top of the giveaway pile and accidentally knocked over a copy of *Captain Corelli's Mandolin*.

It landed in an open position, and a phrase was underlined: "When you fall in love, it is a temporary madness. It erupts like an earthquake..." On that page, my mom had written, "Truth!"

Why had my mom underlined that passage and commented on it? Did she have someone in mind? If so, I couldn't imagine who.

I paged through the novel and noted dozens of lines my mother had underlined and commented on. Was this a habit of hers? I picked up another book from the giveaway stack. My mother had highlighted passages in that book as well.

If all of her books were similarly personalized, how could I possibly give any of them away? They were too precious.

Unfortunately, her collection wouldn't begin to fit into my studio apartment. Maybe I'd have them shipped to a storage unit. It would be enormously expensive, but I had no other choice.

At some point, I'd want to go through every book to see what lines had resonated with my mom. It'd be like reading books through her eyes. Maybe I could get to know her a little better after all.

Chapter Seven

I was double-checking the letters from authors in my slush pile, making sure Bamber hadn't overlooked a hot property, but the pitches were as unsalable as ever. A two-hundred-thousand-word *Game of Thrones* knockoff for tweens? No way. A picture book called *Santa is a Sneak Thief*. What were writers thinking?

A knock on the door interrupted me. It was Bea picking me up for the book club meeting. Time had gotten away from me.

The two of us strolled to the meeting which was held in a nearby cottage called Dune Our Thing. Inside, the *Book of Love* was playing on the sound system, and the book club members—all wearing colorful muumuus and wide brimmed straw hats—were milling around, holding tropical drinks.

"Social hour before the meeting," Bea said.

At the bar, we were offered a choice of either strawberry marga-read-as, purple frosé, Writers' Tears Whiskey or Double Plot Chardonnay.

I'd had my fill of writers' tears, so I chose the chard; Bea went for the purple frosé which was a slushy drink made from pineapple juice, Blue Curacao, and Grenadine. Bea introduced me around, and the members offered their sympathy about my mom's death.

"Claire is a literary agent, just like her mother," Bea said.

Not just like my mom, I thought. We had very different business models.

"How fascinating," said a squeaky-voiced woman named Fawn.

"Claire is a true taste maker," Bea said. "She discovers all the new authors."

"I hope that means new ideas as well," boomed a woman named Vera, who also happened to be Bea's plumber. She had broad shoulders and wore oversized glasses that made her look like an over-caffeinated owl.

Before I had a chance to respond, a bell rang, calling the meeting to order. In unison, the members lifted their glasses and shouted, "Let's get lit!"

It was time to discuss the book, and boy, did the ladies have opinions. Fawn, who'd picked the novel, said, "I apologize. I keep getting sucked in by books that compare themselves to *Gone Girl,* and I'll be honest, this wasn't remotely in the same league."

Vera snorted. "I could have told you that."

"A bland knock-off," someone said.

"Characters with as much personality as paper dolls."

"Figured out the twist by page fifty."

"Page twenty-five for me."

"The authors who try to imitate *Gone Girl* are missing the point," Vera said, her voice as loud as her lime green caftan. "They think it was the incredible twist that set the book apart. But they're wrong. *Gone Girl* was singular because of its one-of-a-kind characters and an author with writing chops. And you know that from the very beginning."

"'When I think of my wife, I always think of her head,'" Bea said, reciting the first line of *Gone Girl*. "Immediately, you know you're in excellent hands. Then Flynn goes on to write, 'She had what the

Victorians would call a finely shaped head. You could imagine the skull quite easily.'"

"Sets up the whole book," Fawn said, nodding.

"A master," Vera said. "Whereas the first lines of *The Missing Fiancé* describe a walk on the beach. Yes, the fiancé is snatched on page three, but first we have to hear about the swell and ebb of the tide."

"And how it undulated." Fawn made a wavy motion with her hand.

"Of course it did," Vera said with a sneer.

Fawn shrunk into her chair. "Again, I apologize for picking it."

"To be fair," Bea said. "It didn't stink. The pacing was brisk. It wasn't boring."

"It went down smooth," said a woman whose lips were stained red from her strawberry margarita. "Like ice milk from Dairy Queen. But it wasn't anything special."

"People loved *Gone Girl* because it was wildly original," Vera said. "Which is ironic since it now has so many imitators."

Bea sighed. "That's the way publishing works. Always trying to replicate success."

Fawn plucked the cherry out of her drink and nibbled it like a bunny. "Isn't that the truth? I'd die happy if I never had to read another World War II novel."

"Amen!" Vera shot up from her chair and raised her arms to the sky like a rapturous preacher. "It's been done to death, and besides, we know how it all shakes out."

After that, the comments came quickly.

"Too many drunk unreliable narrators."

"And the cartoon covers. They're all blurring together."

"Most are deceptive. Looks like a sweet, funny romance on the outside, but on the inside, there are more moans than a porn flick."

"It's so rare to run into a novel that's memorable," Vera said with a pout. "I find myself rereading my favorites. Or streaming shows instead of reading. I never thought I'd prefer to watch TV than read, but sometimes I do. If this continues, one can't help but wonder about the fate of the novel."

"Wow," I said. "As a literary agent, it's fascinating to hear readers' perspectives. I don't get that often."

"Speaking of memorable novels," Bea said. "Claire's father wrote *Galaxy*."

Everyone started talking at once. How much they loved *Galaxy*. How some of them had read it several times. How it made them cry.

Vera slapped her thighs. "When the hell is your father going to write another one?"

That was the seven-figure question, one I'd been asked hundreds of times over the years. I didn't know the answer, but I had my theories. When Harper Lee's *Go Set a Watchman* came out, Meredith was horrified. "She's diluted her legacy!" she said more than once.

Had Meredith discouraged my father from writing again, fearing he'd pen a lousy follow up? I wouldn't doubt it. It was as if my dad's legacy was like the valuable art she kept in storage, and she was terrified of any damage to it. And my meek father was so dependent on Meredith, it wasn't a stretch to imagine he'd listen to whatever she said.

But that's not a story I could tell strangers. Instead, I'd come up with a stock answer.

"My father's writing feeds him so much, he doesn't need the validation of publication," I said.

It was a romantic reply. Art for art's sake! It was also a fairy tale that I'd partially stolen from Salinger. When my dad first reached literary prominence, he was trumpeted as the new Salinger.

"Sounds selfish to me," Vera said.

"Vera!" Fawn said.

"Just saying." Vera was gnawing on a chicken wing. "If you have a gift, you damn well should share it with the world. Not hoard it."

Frankly, I also suspected my father was fearful of his gift and its effects. He was introverted and hated author appearances, although Meredith made him do the most prestigious ones. It was painful to witness him mumbling his way through a ten-page passage in his novel, the same reading he'd done for years.

My dad was also grateful he wasn't often recognized in public. His book jacket showed a thirty-year-old man with a full head of floppy blonde hair and large, soulful eyes. Now, his hair was silver and thinning. His drooping eyelids and bifocals stole some of the soulfulness from his eyes.

The publisher was putting out a commemorative edition of *Galaxy*, and Meredith wanted him to sit for a new author photo—she lapped it up when people recognized him—but in a rare show of defiance, my dad refused.

"I'll pass your comment on to my father," I fibbed.

"You should." Vera pointed her chicken bone at me.

Fawn gave Vera a withering look and said, "Have you ever wanted to follow in your dad's footsteps?"

If she'd asked me when I was a child, the answer would have been yes, yes, yes. I used to scribble in notebooks saying I was going to be just like Daddy when I grew up.

One day, when I was ten, Meredith sat me down and said, "Let me save you a lot of heartache. Your father is a one-of-a-kind writer, and anything you write will always fall woefully short."

I thought she was being mean, but that was before I understood the impact my dad had on the literary world. Meredith was right. If I were ever to write a novel, the comparisons would be tortuous. But I loved books so much, I decided to be a literary agent instead of a writer.

"I'd rather sell novels than write them." That was another pat answer of mine. "More lucrative."

"Doesn't seem fair," Vera said. "Why should someone who sells books make more than someone who writes them?"

"Well, I—"

"You don't have to answer that." Fawn glanced at her watch. "Getting late. Time to choose our next book. Claire, do you have a suggestion? If anyone knows good books, it should be you."

"So glad you asked. I know a wonderful book and it just came out," I said. "*Schooled* by Dani Cline."

Vera frowned. "What's the genre? Can't tell from the title."

"Coming of age," I said. "It's about a young woman attending an all-woman college. She expects to find a supportive environment, but a group of students are very ugly to her. She devises a way to fit in, which ends up being costly."

Fawn clasped her hands together. "I adore coming of age. *To Kill a Mockingbird, Catcher in the Rye, A Tree Grows in Brooklyn.*"

"Gotta admit, I'm a sucker for an academic setting," Vera said.

"Then you'll love it," I said.

"Wonderful," Fawn said. "I'll send out an email tonight to the group so they can order the book in time to read."

The meeting adjourned, and Bea and I walked back to our cottages. A breeze had chased away the day's humidity, but every house on the block hummed with the sound of an air conditioner.

Sprinklers chattered in yards, throwing off rainbows. It was still light out, and the setting sun smeared sherbet stains across the horizon. I had to admit it was stunning. When was the last time I'd observed a sunset in the city?

Bea said, "Isn't *Schooled* that novel you were telling me about? By your editor friend?"

I put a finger to my lips. "Don't tell the others. It'll be fun to see their unbiased reaction to it."

"But how will you feel if the club doesn't like it? Will you take it personally?"

"They'll love it. The book is very clever. And even if a few don't like it, that's fine. Novel tastes are so subjective."

Bea laughed. "Don't I know it. So long as you aren't too thin skinned."

"I'm a literary agent." I pounded my chest. "My skin is as tough as a kiwi."

I said goodbye to Bea and walked around the corner to my mom's cottage. They'll like Dani's book, I thought. I was so fond of Dani, and, in the last few years, she'd been extremely supportive of me.

She and I met shortly after I finished therapy, and I was determined to change the course of my fledgling career. I'd cold called a bunch of editors, trying to arrange lunches. She was one of the few that said yes.

I'll never forget our first lunch. I'd suggested Whole Foods, a complete faux pas. First of all, editors typically select the lunch place because they pay, and they never choose buffets. But Dani was kind and agreed to meet me there.

I was still dressing like a frumpy college student, wearing a sweater, a plaid skirt and... oh my God... clogs. (To this day, I blush when I think about it.)

Dani, on the other hand, wore a camel-colored tweed jacket with gold buttons, her grandmother's Hermes scarf, and a pleated skirt. With her swingy blonde hair and good teeth, she looked like an older version of a cheerleader. Not the bitchy head cheerleader who everyone secretly fears—but the good-natured, athletic one who doesn't mind spending hours on her knees working on posters for the pep rally and always has a smile for everyone.

Outside of Whole Foods, Dani said, "I'm not a bit hungry. Why not forget lunch and go shopping? I know a consignment shop on Madison where all the UES women retire their clothing."

"UES?"

"Upper East Side. Last time I visited, I got this Metier bag." She held up a leather tote for me to see.

That day we prowled the store on Madison, and I received a subtle education on what to wear to a working lunch. The quality of shoes and bags were important, but they shouldn't be flashy. Understatement ruled the day. "It's publishing not fashion," Dani said.

After that day, we became friends, shopping, taking yoga classes, and talking about our lives. In high school, Dani wasn't a cheerleader like I'd assumed; she'd been president of the poetry club.

"A bunch of dateless girls swooning over Emily Dickinson," was how she described it. In other words, at heart, she was a book nerd just like me, and we became even more bonded once we learned we both loved *The Secret History*.

As Dani and I got to know each other better, it became clear why we both identified with the novel.

"Thematically, *The Secret History* is about being an outsider looking in," Dani said once during our frequent shopping dates. "And I felt that way all my life."

"How so?" Dani had the looks and sunny personality of an insider.

"My sisters were all socialites and married very well, but all I wanted to do was hole up in my room with a book," Dani said while we sorted through the clothing racks. "Now, I'm the outlier with the low-paying job. An object of pity. At family gatherings, people are always slipping me envelopes of money."

Not long after we became friends, Dani confessed that she'd been working on a novel since she was eighteen. "Every few months or so, I drag it out and tinker with it," she said. "But don't tell anyone."

"Why not?" I asked.

Dani sighed. "Editors with secret ambitions to be novelists aren't looked kindly upon by their peers. It's almost as if you're implying that being an editor isn't good enough or that it's a means to an end. And God forbid if you get a publishing contract. Everyone assumes it came about because of nepotism."

And what's wrong with that? I thought. So long as it helps sell the book.

"Let me read it."

"It's not ready for anyone else's eyes yet."

For over a year, I kept asking to read the manuscript, and Dani refused. When she finally relented, I got back to her in less than twenty-four hours, saying I loved it and wanted to sell it.

"You read it that fast?"

"I couldn't put it down, and I'm convinced we're looking at significant money here."

By that time, I was already making a name for myself as an agent.

Dani demurred, saying that if she went down that road, she could never go back. I, however, wouldn't give up.

"Did you know Toni Morrison and Margaret Atwood both started out as editors?" I said during one of our lunches.

Dani put down her fork. "I have nothing in common with those two brilliant writers. It's blasphemy for you to compare them to me even in a casual way."

"Fair enough. What about Jill Bialosky? She's written three novels, two memoirs, and a handful of poetry books, and still works as an editor at Norton."

A thoughtful look crossed Dani's face. "I don't know Jill or her books, but I remember hearing about her. That's an impressive body of work."

"And yet despite her publication credits, she still happily edits."

I could tell that the mention of Jill affected Dani, but it was still several weeks before she finally changed her mind, and my nudging had nothing to do with it.

"I'm pregnant," she told me over the phone. A year ago, she'd married Bryan, a fact checker for *The New Yorker*.

"Is that good news?" Dani once told me she was likely never going to have children.

"It's a miracle. I'm not supposed to be able to get pregnant. My uterus has an irregular heart shape, and doctors have told me I'm unlikely to conceive, so I resigned myself to being childless. But they were wrong. I'm pregnant, and I couldn't be happier."

Once her initial elation wore off, Dani started thinking about the practicalities of combining child rearing with editorial work, and it didn't add up.

Editors did very little editing on the job. Their days were spent attending marketing meetings, fielding phone calls from agents, reading pitches, writing rejection letters, and drawing up profit-and-loss statements.

Most editing had to be done at home, which wasn't practical if you had a child who demanded your full attention.

At some point, she phoned me and asked, "Do you really think you could get a decent advance for my novel?"

"No," I said.

"Oh," she said, sounding disappointed.

"It'd be wickedly indecent."

"Ballpark on the filthy lucre?" That was an inside joke between Dani and I. Bunny, a character in *The Secret History*, referred to money as "filthy lucre." It was also Bunny's lust for the lucre that led to his demise.

"One point five mill," I said.

Deep breath. "That's ridiculous."

"You're an editor who's worked with several bestselling authors. It'll get you a lot of publicity. I'm not telling you anything you don't already know."

"And if I wasn't an editor?"

"It's a clever novel. It would still sell." At least, I thought so. Hard to say since I didn't work with garden variety authors. "But not seven figs."

Not even close. That's what I was thinking but there was no upside in saying it aloud.

"I've read my novel so many times I have no objectivity," Dani said. "We both know if it doesn't fly off the shelves, there'll be no follow-up. Do you really think it's ready?"

From the standpoint of marketability, it was beyond ready. Dani, as the author, was an agent's dream, and I'd already come up with a great pitch. When you had those two things in place, the book was the least of it.

But she was asking me about the quality of the book, and I knew if I paused too long, Dani would back out. It was clear she wanted this, and just needed a push from me.

"Every page is brilliant."

"You wouldn't lie to me?"

As Dani's friend, I would never ever lie to her, but now that she was a potential client, the standards for truthfulness had changed. Otherwise, our business relationship wouldn't fly.

"Of course not," I fibbed.

Long, long, long pause from Dani. Finally, she said, "Okay. I'm going to do it... for the baby. A big advance will buy me time to be with him or her."

Tragically, two weeks after I brokered the $1.5 million deal (an amount I predicted), she lost the baby. But the good news was Dani got pregnant again, and now she was almost past the dicey first trimester. Also, it looked as if her book was going to do well, especially since Charmi picked her book. All in all, she made the right decision to pursue publication.

Before going to bed, I texted Dani, telling her about the book club. "I know they're going to love it. But I'll be sure to report back."

I'd pushed Dani into publication, which made me feel more invested than usual in her book's success. Also, I'd done something I was ashamed of. I hadn't told Dani the entire truth about her book. Luckily, she'd probably never discover my deception.

Chapter Eight

Every morning, I checked Publishers Marketplace for Morris's deal with Quince, but it never appeared. I was tempted to contact Quince to see what happened, but resisted the urge because I wasn't a poacher.

After checking emails, I went out to the porch to write my mother's eulogy, but the right words wouldn't come. Her death had mostly gone unacknowledged. No obit in the *Times* or *Publishers Weekly*. I found myself wanting to make up for that in the eulogy, but everything I wrote seemed flat and general, like a minister who delivers a homily for a church member he barely knows.

I looked up from my computer and said, "Mom. I'm so, so sorry. I wish we'd been closer. I've failed you." I glanced about, almost as if I expected her to make an appearance, but, of course, there was no such thing as ghosts.

More blue paint flaked down from the porch ceiling, which reminded me I'd forgotten to ask Bea if she knew a local painter. It was such a small job, I might have trouble finding someone. Was it possible I could do it myself?

I visited the shed to see if there was extra paint inside. *Bingo*. One shelf held paint cans, all labeled. There was white paint for exterior touch-ups and blue for the ceiling of the porch. A small ladder stood in the corner, and a collection of drop cloths were neatly folded on a shelf.

All the equipment was on hand, and it'd be satisfying to check off an item on my to-do list. Had I ever painted a ceiling before? No, but how hard could it be? Not hard at all, according to a YouTube video I watched.

Gull Island had a small hardware store called Nailed It where I was able to pick up a couple of brushes and a roller. I also decided that the porch ceiling would look better if it was painted the same white as the rest of the cottage instead of the odd blue color.

I tuned my mom's portable radio to a jazz station, and I stood on the ladder, enjoying the coolness of a sea breeze and Anita Baker singing "Sweet Love."

"Stop what you're doing. This instant."

It was the old man with the bow tie. He stood on the walkway with his hands on what were surely arthritic hips. Good God, he was everywhere.

Why would he want me to stop painting? And would he ever stop meddling in my life?

He ascended the steps and snapped off my radio. Ballsy of him. Was it too loud? Or maybe he wasn't a jazz fan.

"Did you hear me?"

That's when I noticed he wasn't old. Before, I'd only seen him from a distance, and I assumed he was elderly because of his white hair, old-fashioned way of dressing, and crabby attitude. Up close, he looked to be in his late twenties or early thirties at the most.

Underneath his horn-rimmed spectacles were eyes that were alert and a deep navy blue. His features weren't loose and slack. Instead, he had a strong jaw and well-defined cheekbones. Not bad looking if you liked the grumpy professor type. In fact, some might say he was a hottie.

"What's wrong?" I asked, puzzled.

"Stop painting."

"Why?"

"Because this cottage is in a designated historical district, and you can't make any alterations without the approval of the president of the historical society."

Hottie or not, this Benjamin Button guy was a pain. "Are you the president?"

"Correct."

"And let me guess. You won't approve it here and now."

"I most certainly won't." The man waved away a fly. "There is a well-defined protocol, forms to be filled out. Verbal approvement is not part of that protocol."

"Okay. What kind of hoops do I have to jump through to get approval?"

"Fill out the paperwork, get it notarized, and wait seven to ten business days."

I descended from the ladder. "Why don't you save me the time and effort? In your professional opinion, will it be approved?"

"Highly unlikely."

"Why not?"

"You're painting the ceiling white but, in order to maintain historical integrity, it must remain blue. Haint blue, to be precise."

I put a hand over my brow to shade the sun. "What's a haint?"

"The word is derived from haunt." He spoke slowly and deliberately as if addressing a child. "If you paint your ceiling haint blue, your home will be free of ghosts."

"Ghosts?"

"That's correct."

"But what if I don't want my house to be ghost-free?" I said softly.

"Excuse me? Speak up. You're mumbling."

Suddenly, I was angry. How dare this stranger be so snippy with me? Who did he think he was, thwarting me at every turn? It almost seemed personal.

"What if I want to see a ghost, and this stupid blue ceiling is keeping her away?"

The old man-who-wasn't-old stared at me with a puzzled look in his eyes.

"This is my mother's house, and she died of COVID because she's asthmatic," I shouted. "And I would love to see her again."

All the man's sharp edges seemed to soften at once. He toyed with his bow tie and adjusted his horn-rimmed glasses.

"I'm sorry. I was out of line. Continue painting if you'd like."

"Really?"

Talk about your jarring transformations. What brought that on?

"In fact, let me finish the job for you. It's the least I could do to make up for being so testy."

"That's not necessary," I said.

"It would be ungentlemanly of me not to do it. I'm taller than you and can make quick work of the task."

"But you're wearing a suit and a tie." Albeit a worn seersucker suit that looked like it needed to be retired to the waste bin. As I recalled, he'd been wearing the same outfit when I saw him in that old bookshop.

"I'm an exceedingly adroit painter." He took the roller from me and hopped on the ladder. Even though he talked with the formality of an old man, his painting style revealed a graceful athleticism, as if he played sports. Probably something vaguely preppy like cricket or polo.

"How long has it been since your mother died?" he asked.

"It's been a little over three years. She died in April."

He stopped painting. "What day?"

"April third."

A glazed look came to his eyes. "My wife and brother died four days later on April seventh."

"COVID?"

"No. A car accident."

"I'm sorry."

For the first time, I noticed the air of sadness surrounding him. The slump in his shoulders. The slight downturn of his mouth. The wounded look in his eyes. No wonder he'd changed his mind about the ceiling so quickly. He, too, had lost family members and obviously felt an affinity toward me.

"Thank you. Elizabeth was... irreplaceable. I'm Philip, by the way, and our names were one of the many clues we were destined for each other. We'd known each other since childhood. My brother was twenty years older than me, and we often butted heads, but his loss was also devastating. The grieving process has been the hardest thing I've ever gone through. But I don't have to tell you that."

I nodded, not wanting to explain to Philip that I didn't know my mother well and that our grieving processes were likely very different. For starters, I'd been delaying and denying mine.

I told him I was getting the cottage ready to sell. "Since I can't operate it as an Airbnb anymore," I said, thinking, *thanks to you.*

"Unfortunately, I can't help you with that," he said. "The city council met last night and accepted the historical society's regulations on beach rentals as law. Some of your renters weren't respectful. Parties, loud music, and such. But if you've decided to sell, I'd be glad to recommend a real estate agent."

"Thank you, but my friend Bea is helping me with that. It's for the best that I sell it. That way I won't have to worry about it anymore. All I'll have to do is deal with mom's personal effects. Do you take book donations at your store?"

I'd yet to find a book without any of my mom's markings, but maybe I would.

"I'm sorry. I only deal with rare books. Is there anything else I could help you with? Move furniture perhaps?"

"No. Bea says I can probably sell it furnished."

"I'd like to do something to make up for my rudeness. Perhaps place flowers on your mother's grave?"

"She doesn't have a grave. I'm actually looking for a place to scatter her ashes."

"Were you planning on going out to the ocean?"

"Not the ocean. Too vast. I'm looking for a quiet, peaceful spot. Maybe in a cove."

If I could find the perfect little place to scatter my mother's ashes and hold a lovely memorial service, maybe people wouldn't notice the failings of my eulogy.

"I can help you. I know this area backwards and forwards. All due to my adventures in bird watching. In fact, the other day, I spotted a purple sandpiper near your mother's cottage. I generally always have a pair of binoculars handy. You never know what you might see." His face turned red. "Rather, the island has a varied bird population, so I like to be prepared."

Because you never know when you might spot a double-breasted Yankee bird with a beer bottle in her hand.

I smiled at the notion of Philip being a peeping Tom. Now that I'd met him, the idea seemed absurd. Yet I had the urge to say, "Did you like what you saw?"

Instead, I said, "I'll take you up on your offer."

Time to start checking items off my to-do list so I could get back to the city. This procrastination business had to end.

"Offer?" He looked panicked as if I was proposing something slightly racy.

"To scout locations to scatter my mom's ashes. I'd like a place that's a little remote and not overrun with beach lovers."

"I'd be happy to assist."

***

The next morning, Philip arrived at my doorstep looking like he was about to embark on a safari. He wore a khaki vest with numerous pockets, which contained a map, water bottle, and field notebook. Binoculars hung around his neck, and a pith helmet perched on top of his wavy white hair.

That hair! Such an abundance, and the whiteness was stunning in contrast with his olive skin.

"I barely recognized you without your bow tie," I said as a greeting.

He touched his throat as if doublechecking. "This is my birding attire. But if you find it too casual for the solemnity of occasion, I'd be happy to change."

"It's fine. Look at what I'm wearing." I pointed to my t-shirt that said, "Resting Beach Face."

He squinted at the message and said, "I don't get it."

I wasn't surprised. Philip didn't seem like the type who would know many popular expressions. He was young, but it was almost as if he was from another age all together. Maybe it was a Southern gent thing.

"So, what's the plan?" I asked.

"I've given your request consideration and have settled on Little Gull Island, which is about three miles from the main island. It has several charming coves that are also remote, which I've marked." He withdrew a map and showed me at least eight places that were highlighted. "One of them should be ideal for a private service."

"Wow. You've gone to a lot of trouble."

"It was my pleasure, but visiting all the possible locations could take a few hours. Will that work for you?"

"I cleared the whole day."

"Good. I also took the liberty of preparing a picnic, so we won't go hungry."

My stomach grumbled at the word picnic. "Thanks. That's very kind of you."

"You're most welcome."

Parked in front of the cottage was an elderly blue Volvo station wagon. The chrome V in Volvo had fallen off, and there were patches of salt damage on the body paint. Attached to the top was a battered-looking canoe.

I pointed to it. "Why do you have that?"

"We need it to get to Little Gull Island, which is only accessible by boat."

"Sorry. A canoe is not my kind of boat," I said.

"It isn't?"

"I prefer boats with a movie theater, seven different restaurants, and a housekeeping staff who folds towels into the shape of animals."

He smiled. "I think you mean a ship. And none of those travel to Little Gull Island."

"Is there a ferry?"

"There is, but it only runs on weekends. Would you like to wait until then?"

I nibbled my bottom lip, trying to decide. He'd really gone out of his way for me.

"If it's a matter of stamina, you needn't worry," Philip said. "I'll do the work and you can just relax and float."

I sighed, feeling resigned to my fate. "Is there at least a powder room?" I joked.

Philip blushed; he was the easiest blusher I'd ever met. New York males rarely blushed. Few things embarrassed them.

"I'm afraid there's no powder room. And Little Gull Island lacks facilities as well. But I packed TP should the need arise."

Peeing in the wilderness. Lord knows I wasn't in NYC anymore.

***

As it turned out, it wasn't just peeing in the wilderness. It was peeing in the wilderness with the threat of encountering a feral hog.

On the drive to the canoe launch area, Philip waxed poetically on the beauty of Little Gull Island and ended his description by saying, "Of course, in any natural setting you have to be aware of the potential dangers."

I learned that Little Gull Island was home not just to feral hogs and their razor-sharp tusks, but also to cotton mouths and crocodiles.

"And this is why I live in Manhattan," I said. "We don't have nature. Or there's very little of it. Especially in Midtown where I spend most of my time."

"Manhattan? Really?"

I braced myself for the inevitable big city bashing, but Philip bucked expectations. "Manhattan is one of my favorite places."

"You've visited?"

"Many times. It's one of best places to find rare books, which I collect."

"You mentioned that. And, of course, I was in your shop. Ducking a rare book you tossed." I recalled the cot and old stove. It went along with his ancient car and worn clothes. Rare books must not be very lucrative, and yet, he had an old money air about him.

"I apologize for being less than courteous. I was reading a book that didn't agree with me." He steered his Volvo down a hill which led to a boat launching area.

"How long have you been collecting old books?"

"My grandfather introduced me to birding and rare book dealing when I was twelve, and I got hooked on both."

Philip stopped the car and came around to the passenger side. He opened the door for me, a move so rare that I couldn't recall the last time it happened.

"Please accept my hand so I can help you out."

"I can manage."

He ignored me and thrusted his hand in my direction. I grabbed it, and he smoothly assisted me out of the car.

"What is it you do in the city?" He loosened the bungie cords that were holding the canoe in place.

"Oddly, I'm in the bookselling business too."

"What a coincidence. New or rare?"

"New. I'm a literary agent."

The boat fell to the ground. "Did it break?" I said, almost hoping it had.

"It's fine," he said. "Did you say you were a—"

"Literary agent." I braced myself for his blowback. Some people put literary agents in the same seedy category as used car salespeople or ambulance-chasing lawyers.

To my surprise, Philip got dreamy-eyed. "I'm in awe."

"You are? Wait. Are you a writer?"

Wouldn't that be my luck? Trapped on a remote island with a writer intent on telling me every plot point of his tome.

"No, but I'm a lover of books, and you've devoted your life to them. How noble."

That was not a word I'd heard applied to my profession before. Perhaps Philip, like many people, didn't understand what agents did.

"Thank you. I enjoy my work. But the truth is, sometimes when people ask me about my occupation, I tell a fib."

"You do? Whatever for?" He retrieved two life jackets from his backseat and handed me one.

"Because so many people dream of being a writer or they know someone who wants to be one. And they want me to help them out, and it's awkward to politely decline."

When he saw I was struggling with the life jacket, he tied it for me. I almost said, "I'm a strong capable female who can tie my own life jacket." But honestly, it was a little tricky.

When Philip was done, he said, "I'm intrigued. What fib do you tell people?"

"That I work in hydraulics sales."

"What are hydraulics?"

"Exactly. Most people don't know, and they don't care. Sounds incredibly dull so they change the subject."

"Clever. By the way, I have a nephew who fancies himself as a writer."

Here it comes, I thought. The inevitable spiel about how talented his nephew was. How he was the exception to the rule. How Raymond Carver had nothing on him.

Philip laughed. "No need to look panicked."

"That's your imagination. I'm not the least bit panicked."

"You could have fooled me. Regardless, I can't imagine that Justin's writing would interest you. His book is faddish and frivolous." He swept an arm in the direction of the canoe. "Shall we?"

Philip picked up the canoe and put it over his head to tote it. I grabbed the picnic basket and paddles and followed him to the bank of the creek. The ground tilted slightly, making it easy to slide the canoe into the drink. It landed with a splash, causing rings in the water.

With Philip's assistance, I gingerly boarded. Philip pointed to Little Gull Island, an expanse of green with no sign of civilization. "As you can see, it's not far."

To my surprise, I liked being in a canoe. Philip's paddle sliced through the water as we meandered through creeks and marshes. Grasses swayed in the breeze, and swampy primordial smells rose from the waters. At one point, a fin appeared in the water.

"Shark," I whispered, my heartbeat sounding the alarm. Scenes from *Jaws* flashed in my mind. The canoe would offer no protection. Why had I agreed to this? I could see the headline now, "Shark Devours Literary Shark."

"What's that?' Philip asked.

"Shark," I repeated, feeling dizzy. The fin was getting closer.

"Not a shark," Philip said with a smile. There was a large splash nearby. Two dolphins were jumping in the air like happy children, their slick bodies arched, their snouts curved into smiles.

My fear fled, replaced with delight. "Did you see that. Did you?"

"Your first dolphin sighting?"

"It is!" I felt elated and wished I'd captured it on camera.

We landed the canoe on a seemingly deserted island that looked like an ideal place to film *Naked and Afraid*. Initially, I was a little wary. Every time I heard a rustling sound, my imagination went haywire, conjuring up everything from copperheads to cannibals. Philip, however, was clearly at ease on the island, pointing out birds like herons, plovers, and even a bald eagle.

He led me to his favorite spots on the island: several peaceful coves, a leafy strip of forest which he called a hammock, and a pretty section of marshland. Any of those places he showed me were suitable for a small gathering and ash scattering, but after we were done visiting every place on his map, I was still undecided.

Both of us were hungry so we opted to have our picnic on a lovely stretch of beach littered with sand dollars, shells, and driftwood. Bare trees looked stark against the cloudless sky. There was a sign that said, "Please leave this place as you found it," and previous visitors obviously took the message to heart because there was no sign of humans. All we could hear was the lapping of the waves and an occasional seagull cry.

Philip opened a wicker suitcase that revealed plates, cutlery, and drinking glasses, which I helped him spread out on our blanket. He handed me a cucumber sandwich wrapped in a cloth napkin.

"This is one of the fanciest picnics I've ever attended."

"My mother always says, 'Just because you're outdoors, doesn't mean you have to eat like a savage. She gave us the basket to mark our fifth wedding anniversary, the wood anniversary. It was also our last. We never had the chance to use it. Elizabeth died three days after our anniversary. But it seemed a shame to leave it to gather dust."

"You must miss her terribly."

Philip gazed in the direction of Gull Island which looked massive compared to Little Gull Island. A striped lighthouse, which I'd not seen before, rose up from the middle.

"It's been over three years, and sometimes it feels like only yesterday. Elizabeth knew me so well, she'd say 'bless you' before I sneezed and vice versa. And my brother, John, well, we weren't close because of our age difference and temperaments, but we were blood."

"I'm so sorry about your loss."

Philip had found a piece of driftwood and used it to make circles in the sand. "It changed everything about my life. My hair turned white overnight. And it also altered my relationship with books. I used to be in continual hunt mode, always hoping to find a black tulip."

"What's that?"

"A black tulip is rarest of rare books. Like a first edition of *The Tale of Peter Rabbit* by Beatrix Potter. Supposedly, there are only two-hundred and fifty copies in existence. But after Elizabeth died, I lost my taste for book chasing. For weeks, I had no idea how to spend my time, but then, one day, I picked up a first edition of *As I Lay Dying* by William Faulkner, and I did something highly uncharacteristic with it."

"What's that?"

"I read it. In the past, I'd searched for books, polished them, and displayed them. I also put out a quarterly magazine on rare book collecting, which I sold after my wife's death. But ironically, I rarely read books."

"Why?"

"I've always been more of a numbers person and enjoyed math in school. But now you'll hardly ever catch me without a book in my hand. At first, reading was a distraction. But the more I read, the more I realized that my emotional turmoil wasn't singular. Other people suffered just as profoundly. It was such a relief to know I wasn't alone."

I nodded, remembering how I felt after reading *The Catcher in the Rye*. At the time, I'd assumed I was the only person who felt disillusioned by the world. But Holden, the main character, challenged that theory.

"Grief is such a long process," Philip said. "And as you might have noticed, I'm currently stuck in the anger phase. Much preferable to despair, however, and books are helping me get through."

"I'm glad books have become such a comfort to you."

"I can't believe it took me so long to discover their magic," Philip said. "What is your favorite book?"

Galaxy, my father's book. But I didn't want to talk about that novel because then I'd have to mention that the author was my father. The older I got, the more I disliked standing in his shadow.

"*The Secret History,*" I said. "I used to read it every Christmas as a gift to myself."

"You're such a discerning reader. It must be magnificent."

A few years ago, I'd stopped reading it every Christmas because it was interfering with my work. It was hard to read debut submissions after reading a masterpiece like *The Secret History.* Also, it made me a little sad to read it, because it reminded me of a more innocent time in my reading life.

"Your enthusiasm for reading is infectious," I said, "but, as you mentioned earlier, there's one book you didn't care for." I made a throwing motion.

He dipped his head. "I'm embarrassed you witnessed my outburst. That book had a plot point I didn't like."

"Do tell?" I hadn't noticed what book it was.

"It's not important," he said quickly. "Would you care for another sandwich?"

"No, thank you." He aroused my curiosity. What novel would offend a guy like Philip? He seemed a little buttoned-up. Maybe he ran across some gratuitous sex. Or perhaps a dog died. Even though I didn't have a dog, I couldn't bear to read books that killed them off.

"How about dessert?"

"You have my attention," I said.

Dessert ended up being chocolate-covered pecans, and I got a tutorial on the pronunciation of pecans. Not pee-cans because, according to Philip, that's "what the gardener uses to relieve himself."

"Pih-cons," he said in his lovely Southern accent. It was so modulated, melodic and full of money, but clearly that money was long gone. He seemed to be living in a state of genteel poverty. How was he supporting himself if he spent all day reading?

We finished our lunch, and I glanced around the island, thinking what a lovely spot it was and yet, for some reason, I didn't want to spread my mom's ashes there.

When I told Philip it wasn't quite right, he said, "You've had those ashes for a while. Perhaps you're attached to them. You could always keep them. My mother displays my brother's ashes on the fireplace mantel in a tasteful vase."

I tried to imagine my mom's ashes lingering in my Manhattan apartment for years on end. They couldn't decorate a fireplace mantel because I didn't have one. Honestly, I didn't have anywhere to put her in my home, except the oven, which was too depressing for words.

"No. I have to do something very special with them." Once again, I glanced around at the barren beach. "It's too lonely here."

Like my mom's life, I thought.

She never married or even had a boyfriend that I knew of. She never had any more children and lived in Gull Island's most isolated cul-de-sac. She always said her career was the love of her life.

And yes, my career was also the most important thing in my life, but at least I was making waves. My mom, with her modest boutique literary agency, had barely made a blip.

It was as if the sign on the beach had been her motto: "Please leave this place as you found it." She came and went from this world with hardly a trace.

A tear slipped down my nose, and I roughly swatted it away. Philip was clearly an experienced griever because he presented me with a monogrammed handkerchief. But it was only one tear, hardly deserving of his fancy handkerchief.

"Sorry about that," I said.

"Apologizing for crying is like apologizing for breathing. It's a healthy bodily reaction."

"Did you cry a lot?"

He nodded. "I ordered handkerchiefs in bulk. And by the way, I've compiled a list of books with grief themes. I'd be happy to share it. There's Hemmingway's *A Moveable Feast,* Tolstoy's *The Death of Ivan Ilyich,* and Angelou's *I Know Why the Caged Bird Sings.*"

"Thank you, but no. I'm fine." Last thing I wanted to do was read about death.

"Are you? Because I also have a list of books with denial themes as well. I keep track of every book I've read, and I've categorized them by emotional themes."

"Thanks." Truthfully, the single tear I'd shed was because I felt sorry for my mom. I wished more for her.

"Anyway, I apologize for wasting your time with this trip," I said.

Philip started to pack up the provisions. "Going to Little Gull Island is never a waste. Ever since the tragedy, it's been a refuge for me." He rubbed his chin. "I wonder if there might be an appropriate place for your mother's ashes in Savannah?"

"Will we have to go by canoe?" I teased.

He laughed. "No. It's on dry land. Have you explored Savannah since you've been here?"

I shook my head.

"Then you must! It's the world's most magical city, and it's only a forty-five-minute drive."

"What makes Savannah so special?"

"I couldn't begin to explain. You'll have to see it for yourself."

"Strong hype," I said skeptically.

I was from New York City, after all, a metropolis that had everything. In Manhattan, you could get a mani-pedi at 3 a.m., take a nude yoga class and eat churrasco at La Caverna, a restaurant with stalactites hanging from the ceiling. All in the space of twenty-four hours. How could Savannah possibly compare? Still, it'd be fun to go with Philip. I'd enjoyed the excursion as well as the bookish conversation.

"If you can spare the time, I'd love to visit Savannah," I said.

"I have obligations for the next couple of days. Will Friday work for you?"

"Sounds good." A sudden breeze stole my straw hat, and Philip took after it.

"It's a date," he shouted as he gracefully sprinted to capture the hat. He picked it up and presented it to me, blushing once again. "To be precise, I didn't mean a romantic date."

"I know exactly what you meant, and I'm looking forward."

After returning to Philip's car, my phone buzzed with a text from Dani.

Gobsmacked. Call me!

I wrinkled my nose. Was she good gobsmacked or bad gobsmacked? Without any emojis, there was no way of telling. But I wasn't calling until I got back to my mom's cottage. I'd enjoyed my mini break from work, and besides, I was starting to dread Dani's texts.

Chapter Nine

The good news? Dani's novel made *The New York Times* bestselling list. The not-so-great news? She charted at fifteen, the very last spot, and it was likely due to the prepublication buzz that resulted in preorders.

What came next was more important. Would the book make a steady rise due to word of mouth and remain for a few weeks or—and this was wildly optimistic—join the ranks of those novels that remained on the list for months? Books like *Lessons in Chemistry* or *Where the Crawdads Sing*.

Or would it drop off the list next week, never to be heard from again? Sadly, the last option was the most likely.

As an editor, Dani knew how the system worked, and she'd been extremely pragmatic throughout the process, shrugging at glowing endorsements from important authors and barely reacting to multiple publications that dubbed her novel "most anticipated."

Even when she learned that the *Times* was going to feature her both in the style section and in the Sunday book review, she remained stoic.

"I'm an editor. The *Times* covers publishing, so it's not a big deal."

But making the list changed all that. Clear-eyed editor? Gone. A giddy, giggling author took her place. Now instead of sending me worried texts, Dani sent long rambling messages about how glad she was she'd made the leap to author, because this was clearly what she was meant to do.

Did I try to talk her down from this high? Nope. Like all highs, it was temporary, and I wanted her to savor it. Besides, how was I to know how the book would eventually be received? My fingers were crossed that she'd defy the odds.

In the meantime, I continued to check Publishers Marketplace, looking for Morris's deal with Quince, but it was never there. Was he waiting until September? Possibly, but Quince was such a hot property that even vacationing editors would put aside their Aperol Spritzes to check out the submission.

I also kept up my search for talent, but the dog days of summer were obviously making writers sluggish because I hadn't found anything remotely compelling since I'd been on Gull Island.

When I wasn't trolling for potential clients, I'd sit on the porch every day, staring at my blinking cursor, trying to write the eulogy. Sometimes, I'd force out a few sentences and let them cool on the page for a day. But the next morning, I'd read what I wrote and immediately delete every wooden word. The practice gave me a new respect for writers who faced the vast white space of a Word document daily.

After a half hour or so, I couldn't stand to sit at the computer for one more second, and that's when I went up to the attic and paged through my mom's books, seeing what she'd underlined. So often the lines she noted also resonated with me.

In Nicole Krauss's *The History of Love*, I came across this line which was underlined twice: "Once upon a time there was a boy who loved a girl, and her laughter was a question he wanted to spend his whole life answering."

She seemed to favor book lines about love. Again, my father came to mind, since, as far as I knew, he was the only romantic relationship in her life.

My mother deflected so many of my questions about their relationship, giving me only tidbits. Once, in a rare chatty moment, she said, "So much of what happened between us had to do with *Galaxy*, but when it was finished, so were we. There was nothing more to say."

When I was a teenager, I had this notion that my mother had written *Galaxy*, and I shared my theory with her. She adamantly denied it. "I pointed out weak spots," she said, "but I didn't write a word of that book."

By the time Friday came along, I was ready for a diversion and grateful to go to Savannah with Philip. On the drive over, he repeated his claim that the city had to be experienced to be believed. Turned out, he wasn't exaggerating.

It didn't matter where we went—the damp cobblestone streets of River Street, the shaded brick of Jones Street, or the patched ivy ground cover of Pulaski Square—the gorgeousness of the city pummeled us. I'd heard people say, "they were drunk with beauty," well, I was knee-walking, room-spinning sloshed with it.

Live oaks festooned with Spanish moss formed tunnels of green on nearly every street and lent an evocative romance to the entire city. A dumpster could look appealing under the drippy shade of those oaks.

But those trees shaded not just dumpsters, but some of the most beautiful buildings I'd ever seen. Savannah was a mishmash of architectural wonders, everything from the arches and domes of Romanesque revival to the turrets of the Second French Empire to the gabled roofs of the Italiante style.

Along with Savannah's beauty came a rich literary history, and Philip planned a tour around them. We walked in the charming historic district to see poet Conrad Aiken's childhood home. Aiken was a mentor to Emily Dickinson, but he himself was an extremely accomplished writer and was the first Georgian to ever win the Pulitzer.

We also toured the notorious Mercer House featured in *Midnight in the Garden of Good and Evil.*

"Or 'the book' as it's called in Savannah," Philip said. "If Savannah were a firefly, the author, John Berendt would be the jar. He completely captured the character of the city, and his book increased tourism to Savannah by forty percent. That's the power of an excellent story."

Flannery O'Connor's childhood home was also on the tour. It's where the author taught a chicken to walk backwards and read Grimm's Fairy Tales to her friends.

"Didn't I tell you Savannah was spectacular?" Philip said as we rested on a bench in Chippewa Square, a.k.a. Forest Gump Square after a long morning of touring.

"You did. But being a New Yorker, I was skeptical."

"Savannah has seduced plenty of Manhattanites. Untold New Yorkers came here during the pandemic and happily made it their home."

But does Savannah have naked yoga? I wanted to tease. But saying the word naked would most likely make the ever-so-proper Philip blush. I'd be surprised if he'd had ever used the word naked in his life. Likely, he'd say unclothed or in the buff.

A convertible hearse zoomed by. It was packed with laughing tourists.

"Ghost tour," Philip said. "Some say Savannah is the most haunted city in the United States. It certainly is for me. Memories of Elizabeth and John are embroidered into the city. There was a time I couldn't bear to come here."

"I hope this visit hasn't been painful for you."

"No. It's been highly enjoyable."

"Will you ever return here to live?"

"One day maybe," he said. "I miss the history and energy of Savannah, but after the tragedy, I wanted to be away from everyone, so I moved to Gull Island. Family and friends were worried I was becoming a hermit. To them, it was unnatural to crave so much solitude. But, as it turned out, time alone with my thoughts was exactly what I needed."

"Really?" I didn't care to be alone with my thoughts. They were terrible company, putting their dirty feet on the furniture and complaining endlessly about their host.

"Grief is a monster," Philip said. "But when you spend enough time alone with it, it loses some of its claws, and even gives you glimmers of wisdom. Have you read O'Connor's 'A Good Man is Hard to Find'?"

"In high school."

"Me too. I used to think it was nothing more than a creepy Southern gothic. But recently, I reread it, and it was a different experience. At the end of the story, when the cantankerous Grandmother is facing death, she has an epiphany about her shortcomings. The Misfit, who kills her, says, 'She would of been a good woman if there had been somebody there to shoot her every minute of her life.'"

I winced.

"Grief is like the Misfit's gun. It aims its ominous barrel at you every day as if to say, 'Life is brief. What do you want to be remembered for?'"

"And how would you answer that question?" I said, genuinely wanting to know.

Philip gave me a sad smile. "Not sure yet. But I'm always thinking about it. Mostly, I'd like to be a better man than I was before their deaths. There were times my behavior wasn't always admirable."

"Hard to believe."

He arched one eyebrow. "You'd be surprised."

"Any hints?"

"I'd rather not. I fear you would find my behavior deplorable."

I didn't know Philip well, but it was difficult to imagine him doing anything wrong, except maybe jaywalking or a parking violation, and those crimes were far from deplorable.

"What about you?" Philip asked. "What would you like your legacy to be?"

Easy. All of my life, I always wanted to make noise. Not a squeak, but a roar, and being the number one dealmaker in debuts would help me accomplish that.

Everyone in the industry would respect me, and even Meredith might be impressed. But that's not the self-serving answer I gave Philip. I said, "Continue to discover new voices."

"So admirable," Philip said. "To make a profound difference in the literature world."

I glanced away guiltily. Philip was making my job sound a lot more selfless than it really was.

After our busy morning, we were both starved. I told Philip I wanted to take him out to lunch as a thank you for all his help. "Absolutely not," he said. "It was my pleasure. I shall pick up the bill."

His tone was resolute, so I didn't argue. Instead, I planned to slip the server my credit card without Philip knowing.

For our lunch, Philip chose the Olde Pink House which was in an eighteenth-century Georgian mansion with sumptuous décor. Hand-painted frescoes and ornate framed portraits of historical figures graced the walls, and fireplaces were found in every one of the wood-planked dining rooms.

I ordered Southern sushi: shrimp and grits rolled in coconut nori. Philip took a long time with the menu. Was he trying to suss out the cheapest thing? Finally, he settled on shrimp and grits with collards.

We were tucking into our meals when a waiter with longish, wavy blonde hair stopped by our table. He resembled the epitome of a pretty boy pop star with long lashes and a full bottom lip.

"Uncle Phil?" he said.

"Justin," Philip said heartily. "What a fortunate surprise. If I'd known you'd be working today, I'd have asked to sit in your section."

"I wasn't supposed to be here, but I got called in." Justin's gaze flitted in my direction.

"Forgive me," Philip said, as if forgetting I was there. "This is Claire. A friend."

Justin smiled as if that was the best news he'd heard all day and extended his hand. "It's a pleasure to meet Uncle Philip's girlfriend."

Philip blushed furiously. "Claire's not my girlfriend," he sputtered. "I barely know her."

"He picked me up hitch hiking just five minutes ago," I said with a straight face.

Justin laughed, and that's when I saw the resemblance between him and his uncle. Same pale blue eyes, same strong jaw, same abundant hair. Looking at Justin made me realize how much Philip played down his good looks with his outdated glasses and fusty way of dressing.

"I'm showing Claire around Savannah," Philip said. 'She's never been before."

"Where are you from?" Justin asked.

"Manhattan."

Justin lit up. "One of my favorite places besides Savannah, and my girlfriend used to live there. What do you do in Manhattan?"

"She's in sales," Philip said before I could answer. "Hydraulics, to be precise."

What? Then I remembered. Justin must be the writer, and Philip was protecting me from him. Chivalrous but unnecessary. Philip had been so kind to me, the least I could do was to hear about his nephew's novel, as terribly ill-conceived as it might be.

"Hydraulics?" Justin said. "What kind? Pumps, cylinders, valves?"

I found myself tongue-tied. No one had asked me that before. Usually, any mention of hydraulics was a total conversation stopper.

"All of the above," Philip said. "But Claire's on holiday and would rather not talk shop."

"Sorry," Justin said. "I'm kind of a gadget guy, and it sounds like an interesting job."

"Beyond interesting," I said, trying not to laugh. "People are always peppering me with questions about my work."

Justin had to see to his tables, and once he was gone, I said, "Who knew anyone would be interested in hydraulics?"

Philip smiled. "That's Justin. Mr. Curiosity we used to call him as a child. Intrigued about everything."

"He's the writer?"

"Yes, indeed. He's also my brother John's child. John was fifty-three when he died. I was the *oops* child who came a couple of decades later."

"How's Justin coping with his dad's death?"

"With difficulty. I'm trying to fill in the gap best as I can."

"He's so handsome." *Like you,* I thought. "And honestly, I'd be happy to hear about his book."

Philip cut a jumbo shrimp in half. "No, you wouldn't. As I said, he's told me about it, and it sounds faddish and frivolous. His father was a poet who published several chapbooks. John would have been appalled."

"Is his novel that bad? Now I'm curious."

"I've not read it, but the premise of the book is all flash, no substance. Justin's convinced there's a market for it. As if that's the primary reason to write a book." Philip chortled at the absurdity.

I chased the last bit of rice around my plate and said, "I'll let you in on a little secret. Marketability is not the worst reason to write a book. Publishers, and agents all have to eat."

"And authors too."

"Authors what?"

"Have to eat."

"Sure they do," I said, feeling my cheeks heat up.

"And yes I realize that publishing is business, buy Justin has only been writing for a year or two, which means he's hardly mastered his craft. He needs to let his abilities slowly grow and unfold. I tell him, 'Redwoods don't soar to the heavens overnight.' But he's impatient. Wants to make his mark on the world quickly. Hard to blame him. I had the same desire at his age."

And I'm still obsessed with that desire.

"Pitch it to me," I said without thinking.

"What?"

"I mean, tell me what Justin's book is about."

"It's almost embarrassing to say."

"You're among friends."

Philip took a sip of water as if gearing up for the tale. "Last summer, Justin was a gopher for these two women—I can't remember their names—but they came to Savannah to film several episodes of a television show about renovating homes. Long story short, he wrote a book about his dramatic dealings with them. One kept making passes at him, and the pair were always squabbling. It sounds like a soap opera."

I kept my expression neutral even though I found myself getting more intrigued by the second. "What are the names of the women?"

"They had alliterative names. Cathy and Katy? No. Mary and Molly? No. Ummm—"

"Lila and Lola?"

"That's it. You're familiar?"

I dabbed my lips with a napkin to disguise my expression of delight. "I might have heard of them."

In fact, *Lila and Lola* was one of the few shows I watched. And I wasn't alone. The entire country was obsessed with the pair, who were the female version of the *Property Brothers*.

"I've never heard of them," Philip said. "But supposedly they're enjoying their fifteen minutes of fame."

I couldn't believe my luck. It was as if someone had dumped hundreds of rubies on my lap and said, "All yours, Claire."

Who cared about Quince? Justin's novel, if it was halfway decent, could easily make me the number one debut dealmaker. It had everything: a photogenic and personable author, dishy subject matter, and a great pitch. It was *The Devil Wears Prada* in the real estate world. Also, there were two villains, which meant twice the fun.

"Has he talked with any literary agents?" I was trying to hide my eagerness.

"No. I've discouraged him, and so far, he's listened. But frankly, I don't know if his patience will last. Justin loves his uncle, but he's also headstrong."

And there was my dilemma. Philip obviously didn't approve, but a deal like this was too lucrative to pass up. Someone was going to rep Justin. Might as well be me.

"Will you excuse me? I need to use the powder room."

I left the table and kept my eyes out for Justin. While looking for him, I spotted our waiter and told him I wanted to pay the bill.

"There won't be a bill. Justin is taking care of it."

Had Justin paid because he knew how much Philip was struggling?

"Have you seen Justin?" I asked.

The waiter pointed to a charming bar where I found Justin picking up an order of gimlets.

"Well, hello again," he said.

I glanced over my shoulder, looking for any sign of Philip. "Let me make this quick. Your uncle lied to you. I don't sell hydraulics. I don't even know what hydraulics are, nor do I care to learn. I'm a literary agent."

He smiled. "Wow. That's even more interesting than hydraulics."

"Your uncle told me about your project, and I'd like to see the manuscript. Is that possible?"

Justin was so surprised he nearly capsized his drink tray. "Are you kidding? I'd love that. Except, well...My uncle thinks—"

"Never mind that. He doesn't know publishing like I do." I handed him one of my cards. "Email the manuscript to me when you get off work."

"Will do."

I felt a twinge of guilt for going behind Philip's back. He'd been kind to me, and we meshed well together. But it was obvious that Justin was jonesing for a book deal, and, if his writing was passable, I was just the person who could give it to him.

Chapter Ten

After my trip to Savannah, I danced to techno music to rid myself of the extra energy I'd picked up after hearing about Justin's book.

Number one, number one, number one.

It might actually happen. Numerous moving parts would have to fall into place, but I felt a familiar twinge of expectation in my belly. Some people's knees predicted rain, but my solar plexus often sensed impending seven-figure deals.

Once I was calmer, I went back to the attic. I remembered seeing *Midnight in the Garden of Good and Evil* on my mother's bookshelf, and I wanted to check it out. She'd underlined passages on almost every page of the book, and I could see why. The prose was as rich and atmospheric as the city it was set in.

I came across a section about aristocrats and their lack of ambition. The author wrote: "It's only the trappings of aristocracy I find worthwhile... the very things they have to sell when the money runs out. And it always does. Then all they're left with is their lovely manners."

Philip to a tee, I thought. He did seem to lack ambition, reading all day in a dimly-lit store that also served as his living quarters. *But he's grieving*, I reminded myself. Yet, it had been over three years since the car accident. How was he supporting himself? Selling off the occasional rare book? He'd hinted at a shady past. Had he done something that prevented him from being gainfully employed?

Nah, not Philip, I thought. Too sweet.

My phone beeped.

Don't forget. Book Club tonight. See you at 5.

The message was from Bea. Had it only been a week since the last one? Time seemed to move much slower at the beach. Anyway, I couldn't wait to hear what the ladies thought of Dani's novel.

***

I opened the front door and a lovely breeze, tinged with salt, seaweed, and coconut greeted me along with Bea. We walked to book club, and I felt light and carefree in my airy summer clothes, letting the wind have its way with my hair and skirt.

When we arrived at Vera's cottage, the Krusty Krab, she opened the door wearing a gas mask.

"What's wrong?" I said, feeling alarmed. "Is there some kind of leak or pollution issue?"

Bea put a steadying hand on my arm and whispered, "Remember. It's all in good fun."

"Bad Moon on the Rise" was playing. The women were drinking red cocktails.

"Stormy Weathers," Bea said. "Try one. They're yummy."

A couple of women had clothespins attached to the bridge of their glasses. For a minute, I was flummoxed, but when I saw a member drop a copy of Dani's book into a canister hand-labeled "hazardous material," I finally got it.

They thought Dani's book stunk.

Fine. They weren't the target readers obviously. No big deal. I could handle this.

"Where to begin with this one?" Vera said, shaking her head as the discussion began.

"How about the metaphors?" said one of the members.

A collective groan filled the room.

"They had the precision of a drunk dog peeing on a grand piano," Vera said.

A woman raised her hand. Her kind blue eyes, pink cheeks, and fluffy white hair reminded me of Mrs. Claus. Hopefully, she was going to buck the negative trend with gushing praise.

"Yes, Penny?" Vera said.

"Generally, I'm on board for a book that mocks hyper intellectualism, but this one came across as didactic to the extreme," Penny said.

What does that even mean?

And on the criticism went: ridiculous dialogue, unlikable characters, plodding storyline.

Bea, likely out of kindness, held back, but everyone else delighted in the evisceration.

"We've talked about the negatives," Bea finally said. "What about the positives?"

"It was inventive," Fawn said. I remembered her from the last meeting, and she seemed to be the nicest one in the club. "So clever to start chapters with a syllabus and to capture how pretentious academic writing can be."

"And the author is photogenic," Penny offered.

"But ultimately it failed," Vera said with her overly loud voice. "The writer was more concerned with being clever than intriguing the reader."

Everyone nodded in agreement.

"Thanks for the great book suggestion, Claire," Vera said.

Was she being sarcastic?

"I thought you hated it," I said.

"With every fiber of my being," Vera said. "But as everyone knows, the stinkers are sometimes more fun to discuss than the winners. Hope your feelings aren't hurt too terribly."

"Not at all," I fibbed.

Fawn pointed at me. "I don't think her feelings are hurt one smidge. This was a test, wasn't it, Claire?"

I cast a worried glance in Bea's direction, and she gave a slight shrug of her shoulders.

"The book seems like it would be a wonderful read," Fawn continued. "Fancy endorsements from famous authors and a beautiful cover. It's my guess that Claire thought we'd be fooled into thinking the emperor's wearing clothes. Did we pass your test?"

I forced a smile on my face. "With flying colors."

"The author truly is a lovely young woman," Bea said, gazing at the cover.

"Who wrote a boring and confusing book," Vera said. "Likely she'll never see publication again."

Don't say that.

I knew Dani considered this to be the beginning of her career as a writer, not the end. There was so much at stake. After all the buzz her book got, it would be extremely difficult for her to go back to being an editor without feeling like a laughingstock.

The meeting eventually petered out, and I couldn't wait to leave. Walking home, the air was sticky and still, as if the ocean breezes were taking a dinner break. My feeling of lightness was over; I felt like I was slogging through a sauna. Bea asked, "Are you upset?"

Not just upset. I was devastated for Dani.

"I hope they're wrong. The novel just debuted on *The New York Times* bestseller list this week. It has to do well."

"Well, if it made the list, that's encouraging."

"It's good news, but that doesn't mean the publisher has a hit on its hands. Some books only sell a few thousand preorder copies and make the list. Dani's sales need to be insanely strong."

Bea had not weighed in on the book, which said as much about her opinion of it as the ladies' vocal bashing.

"Did you love the book, Claire?" Bea's voice was so soft it could barely be heard over the cicadas who were beginning their nightly concert.

"Of course!" I said, perhaps a bit too forcefully. It was so humid my shirt was clinging to me. I pulled it away from my body to let in a little air.

"I know you specialize in debut authors, Claire, and I'm sure it's exciting to discover new voices, but a novel is an extremely complicated piece of work. It takes years to master the art of it, and it rarely happens on a writer's first try. Naturals are few and far between. I don't know of any."

"What about my dad?" The sun was beginning its technicolor dive into the sea, leaving splashes of pink and yellow in its wake. Even while agitated, I appreciated the beauty.

"Maybe your dad is one of those few rare naturals, but he still had plenty of help from Glenda. So, yes, debut writers who have tireless advocates like your mom can sometimes produce a wonderful novel, but have you ever wondered if he could have written it without her?"

"So many times." Particularly since he'd never written a follow-up.

"Glenda once told me she felt like she ruined your father by making him too dependent on her. When she started agenting, she was determined to avoid making that mistake again."

"But I thought she was a nurturing agent."

"Glenda was always supportive, but her whole agency philosophy was about empowering her clients."

"Empowering?" I scratched a mosquito welt on my arm. "How so?"

"I have a letter she wrote me that will show you exactly what it means. I'll dig it out and share it with you."

"Thanks."

"And fingers crossed for the success of Dani's book. There were many witty passages."

We arrived at Bea's cottage, and I was glad because I didn't want to talk about Dani and her book anymore.

"See you tomorrow?" Bea asked.

"The usual time." After Bea finished her writing day, she and I usually had a happy hour on her porch together.

When I got home, I locked the door behind me. The evening was disappointing, and when it was time to tell Dani about the book club's reaction, I was going to have to lie.

It would be one of several lies I'd told her since she'd become my client. I lied to her about the Gull Island bookstore stocking her book, and I lied and told her that people were reading her book on the beach. But that wasn't the biggest lie of all.

I trotted up to the attic and sought out the last photo of my mother and me in a Chelsea restaurant, taken just before the pandemic. We didn't resemble each other much. I looked like the stylish uber-agent I was becoming, and my mom looked like an older version of me before I became a success. Her hair was curly and brown, and she didn't bother to cover up her freckles with foundation.

Meredith always described my mom as frumpy, but it wasn't a fair description. In the photo, my mom looked pretty with luminous skin and large inquisitive eyes beneath the lenses of her glasses. The waiter who took our photo flirted with her.

"Mom, I did a crap thing," I said to the photo.

In my head, I imagined her saying, *I'm sure it's not as bad as you think, Claire.*

"Yes it is. Here's the ugly truth: I never read Dani's entire book. I stopped about fifty pages in and skipped to the ending."

Was I the only agent who'd ever done that? Not at all. Early in my career, I read an interview with a famous agent who said, "If the first fifty pages work, you can sell it."

I always remembered that advice, and it's how I approached manuscripts. It was a strategy that worked for me. If the author and the pitch were appealing enough, and the first fifty pages held up, that's all you needed.

Besides, it wasn't just agents who didn't read every page. In auction situations, it simply wasn't possible that all the editors involved had time to set aside their responsibilities and read a novel that they might not even acquire.

But Dani was more than a client, she was also my friend, and she'd been concerned about the flow of the novel. Particularly she wanted to avoid the saggy middle. I shouldn't have lied to her and told her I'd read every page. I'd done it because I knew I could get her a great deal regardless of the middle.

"I bet you always read your clients' books, cover to cover," I said to my mom's photograph.

Whether or not Dani would still love me if her book tanked was questionable. Right now, I was still a miracle worker, but that could change at any time. One day, she might turn into a Wendy, just not quite as crazy.

"Please let her book do well," I whispered. I didn't want to lose the best friend I ever had.

And maybe the book club was wrong. This was an unsophisticated beach town, after all, and they were older women. Maybe Dani's book would appeal to a different type of reader.

Like Hazel.

When I brokered deals, I always thought about a young woman I'd once seen in the Strand Bookstore back home. She had tangled red hair and wore unlaced Doc Martens. Her skin was milky white save for an Edgar Allan Poe tattoo on her forearm, and she stood over the new releases table, reading one of the first books I'd ever sold.

I didn't know her name, but I dubbed her Hazel and invented details about her: Hazel had an English lit degree and worked in a hipster coffee shop in the East Village—one with chipped mugs and threadbare oriental rugs.

She had a love-hate relationship with Sally Rooney, wrote maudlin poetry, but first and foremost, she was a reader. Books were everywhere in her studio apartment, towering on the non-functional radiator, tucked under the single bed, piled beside the rusted claw tub.

Hazel devoured the kind of books my clients wrote. She'd read about the book deal in the *Times* or *Book Riot,* and for months, she'd be anxiously waiting for the book to come out.

When pub day finally came, she'd go to the Strand, the very bookstore where I first spotted her. Outside, the store's red awning boasted, "16 miles of books," yet Hazel only wanted one. Once inside, she'd scan the tables until she spotted it.

After scooping it up, she couldn't wait to take it home to her apartment in some transitional neighborhood like Bushwick or Throgs Neck. As soon as she arrived, she'd crack the spine and take a long, luxurious whiff of the pages. Finally, she'd read the first line, which was like the lobby of a five-star hotel, shimmering with the promise of more riches inside.

And even if Hazel didn't love the book, it wasn't a total loss for her, because it wasn't just the reading experience she was paying for. Instead, it was the months of anticipation leading up to the purchase and the possibility of being one of the first to discover a promising new author.

Just thinking about Hazel made me feel better. I'd bet a bottle of Don Julio tequila that she'd fallen in love with Dani's book, and she wouldn't be the only one. There were thousands of Hazels out there who lived in hip, urban areas, not sleepy beach towns, and they, hopefully, would make Dani's book a success.

Chapter Eleven

Justin's book arrived in my inbox, and it didn't disappoint. The first couple of chapters were filled with hysterical inside details about a lifestyle couple who pushed a just-folks brand to the public but were total jerks in private. As a bonus, the writing was even better than what was required for a book like this. Justin was no Donna Tartt, but he could turn a phrase.

As soon as I finished reading, I called and asked to meet him in person. Justin sounded enthusiastic on the phone, but there was also some tentativeness in his voice. Whatever reservations he might have, I would make them disappear.

"I'll have some HVAC repairmen working at my house all day," he said when I suggested getting coffee. "Would you mind coming here?"

Would I mind? I'd travel anywhere if it meant I could sign him.

For over a week, I'd been schlepping around in beach clothes, but the next morning I transformed myself back into the Pitch Queen. I contoured my cheeks to give them the illusion of sharper bones, and I painted my lips their customary power red. I tamed my hair with a flat iron, shimmied into my pencil skirt, and slipped into my pumps.

Bea had been maintaining my mom's powder blue VW bug, so I was able to drive it to Savannah. I'd expected Justin to live in some humble, young person abode, but Google Maps delivered me to a grand house on Gaston Street. Wrong address? Nope. An HVAC repair van was parked outside.

Surely, Justin didn't own this majestic, three-story masonry beauty with three triple piazzas and etched glass windows. A plaque outside said the house had been built in 1852. Maybe Justin lived in a carriage house or rented one of the rooms.

I rang the bell, which filled the air with impressive *gongs* and *bongs*. The door swung open, and there stood Justin, even more handsome than I remembered. Today, he wore horn-rimmed glasses like Philip, lending a serious note to his poster-boy appeal. His impressive mane of wheat-colored hair picked up the sunlight, and the doorway framed his lanky limbs.

Instagram eye candy, I thought.

I threw back my shoulders, lifted my chin, and turned up my literary agent wattage. "Are you ready to be a star?"

Justin blinked and his lips parted, looking both stunned and intrigued by my question. He said, "Well, I don't know about that."

"I do," I said with the confidence of someone who had the full force of dozens of successful pitches beneath my wings.

I expected Justin to lead me to some lowly servant room, but instead he showed me to the parlor with swoopy, royal-blue curtains, ornate mirrors, and formal furniture that looked like it had escaped from Buckingham Palace. A crystal pitcher of iced tea, watercress sandwiches and sugar cookies awaited us.

"Did you prepare this?"

He nodded. "I had good home training."

"Impressive pile of bricks you have here." Especially for a person who worked as a waiter.

"Thanks, but it's not mine. I'm house sitting."

"Cushy work," I said. "But I think your house sitting days are over. Are you ready to get a book deal?"

"It makes me shiver just thinking about it."

"Good," I said as we perched on a pair of spindly chairs. "Because I'm in the shiver business. Let's talk about the wonderful future in store for you, starting with film rights. Who do you see playing the two lead characters?"

He covered his face with his hands, as if embarrassed. "I've never thought about it."

"Liar," I said with a smile. "Everyone who writes a book thinks about the movie casting. You're not an exception."

"Okay. I have thought about it a little." Justin, like his uncle, was an easy blusher. Right now, he looked as if he'd been sitting in front of a fireplace for hours or tippling on whiskey. "How about Jennifer Lawrence and Emma Stone?"

"Perfect! I'll get in touch with both."

He laughed.

"You think I'm joking? I work with an amazing film agent who will pass the book onto them. With the juicy characters you've created, I wouldn't be surprised if both want in."

He pushed his long bangs out of his face, a winning gesture. "This is so... heady."

"We're just getting started."

I launched into my spin, painting a future that would make an author swoon: *The New York Times* style section feature, morning show appearances, Reese's Book Club, and more. Everything I said was in the realm of possibility. Justin had written a book that would create geysers of excitement.

And yet, the more I talked, the more distracted he became, shaking his leg and nibbling his lip. Was I saying the wrong things?

"I feel like I've landed in the metaverse," Justin said.

"But in your case, everything is real."

So why aren't you smiling?

Justin kept stirring his iced tea and staring into his glass instead of meeting my eye.

"Something's bugging you. Whatever it is. I'll fix it."

"Well, you praised a lot of things about the book, but you haven't said anything about the writing quality."

Yikes. How could I have forgotten? Authors always wanted to be praised for their writing, even though it was sometimes the least important thing when it came to sales. For instance, few people have praised the prose of *Fifty Shades of Grey,* but that didn't get in the way of its mega success.

"Forgive me. That was a grave omission! Your writing is sharp, wickedly funny, and most of all… what's the description I'm searching for?"

Masterful was laying it on too thick. Singular was too vague…

"Your book is a new and original voice for the ages," I said.

Justin smiled. "My dad was a poet, and he died a few years ago, and good writing was important to him. He's not around anymore. But I'd like to imagine he'd be proud."

Honestly, who could define good writing? Flowery prose overwhelmed some. Others disliked spare writing. Justin's writing was several notches above serviceable. Would it have passed the dad test? Good poets typically chose words as carefully as a Michelin chef chooses heirloom tomatoes, so maybe not. But who could really say?

"Obviously I can't speak for you dad, but I feel certain he'd be happy."

Justin, once again, revealed his spotlight-bright smile. I must have said the right thing. "I guess you're offering to be my agent."

Offering? I'm begging. I'm drooling. I'm holding a cardboard sign that says, "Will work for your signature." But it didn't pay off to come across as needy.

"I'd be elated to be your agent."

"What about revisions?"

"I'll let an editor worry about that, but it's in great shape."

Not that I'd read the whole thing, but I didn't need to. Now that I had Bamber, she could read it and prepare a report. The first two chapters were solid, the concept was killer, and the author was swoony handsome. That reminded me. I needed to ask Justin for a photo to send out with the pitch.

"I can't believe this. Uncle Philip hated the idea of the book. He thinks it's too cheesy and commercial."

And that's what I love about it.

Still, my stomach dropped slightly. Philip's disapproval was the only downside in what was probably going to be the biggest deal of my life.

"Commercial is not a dirty word. It just means that lots of people are going to read it. What's wrong with that?"

Justin propped his chin on the palm of his hand. "When I told Uncle Phil it would probably appeal to a lot of people, he said, 'So did pet rocks. But what value did they bring to the world?'"

"What about amusement? Isn't that a value?"

"Not to Uncle Phil. He takes a dim view of anything that's popular."

"Maybe he hasn't considered the bigger themes of your book, like powerful people taking advantage of others. Or the discrepancies between public and personal identity. Those are fascinating issues that make people think."

"I hadn't considered that." Justin widened his innocent blue eyes, and he stroked a sculpted cheek that still carried the perfect touch of baby fat. The kid was going to break every female heart on BookTok.

"Because that's my job not yours."

He took off his glasses and twirled one of the arms. "So, you don't think my book will be faddish?"

Considering it was based on interactions with reality stars, the answer was *hell, yes* but being honest was no way to win clients.

"It's impossible to say how a novel will be received. Some books might seem faddish, but if the themes are universal, the novel tends to have staying power."

Justin still didn't look convinced. "Can you give me an example?"

"Well, there's uh... *Galaxy*." The title shot out of my mouth before I could stop it.

"*Galaxy*?" Justin reared back in his chair as if I'd heaved a medicine ball his way. "Are you saying my book's comparable?"

Not at all. *Galaxy* expertly teased out themes of alienation and the meaning of love. It was the work of an author with incredible natural talent, and its prose put the reader under a seductive spell. Justin's prose, on the other hand, was much clumsier, like a teenager who fumbles with a bra clasp.

But who cared? I compared debut novels with great novels all the time. I'd just never used my father's novel before. Even though it made me feel slightly dirty, I was also caught up in the chase.

"Your book and *Galaxy* both use colloquial language. They're both coming-of-age stories. They both capture a specific moment in time."

That was it for the most part. Other than those similarities, *Galaxy* and Justin's novel were as different as Picasso and a paint-by-number work.

Justin let out a low whistle. "I was assigned to read *Galaxy* in school but only read the SparkNotes. Remind me what it's about?"

"It's the unlikely love story between two teenagers who meet in a physical rehab center. Dawn is a popular cheerleader who is learning to walk after a car accident, and Mark, an awkward foster kid, works at the center doing janitorial work."

"Why is it called *Galaxy*?"

"Because they live in two different worlds, but throughout the novel, Mark always claims he's literally from a different galaxy."

"An alien?"

"Yes. Although, of course, no one believes him. Yet it's ambiguous. Maybe he is. At the end, he disappears, and so does she."

"Has it been made into a movie?"

"Not yet." Meredith felt it would ruin the novel's legacy to turn it into a film. "Anyway, I'll use the *Galaxy* comparison when I pitch to editors."

Justin's forehead crinkled with doubt. "Isn't that going too far? I mean... *Galaxy*. That's a big deal. You might as well compare my book to *Catcher in the Rye*. No one will believe you."

"Oh, yes, they will."

"What makes you think so?"

"Because I'm the daughter of the author."

"What?" The word sounded like the yowl of a cat. "Does Uncle Phil know that?"

"He doesn't, and there's no need to tell him right now. In fact, I'd rather you didn't mention our business relationship to him until I sell your book."

By that time, I'd be long gone from Gull Island, and Philip, much as I liked him, would be a pleasant but distant memory.

"*Galaxy*," Justin said, his face filled with wonder.

Now that he was punch drunk with my praise, it was time to seal the deal. "I'd like to send my agent/client agreement out today."

"Sounds good to me."

Great. Everything I dreamed of was finally coming true. I imagined myself wearing one of those foam hands and shouting into Morris's face: "I'm number one! I'm number one!"

Childish? Yes. But also exhilarating.

"I'm going to contact editors right away."

Philip wouldn't be happy with this news. But maybe a million-dollar deal might make him think twice about the value of Justin's book, considering money was scarce in the family. At least that's what I was counting on.

Chapter Twelve

Great news was meant to be shared, but not with Bea, and certainly not after the book club disaster. I was afraid she'd ask me too many questions about the nature of Justin's deal.

It was hard for an established author like Bea to understand that debut authors were different animals. Likely, there were crumbs of resentment. When you're a seasoned pro, it can't be fun to watch a greenhorn command large sums of money that took you years to achieve.

As soon as I left Justin, I went back to the cottage, shucked off my pinchy shoes and pencil skirt, and changed into shorts and a t-shirt that said, "The lower the latitude, the better my attitude."

Then I fetched myself a generous pour of pinot grigio, ordered Alexa to play Jimmy Buffett, and called Bamber, who was appropriately thrilled for me.

"You are within a hairbreadth's distance of being the number one dealmaker in debuts," she said.

"Looks that way." I still wondered what had happened with Morris and Quince, but that deal could pop up at any moment. That's why it was important to get a contract for Justin's book ASAP.

"I wonder what they'll call you after you make number one," Bamber said. "The Pitch Goddess?"

I laughed, lapping up her enthusiasm like it was my favorite lavender latte, which I hadn't enjoyed since I'd been on Gull Island.

"There's just one little wrinkle." I told her about Philip. Mostly because I wanted Bamber to soothe my guilt, and she didn't disappoint.

"Who cares what he thinks? He's nobody to you, right?"

"Well, I wouldn't say *that*. He's been sweet to me."

"Million-dollar-deal sweet? Number-one-in-debut sweet?"

"Bamber? Who knew you had such a Machiavellian side?" I was amused but also a little shocked.

She let out a cackle. "I'm just putting things in perspective... Oh wait. Is there something going on between the two of you?"

"Absolutely not. I'm too busy for a boyfriend, and he's still mourning his late wife. Not to mention he's geographically undesirable. In other words, there's no way that he and I... Well, you have it wrong."

There was a long pause.

"Bamber?"

"You're protesting a lot. Does that mean you like him?"

"As I said, he's nice, but we're so different and... Okay. Maybe I like him a little."

Saying it aloud made me realize it was true. It was so easy to be around Philip, and I loved our discussions. They went far beyond small talk. Yes, Philip could be fusty, musty, and more old-fashioned than a rotary phone, but his wise view on life stirred a longing in me. I couldn't put my finger on it exactly.

"But surely you don't like him enough to blow this deal," Bamber said.

I went back to the fridge and topped off my wine. "Hey, there's few people I like that much. And besides, I'm not doing anything wrong. Yes, maybe I did go behind Philip's back, but it's just business. He doesn't understand books like Justin's. He's an antiquarian book dealer and reads all these classics. He's worried Justin's book will be a flash-in-the pan."

The more I talked, the more uncomfortable I felt. Philip's opinion did actually matter to me… a lot. He was a guy who'd been dealt a deck of jokers and survived, and suddenly, I felt protective over him.

"In the book world, how long is a flash-in-the-pan?" Bamber asked. "A year?"

I laughed. "I wish."

"Six months?"

"Try six weeks. I don't mean it'll go out of print by then. With ebooks, that doesn't happen anymore. But six weeks is when sales will fall off. It'll probably make the list. Maybe at number ten. If we're lucky, it'll hover there for a couple weeks and then it will drop off completely. After that, it's done."

"Sobering." Bamber's voice lost some of its bravado. "Considering most authors take years to write their novels."

"We live in a disposable society, and books aren't immune. But you can't tell a writer that because—"

"They can't handle it," Bamber said, finishing my sentence.

"You're a quick study. And Justin, of course, will be paid handsomely for the time he spent on the book."

"Exactly. Who can complain about a million dollars?"

Plenty of authors. They were thrilled at first, but after publication, so many felt let down. Which reminded me.

"Anything going on with Wendy?" I pushed open the kitchen windows to let in the sea air.

Bamber paused. "The usual drama. But I'm handling it."

"She's not a client; she shouldn't be calling the office." I felt bad about Wendy and was tempted to ask for details, but no… I'd just get upset. "Thanks for doing a great job. I appreciate it."

"My pleasure. Anything for the Pitch Goddess."

"Enough," I said, not really meaning it. "I'm going to send you Justin's book, and I need you to read it immediately and write a report. Weaknesses, strengths etc. There's a document in the cloud that'll help you."

"Can't wait," Bamber said. "I'm going to read my first seven-figure book. I have the best job in the world."

The second-best job, I thought. I couldn't imagine any job more thrilling than mine.

***

As the afternoon bled into the evening, I started to feel increasingly worse about going behind Philip's back until I couldn't take it anymore. I went out on the porch in my bare feet—a new habit I was enjoying—and called him to fess up.

"I was just about to contact you," he said before I had a chance to speak. "I've thought of a wonderful final resting spot for your mother. Bonaventure. It's a famous cemetery. Johnny Mercer, Conrad Aiken, and Noble Jones are all buried there."

"Cemetery?" I said, sitting on one of the Adirondack chairs and putting my feet up on the other. "I don't think so."

"It's not your typical cemetery. It's located on the bluff of the Wilmington River with plenty of picturesque places to scatter ashes. You can see ships going by. I'd be happy to take you there. The weather tomorrow is supposed to be delightful. A cool front's coming in."

Delightful? What man his age talked like that? Only one that I knew of, and frankly, I was feeling charmed.

"You're so kind to be thinking of me, and I'd like to go tomorrow, but..." I sighed. "In the interest of honesty, there's something I need to tell you. It's about your nephew."

He chuckled softly. "I already know. Justin called me right after you left him."

So why do you sound amused, I thought. It was the last reaction I expected.

"Justin told you? I asked him not to."

"He couldn't help himself, and frankly, I'm thrilled for him."

"But I went behind your back. That's why I called. To ask forgiveness."

"Thank God you pursued the project. I feel terrible that I was dismissive of Justin's work. Clearly, it has a great deal of literary merit if a discerning agent like yourself wants to represent it."

"Excuse me?"

"Justin's girlfriend, who is also a writer, did some research and apparently, you're one of the top agents in New York City. I'm told your agency represents Pulitzer and Nobel Prize winners."

."Hold up. That's not me. My boss Kippy represents those authors."

"You're young. In time, you'll have your own prize winners."

Not likely. My business model was completely different than Kippy's.

"Maybe even Justin will win a literary prize," Philip said.

Had Justin told Philip about my *Galaxy* comparison? Probably. He'd spilled everything else. "To be honest, debut authors rarely win Pulitzers or Nobel prizes."

"Sorry! I'm getting carried away. I'm simply bursting with pride. The death of his father has been hard on Justin, and your interest in his book has been such a confidence booster. Thank you so much. You, Claire Wyld, are a true person of the book."

"Sweet of you to say," I said. "But I'm not sure I deserve—"

"You're entirely too modest. I can't wait to read his novel. I clearly underestimated it."

"Don't read it now," I said quickly. "Wait until it's been edited."

"Of course. Although, it's tempting to cheat and take a peek. Anyway, about Bonaventure—"

"I would love to go. It'll be my last day in Georgia." That made me unexpectedly sad, even though I was eventually coming back to sell the cottage and hold the memorial service. "The day after tomorrow, I'm leaving for the city to sell Justin's book."

After our call ended, I stayed out on the porch to watch the sunset, another new habit I enjoyed. Did coastal people ever tire of these nightly shows? I could imagine Bea saying, "Told ya you'd like Gull Island."

Maybe I did but only in small doses. Soon I'd be more than happy to go back to Manhattan and forget all about Instagram-worthy sunrises, barefoot living, and breezy porches. But I had to admit my time on Gull Island gave me a much-needed pause. One I hadn't realized I'd needed.

***

The next morning, my mother's porch floorboards creaked at five minutes to nine. I figured it was Philip, but he didn't ring the bell. Was it just the house settling? Five minutes later, the bell made its *bing bong* sound, and I opened the door to see Philip.

"How long have you been on the porch?"

"Exactly five minutes." Philip was garbed in his usual uniform of threadbare seersucker suit, bow tie, and khakis. The bowtie color always varied. Today's hue was marigold yellow.

"I thought so. Why didn't you ring the bell?"

"Because being early can sometimes be as annoying as being late. I make it a point to be exactly on time."

I laughed. "I thought I was the only one that did that. Punctuality is practically a religion for me."

Philip smiled and offered his arm. "Shall we?"

"Gotta admit it, I'm getting used to this Southern gentleman jazz."

"I'm happy you appreciate it. Elizabeth sometimes thought it was too contrived. I recall her saying, 'Just once, I'd like you to belch without saying excuse me. It's like you're not human.'"

That was the first time he'd ever said anything less than glowing about his wife. Philip shook his head as if realizing what had come out of his mouth. "Of course, when you've been married a while, occasionally there are habits that grate." He opened his car door for me.

"I imagine," I said. Not that I had any personal experience with marriage. I'd dated several men but none of my romantic relationships lasted more than a couple of months. Again, an existence spent serving books didn't allow for much of a love life.

Philip buckled himself into his Volvo. "But Elizabeth and I always smoothed over those rare rough spots. All in all, we were very appreciative of each other."

"Must be nice to have so many good memories."

"Thousands. Some people are high school sweethearts, but we were preschool sweethearts, bonding with each other in the pea gravel box."

"*P-e-e* gravel?" I wrinkled my nose.

"No, *p-e-a*. Like a sand box but supposedly safer." Philip pulled down his window shade. "Yet, no matter how well we know a person, there're always hidden aspects."

"True," I said, wondering what he was getting at.

"Some people have so much of themselves curdling and roiling below the surface."

Interesting verb choices. "Is there someone specific you're thinking of?" *Like me,* I wondered.

"Absolutely not."

I raised my eyebrows. As Bamber would say, he was protesting too much.

"That's why I love novels. You know exactly what the characters are thinking." Philip's eyes narrowed. "Except when you're dealing with an unreliable narrator. Which, by the way, is my least favorite type of character. Too shifty. I like to know who I'm dealing with." He sounded almost angry.

"I hear you," I said, feeling more nervous with every passing second.

"I also value authenticity in people," he said.

Oh, no. Where was this going?

"That's why I like you."

Authentic? Me? I hadn't expected that.

"For instance, I very much appreciated you telling me you signed Justin."

A rare moment of honesty on my part. But there were other things about me he didn't know. If our interactions were scenes in a novel, and Philip could read my thoughts, it's possible he'd toss the book against the wall, saying, "That Claire character is a fraud!"

"Thanks," I said. "But I'm hardly a saint."

"Who is?"

Maybe you, I thought. Besides Bea, he was one of the most decent people I'd ever met.

We arrived at Bonaventure, and as promised, it was beautiful but sacred. The ubiquitous and trailing grey Spanish moss matched the color of the gravestones and looked like the lifeless hair of the departed. Stories seemed to whisper from every stone angel, every carved monument, and every ornately-decorated tomb.

"Where death and beauty meets," Philip whispered. Bonaventure inspired that sort of reverence. You couldn't ever imagine shouting or laughing on these grounds. I was self-conscious of every footfall, every inhale and exhale of breath.

A breath that will one day still.

That was the message of the residents of Bonaventure: "You, with your beating heart, will one day share our fates."

We visited Johnny Mercer's grave, which was marked with a bench that listed his most iconic songs. I found myself softly whistling "Moon River."

Philip was mute, staring off into the distance.

"Are you okay?"

He shook his head.

"Is there anything I can—"

"I love 'Moon River.' The day before Elizabeth died, we were outside on the deck, and I was singing it to her." His eyes were hazy with tears.

"You must cherish those lovely memories."

He shook his head. "Not this particular memory. It was miserable."

"What happened?'

"I was singing that song, feeling so content, when Elizabeth…" He touched his throat and shook his head.

"I'm listening."

"She told me she was having an affair with my brother John."

Did I hear him correctly? Dear Lord, I hoped I hadn't. "Did you just say—"

"I did, and I'm not sure why I blurted that out."

"But I was under the impression—"

"That my marriage was perfect?" He twisted the simple gold wedding band on his finger. "I thought so too, until that evening when she told me she didn't love me anymore. I had no inkling, and she replied, 'That's the problem in a nutshell. You're living in a fantasy world. We haven't been happy for years.'"

"Oh my God. That must have been devastating."

"She also said, 'I'm not sure I was ever happy. I agreed to this marriage because everyone seemed to expect it of me. I'm not sure I've ever loved you.'"

I could barely force out any words. "No! And with your own brother? Wasn't he a lot older than her?"

"By over twenty years." Philip's fingers parted his longish hair. "She was my wife for five years. But, looking back, even though I slept by her side every night, it's as if we were strangers. There's something so frightening about that. The outside world is a challenging place, always changing, always surprising us, and often not in a positive way. When you're home, you crave stability. You want your spouse to be a known quality. But she wasn't. And neither was my brother."

"This is awful... Philip. I'm so sorry."

He took off his glasses, making his eyes look naked and defenseless. "She and John were going to leave Savannah and start a new life in Beaufort. They were on their way there to look for a love nest when the accident happened. A head-on collision with a driver who was trying to pass on a two-lane road."

I shook my head, unable to process the pain he'd undergone.

"And as you might imagine, their affair complicated my grieving process. One minute, I was furious at them." He gritted his teeth and let out an actual growl. "The next minute, I was weak with sadness. Other times, I would make myself sick, imagining them entangled together. It's been so—"

Philip's phone rang with a tone that sounded like the jingle of a landline. "My apologies, but if I don't take this, it'll just keep ringing and ringing."

"Of course," I said, patting his shoulder.

"I'm sorry, Mother, I'm occupied at the moment. May I return your call later? Oh... Yes. Of course. That would be wonderful. I'll see you tomorrow night."

He pocketed his phone and said, "My mother called to remind me that tomorrow night is John's birthday, and she wants us to spend the evening together. Reminiscing."

"Does she know about—?"

"Absolutely not! No one knows. Not her. Not Justin and no one in Elizabeth's family either."

"But they died together. Did anyone suspect?"

"I lied and told everyone that they were on a shopping excursion, and that John was helping Elizabeth pick out an anniversary present from a rare book shop in Beaufort. Because of their age difference, nobody has ever been suspicious."

Despite signs forbidding it, I sat down on Johnny Mercer's stone bench. "So all this time, you've had to pretend your heart wasn't broken by both of them?"

Philip sat beside me. "It would just make their grief more difficult and sully their memories. I didn't want their mistakes to define their entire lives."

"That was so kind and generous," I said, meaning it. I'd never met someone quite like Philip. His moral compass seemed to be more developed than most people's.

"Not really. I can't tell you how many times I wanted to say, 'Let me tell you the truth about your precious Elizabeth or your darling John.' Especially to my mother, who couldn't hide which son she preferred. She'd always favored her eldest personable son over her introverted, bird-watching youngest child. I also reminded her too much of my grandfather, who could be stern and disapproved of my father, who was charming but a bit of a wastrel."

"I'm sorry."

I knew what it felt like to have a parent express obvious dislike. Meredith never said it out loud, but I was aware she had trouble tolerating me because I reminded her too much of my mom.

"I have my moments of intense anger. Sadly, you witnessed one of those. That day you came into the historical society."

"And you threw the book?"

"It was *Madame Bovary*. Not sure if you're familiar with the plot but—"

"Yes. I had to read it in college. It's about adultery."

Philip grunted. "I'd never read it before. I didn't know that it was going to blindside me. Anyway, thanks for listening to my confession. I guess I needed to say it to someone."

"I'll never repeat it."

"Thank you." He put a finger to his temple. "I confess, I have an urge to hug you. But surely that's inappropriate."

"Hug away," I said.

He embraced me, and we fit together well, as if his arms were especially designed to engulf my form. Philip must have felt similarly because he hugged me a little longer than I would have expected.

"Thank you," he said. "I can't remember the last time I've had close human contact."

"I don't get many hugs myself."

Bea always hugged me when she saw me, and her embraces were exuberant and satisfying. Meredith wasn't a hugger, and my dad's hugs were stiff and brief.

"A shame," Philip said.

He brushed aside my hair and took a long look at my face, as if counting my freckles. I could barely breathe, thinking his attentive gaze felt more intimate than any physical contact. I was certain he'd kiss me, but suddenly, he looked away. "I'm sorry for staring. I lost myself for a moment."

I didn't know what to say. I'd been looking forward to the heat of his lips on mine, and his sudden cooling confused me.

"For a second, I thought maybe you were going to—"

"Kiss you? No. That would be unwise. I'm not ready for a new relationship. Especially with someone who doesn't even live in the same city and is leaving tomorrow."

"You're right." I'd been so surprised to find myself physically drawn to Philip, and my hormones had momentarily clouded my thinking. I didn't have time for a long-distance relationship.

Besides, there was so much Philip didn't know about me. And we were too different. He was like a sweet meandering donkey, living a thoughtful but slow-paced life, and I was a thoroughbred horse with blinders, not allowing any distraction in my quest to win the race.

"We're in agreement then?" Philip said.

"Yes," I said softly and a tad reluctantly.

"Glad we have that settled." Philip dug in his trouser pocket and produced a battered gold pocket watch of all things. I thought watches like that only existed in period films or antique stores. "It's late. Ready to go back?"

We made the usual small talk on the drive home. I told Philip that, so far, Bonaventure seemed like the best place for my mom's ashes, but I needed to think about it some more.

If you listened to our conversation, it would seem as if Philip had never almost kissed me, but the memory hadn't been excised. My lips were still pulsing at the missed opportunity.

As usual, when we arrived at my mom's cottage, Philip trotted around to the passenger side to open the door for me. I thanked him for all he'd done, and he said, "You're most welcome," and quickly returned to his car.

I watched his Volvo drive away, thinking it was wise that we hadn't lost our heads. Yet, the idea of never seeing him again made me feel sadder than I had felt in a long while.

Chapter Thirteen

Whenever uncomfortable emotions threaten to stir, I shoo them away like fruit flies hovering over a glass of Riesling. Soon as I got home, I called Bamber to check in but mostly to distract myself.

"I was just about to call you," she said.

"What's going on?"

"I finished Justin's book and the reader report."

"Great. Email me the reader report." Now that I had an assistant, clients' books would always be read. Happy day! Finally, I could feel better about myself.

"Will do. It's a fun novel, especially in the beginning, but..."

"Go on."

"Well, I hate to say this, but after a while, the wheels start coming off."

"What do you mean?"

"It gets repetitive, and one event doesn't seem connected to the next. There were still some funny moments, but overall, it was rough sledding."

I plopped my backside into a cushioned wicker chair in the living room. "What chapter did it start going sour for you?"

"Eight."

Not bad, I thought. *Not bad at all*. Sometimes novels started falling apart as early as chapter three, which wasn't a deal killer if the chapters were long enough.

"I'm just one reader so I could be wrong," Bamber said. "How did you feel?"

"Like it's ready to go out. Any uneven spots an editor will iron out."

Maybe. If we're lucky.

"Oh. That's good," Bamber said, sounding a little uncertain. "I always hear that editors don't edit anymore, so I assumed Justin would need to do another draft or two."

Not with a hot property like this, I thought. Besides, Justin was telling a story about reality stars. The bar was low on that kind of writing, and everyone knew it.

"Thanks for weighing in." I kicked off my flip flops. "I always appreciate another set of eyes. Anyway, I'll be in the office the day after tomorrow so I can get this deal off the ground."

My phone beeped with another call. *Dani.* I switched over. She was crying.

"My book dropped off the bestselling list. Sales are sinking, although I don't know how much. Will you call my editor and ask?"

It started to rain, battering the tin roof of the cottage. "Dani. I'm not sure that would be helpful information. The book is still new. There's no telling what might—"

"Don't patronize me. I'm not the usual clueless author. Knowledge is power." I heard the television in the background. Beeps and claps. Was she watching a game show?

"How is it power? What can you possibly do to affect book sales? There is one thing, however, within your power. Writing. Quit stressing over this one and write the next one."

My advice to Dani wasn't new. It was something I'd said many times to panicky authors.

"Bullshit," she said, spitting out the word. If our conversation was taking place in person, I would have gotten wet. Also, that was the first curse word I'd ever heard her say. "There won't be a next one. You and I both know that. The publisher overpaid, and they won't ever touch me again."

She wasn't wrong, but I didn't want to go there. Time to change gears. "Dani. Please calm down. Think about the baby. This stress can't be good for you."

Long pause. "You're right. I'm sorry. I don't know why I'm acting this way." Her voice got ragged, on the verge of tears. It's just… I'm regretting this. The book wasn't ready. The reader reviews aren't great."

"You're reading reviews? Haven't we talked about this?"

"I know! I used to say the same to my authors, but it's so hard not to. A lot of them are saying the middle is muddled. Do you feel like the middle was muddled?"

"As I've told you before, I loved the book, cover to cover," I said, lying as smoothly as ever. Too late to admit my laxity now. Who would benefit?

"I know. I know… I just… The reviews are so scathing. It's like everyone agrees."

"Not everyone. You had dozens of fabulous pre-pub reviews."

"From authors I know. They weren't sincere."

"Early Goodreads reviewers raved."

"Early Goodreads reviewers get free books, and we both know there's an unspoken agreement with the publisher: 'Write a glowing review, and we'll continue to send you advance copies of our novels.'"

"Dani. You're being so cynical."

"I can't help it. I know how this business works. And everyone is saying the same thing about the middle."

"I loved the middle."

"Which parts?" Her voice was hungry for reassurance.

I glanced out the window at the sheets of rain coming down. "You're putting me on the spot. I read so much it's hard to remember specifics."

"You're right. I'm sorry. I was just wondering… Were there too many scenes that took place in the quad?"

"The quad scenes were among my favorites! Surely, I've complimented you on those scenes."

The television in the background was now playing dramatic music. Soap opera? Did those even exist anymore?

"Dani?"

"Sorry," she said in a wooden voice. "I'm just distracted and feeling so poorly."

"All this stress isn't good for you. Take care of yourself and the baby! Promise me?"

"You're right. Thanks for the pep talk. You're the best." She didn't sound quite as sincere as usual, but that was to be expected.

Poor Dani. The combination of a difficult pregnancy, fear of losing the baby, and debut author nerves was getting to her. The latter, by the way, should be recognized as a temporary psychological disorder. It was so common among writers.

Chapter Fourteen

Truth? The allures of coastal life were wearing me down with a seductive whisper campaign. For the last few days, I'd been having stray thoughts like, *I wish I had a porch swing,* or *I like the sound of frogs and crickets at night.* If I stayed any longer, I might get the violent urge to open a bakery or buy a crumbling Victorian house and start my own bed-and-breakfast, serving homemade scones in beribboned baskets.

Or throw myself into a full-blown relationship with an aimless antiquarian book dealer.

Time to go back to real life in Manhattan where such preposterous thoughts would swiftly throw themselves off the Brooklyn Bridge and die.

The next morning, while I was packing for my trip home, I got a text from Philip.

I have a parting gift for you. May I drop it off sometime today?

I considered ignoring the text. We'd already said our goodbyes, and I'd shifted back into practical mode. Yet I found myself typing, *I leave for the airport at three.*

Is now convenient?

Again, I should say no, but I'd already cracked open the door. Might as well swing it open.

Sure. Come on.

I'll be there directly.

Five minutes later, he was at my door, holding a bag of chocolate-covered pecans. "I couldn't let you go back to New York without a souvenir."

Philip's hair was mussed, his white shirt was misbuttoned, and his bowtie was AWOL.

"Thank you. Are you okay? You look—"

"Slovenly, I know."

That wasn't the word I'd use. He looked sweet and vulnerable and very young. I'd been prepared to swiftly send him on his way, but his unguarded appearance softened me.

"The fact is, I stayed up all night," he said.

Worrying over me?

"Reading a novel. A wonderful, life-affirming novel which I read cover-to-cover last night. When I finished, I felt completely different. Hopeful and lighter. Like I'd shucked off a jacket with stones sewn into the pocket."

I cocked my head, confused. *Where is he going with this?*

"I've read a lot of novels since the tragedy, and all have contributed to my healing in one way or another. But this one topped them all. It's amazing how a simple love story between two very different people could affect my world view so much. But then again…" He paused and trained his gaze on me. "'Our identity, which feels so solid, is only a fable that we tell ourselves over and over.'"

What? Philip's last sentence was a quote from *Galaxy,* and it was one of my favorite lines.

"You read my father's book?"

"Justin told me you're Peter Wyld's daughter, and I've never read *Galaxy*. But I'm so glad I did. It was glorious."

My jaw tightened. This was a fan-boy moment. Nothing more. Talk about feeling disappointed. How many times in my life did I have to listen to people rave about my father's talents?

"So kind of you to say. I'll pass on the praise to my dad." It was a stock phrase I'd used hundreds of times. "Now if you don't mind, I need to—"

Philip touched me on the shoulder. "Claire. I'm not here to rhapsodize over your father's book. I'm here to tell you that *Galaxy* was so moving it shifted something within me. I made a mistake yesterday, pulling back. I wanted to kiss you, and I think you wanted to kiss me but—"

"You made the right decision. There are some very good reasons why we shouldn't—"

"Claire."

The look on his face was tender, it undid me.

Suddenly, I moved closer, and before I knew it, his mouth was on mine. I relaxed into the moment because I'd wanted it since our last encounter. And what a kiss it was. Not the kind I'd expected from a buttoned-up man who favored bow ties. It was *From Here to Eternity* meets *The Notebook* meets *Lady and the Tramp*.

When we pulled away, Philip touched my cheek and said, "And what were the reasons we shouldn't be together?"

"I don't remember," I said breathlessly. I was still intoxicated from the kiss.

"Neither do I."

"Oops. I just recalled. The geographical issue. I'm leaving for New York today."

"Might have been an obstacle before the advent of the airplane and train. But maybe not so much anymore."

"Right you are," I said, and we started kissing again.

We spent the next couple of hours on the cottage's porch, swinging on the glider, kissing until our lips were sore and talking intimately about our families. Philip's father died of a heart attack when Philip was only ten.

"My grandfather ended up being my biggest role model. He gave me the gift of appreciation for numbers, birds, and rare books. Not to mention, bow ties."

He was also the only person Philip felt close to in the family. According to him, every female in the world, including his mother, was worshipful of his older brother John. His poetry, tweed jackets, and Lord Byron curls enchanted them all.

"I was always trying to gain my mother's approval, but nothing I did mattered," Philip said. "The world revolved around her eldest son. My mother would never say it, but I'm sure she wished it'd been me in that car instead of John."

"And yet you resisted the temptation to taint his memory."

Philip abruptly stopped the motion of the glider with his shoe. "Who would benefit from that? Forgiveness is my goal, and I have a list of books that are helping me with that: *Crime and Punishment, Jane Eyre,* and *The Bluest Eye* to name a few."

After discussing his family dynamics, we moved onto mine. Philip wanted to know what it was like to have Peter Wyld as my father.

It was a question I'd been asked many times over. I always lied, painting an idyllic childhood with a clever father who adored me. But I couldn't do that with Philip.

Before answering, I opened the bag of chocolate pecans and handed Philip one and bit into my own. "My dad isn't an easy man to get to know. He reads all the time, and that's what he likes to talk about. He avoids personal topics."

"And yet he wrote such a wise book."

"My boss Kippy once said it's not unusual for writers to craft emotional experiences and convey wisdom that seem out of their range. Her clients are proof of that. They write beautiful, assured novels that win prizes, but in person they can often be neurotic and insecure."

I thought about all the authors who visited the office, fretting over everything from sales to reviews to marketing budgets.

"Maybe art brings out the best in people?" Philip said.

Or sometimes the worst, I thought, thinking of Wendy and some other clients. But I didn't want to sully Philip's optimistic view. It was one of the things I liked most about him.

He squeezed my hand. "I'm envious of you. How magical it must be to work with people who can change minds and hearts. Who can show those who are in despair that there's hope."

Such a wildly romantic view of authors. And yet, it was almost contagious. A part of me really wanted to live up to his ideal of me as a person who discovered and championed new and important voices. But then again, I'd tried that at the beginning of my career and nearly starved.

I glanced at my phone to check the time. "It's late. I'm sorry but I need to finish packing."

"Of course. I've kept you too long. Do you need a ride to the airport?"

"No. A friend is taking me."

And there it was: the geographical issue. It was like a toddler who wedged himself between his parents in bed, saying, "Don't forget about me!"

"As it so happens, I'm going to London in two weeks to sell more of my collection. I could stop in New York for a couple of days beforehand. There's a friend I can stay with. Would you like me to—"

"I'd love to see you. And, at some point, I have to return to Georgia to finish getting the cottage ready for sale and to hold my mom's memorial service."

We'd temporarily tabled the geographical issue, but we both knew it'd be back. And in the meantime, we'd be answering those age-old questions: does absence make the heart grow fonder? Or would our relationship be a case of "out-of-sight, out of mind?

Frankly, I suspected the former. Philip wasn't gone yet, and I was already missing him.

Chapter Fifteen

After my return to Manhattan, for the first couple of days, I couldn't stop thinking about Philip. I also missed Bea, sunsets, and even the subpar coffee at Plain Jane Java. My usual lavender latte now seemed a little too flowery and sweet.

But, by the third day, it was almost as if I'd not been at Gull Island at all. I was back to being Claire Wyld uber agent, and my every waking moment was focused on pitching Justin's book. I also kept checking Publishers Marketplace, half expecting Morris to slide in with Quince's deal, but it never happened.

Justin's book went to auction, and just as I anticipated, the winner paid seven figures. At the end of the day, I submitted the deal to Publishers Marketplace. At some point, I'd be listed as the number one dealmaker in debuts. That's when it would be real for me.

To celebrate Justin's deal, Rebecca brought a rainbow explosion cake from the Flour Shop. When she cut into it, sprinkles tumbled out. There was also Moet champagne to wash it down. Rebecca and Bamber toasted me with crystal flutes.

"Poor, old Morris," Rebecca said. "Don't you know he has steam curling out of his ears. If he has any class, he'll send you a congratulatory email."

"Doubt that," I said. "He's been AWOL for a couple of weeks."

"Some publishing people ditch their jobs in August. He'll regret it once he gets back to work," Rebecca said.

Morris didn't seem like the type to ignore his career for even a day; like myself, he was a perpetually circling shark. Was it possible we'd both been wrong about Quince's novel, and no one was biting? Sometimes it happened.

Bamber had been refreshing her phone every few seconds, waiting for the deal to post, and just as I was cutting myself another piece of cake, she said, "It's up!"

"Awesome," Rebecca said. "Read it to us."

Bamber cleared her throat and sucked in her stomach as if she were about to perform: "Justin Habersham's YOUR PLACE OR MINE, based on his real-life experience working with reality stars Lila and Lola, is pitched as *The Devil Wears Prada* meets *The Proposal*. It's filled with dishy details about celebrities behaving badly but it's also a tender and humorous coming-of-age story reminiscent of *Galaxy*. To Atria in a major deal by Claire Wyld at Prestige Literary."

"Wickedly amazing pitch, my queen." Rebecca gave me a high-five.

Bamber held back and looked a little pale. Maybe it was the excitement or possibly the champagne.

"You okay, Bamber?"

"I'm fine. I was just caught by surprise… You compared Justin's book to *Galaxy?*"

"It's a bit of a stretch but pitches are all about exaggeration."

"True that," Rebecca said. "I compare every kid novel to *Because of Winn Dixie*. Even if it's set in outer space."

We both laughed, but Bamber didn't join in.

"I love *Galaxy*, and Justin's novel is nothing like it." Bamber's arms were folded over her narrow torso, and her lips were a thin line, as if she were holding back even stronger words.

"Come on. There are loose similarities between the two," I said.

"No," Bamber said vehemently. "There aren't, and it cheapens your father's brilliant novel to say so."

I stared at Bamber, wondering what had gotten into her. Where was that worshipful assistant that I knew and loved?

Kippy swept in, traveling in a cloud of perfume that evoked the lobby of the Four Seasons or the orchid-infused air of Guerlain Spa.

"In my office, Claire." She waved nails so pearly they seemed to leave a glowing trail in their wake.

"Coming," I said. Dealing with Bamber would have to wait.

I sat across from Kippy, thinking, as always, that she was too glamorous for an office setting. I could easily imagine her willowy frame astride an Arabian horse. Or draped in taffeta in an old-timey nightclub, ciggie in hand, looking slightly bored.

Kippy arranged herself on her swivel chair and pumped a dollop of lotion into her palms, spreading it over her long fingers. "I have wonderful news, my sparkling Pitch Queen. *Culture* magazine called. They want to do a profile on the two of us. The new guard and the old guard. It'll be their cover story."

"Shut the door!" I said.

Kippy glanced at her already closed door and said, "Is that slang?"

"Yes. I'm sorry." Usually, I tried to be more refined around Kippy. "It's just... wow."

Culture was one of Meredith's favorite publications. I couldn't wait for her to see me on the cover.

"They'd like to speak to clients as well," Kippy said.

"How many?" I asked warily.

"Just one from each of our lists. It's hard to choose, but I think I'll have to go with Emily." Emily was Kippy's Nobel Prize winner. "And you?"

"Justin," I said quickly. At the moment, he was my happiest author. Clients were always their most effusive just after a deal was struck.

"But his book isn't out yet. Didn't one of your authors just make the list?"

"Dani, yes, but she has a problematic pregnancy and hasn't been well." I'd not heard from Dani since I'd been back in New York, and I was afraid to call her for fear she was going to start blaming me for her unimpressive book sales.

"Justin it is. Send me contact info, and I'll forward it to the reporter."

"Okay."

Kippy started to tap on the keyboard of her computer which I took as a signal to leave. I reluctantly stood.

"I almost forgot," she said. "When the reporter calls for the interview, I'm going to reveal some inside information."

"What's that?"

"I'm making you a partner in the agency."

"Oh my God, Kippy, thank you."

"I've been in this business a long while, and I've never seen an agent rise so quickly. And I'd much rather have you stay here then fly off and put up your own shingle."

And there it was. I'd finally gotten almost everything I wanted and worked for. But the cherry on the hot fudge sundae would be that moment when my name finally appeared on the Publishers Marketplace site as the number one dealmaker in debuts. Even though the deal had been listed, the rankings of agents had yet to be updated.

Kippy gasped. "Look at the time. I must go. Lunch with Libby."

"Libby?" I thought I was familiar with all of Kippy's nicknames for her authors. "Is she a new client?"

Kippy laughed. "No. Libby's my daughter."

I was momentarily dumbfounded. I knew Kippy had once been married to a *New York Times* sports journalist named Tom, but they'd divorced at least ten years ago. I had no idea they shared a daughter.

"I didn't realize you had children."

"Just the one daughter," Kippy said briskly, as if a single child was easy to overlook. "Libby lives in LA and has a busy dermatology practice, so I don't see her that often."

"Oh," I said softly.

"We've never been particularly close. She was more of a daddy's girl. Still is."

How is it possible that I'd worked for Kippy for eight years and not known she had a daughter? She never talked about Libby. Odd, because Kippy was one of the most nurturing people I knew. At least when it came to her clients.

Kippy must have guessed my thoughts because she said, "The book life demands so much of us. At some point, we make a choice."

I glanced around her office at all the photos of her glittering clients. It was a life anyone would envy, including me.

"Like me, you've chosen the book life," Kippy said with a smile, "but unlike me, you wisely made the choice early on."

Before marriage and children. That was left unsaid.

Had I made that choice? Most people would probably say yes, especially now that I was going to be a partner. Yet, completely ruling out a husband and kids at age twenty-five seemed a little premature.

Especially now that you've met someone you really like.

All the same, as I stood in Kippy's office, still light-headed from her partnership offer, Philip and Gull Island seemed so far away.

Chapter Sixteen

After my meeting with Kippy, I decided to do something I never did: Leave work early. There was plenty to do—acknowledge congratulatory emails, answer client correspondences, and read slush that Bamber had pre-screened. But I was high from the champagne and my upcoming promotion, and I wanted to relish both before I chained myself to my computer or phone.

Before leaving, I poked my head into Bamber's office to see if she was still stewing about Justin's deal. She wasn't at her desk, and because she always ate in the office, I knew she wasn't out to lunch. She probably needed some cooling off time. Likely she'd be back soon, spilling over with apologies.

A bit of glitter in Bamber's wastepaper basket caught my eye. It shone from a handmade card with a loving cup on the cover. On the bottom she'd written, *To my hero, Claire.* Her handwriting was so beautiful it looked like calligraphy, and the loving cup was well-rendered. It was obvious she'd spent some time on it, and yet she'd thrown it away.

I felt a twinge of regret. Had I permanently fallen from grace in her eyes? Or was she simply having a bad moment?

"It's just the way publishing works," I said to her empty office. "I thought you understood that."

I left the office and walked for blocks, mostly oblivious to the pinching of my high heels and the drizzle that dotted my head. I found myself in front of the Strand Bookstore and was more than happy to duck in and leisurely browse.

I wandered through the aisles, glancing at the new release tables, recognizing many books from deals I'd read about in Publishers Marketplace.

In the Staff Picks, I was surprised to see Bea's latest title. The Strand's picks tended to be more highbrow. The shelf talker said, "Technically a beach read but transcends the genre. Trust me on this."

I picked up Bea's book, and that's when I saw her: Hazel.

She stood in front of a display table. I glanced down at her feet. She wore Doc Martens. Just like last time. Her hair was a different color—emerald-green instead of red—but the Edgar Allen Poe tattoo on her arm assured me it was the same woman.

Dani's book was on the table, and I grabbed it. Casually, I said to her, "This one looks intriguing. I don't suppose you've read it?"

"Read it the first day it came out," she said.

I knew it! Hazel was the ideal reader for the books I sold. Not the book club ladies. Not the people who read on the beach at Gull Island.

"And?" I said, waiting for a slew of accolades.

"I bought it after reading the first chapter, which was clever. And it was compared to *The Secret History,* a favorite novel of mine."

"Mine too," I said.

She tugged on a hoop earring. "But there was no comparison. I mean, the author had some potential, but the middle was a mess. I marked it "Did Not Finish" on Goodreads. Usually, I put DNF books on the curb outside my apartment, but I didn't want to subject anyone to it."

"Really? I've read so much about it, so I assumed—"

"I can't tell you how many times I've been duped by hot book hype, and I hate that because I'm a special ed teacher, and books are a luxury for me. Every once in a great while, a debut novel will live up to its press, and I'll be swept up in an astonishing story. And that story will remind me of how much I love books and why I keep spending money on hardcovers, but, these days, it's so frigging rare to find compelling novels."

I had the urge to defend publishing and say, "Hey. We're all looking for great books, but it's tough. Publishing would go broke if they only published masterpieces." But instead, I said, "That must be disappointing."

"It is, but I'm finally wising up. By the way, the one in your hand is a good one." She pointed at Bea's book. "I don't usually read beach books, but it was a staff pick, so I gave it a go. Didn't disappoint. More thoughtful than the usual beach read and the story... Wow. Couldn't put it down."

"Thanks for the tip. I'll buy it."

Bea's publisher always sent me copies of her books, but I always gave them to a woman in my building who was a fan. I didn't own any copies of my own.

"Nice chatting with you. I'm Claire, by the way."

"I'm Faith. Happy reading."

After Faith moved on, I picked up Dani's book and studied her author photo. Dani was a powerful editor who'd participated in many high-stake deals, but in the photo, she looked about sixteen. There was a hopefulness in her eyes that seemed to say to the reader, "Please love my book."

Isn't that what every writer wanted? And in my experience, most debut writers wanted praise more than they wanted the truth. I adored Dani, and I'd given her what I thought she wanted, but it was possible I'd been wrong.

Chapter Seventeen

It was three days since Justin's deal had been posted, and Publishers Marketplace had yet to list me as the number one dealmaker in debuts. I was still number two just below Morris. What was the delay? I'd waited so long for the honor I was losing patience.

Meanwhile, Bamber hadn't come to work since the celebration of the deal. When I called her phone, it went to voicemail. My emails to her went unanswered.

Obviously, she wasn't planning to return to the agency. My feelings were mixed. Part of me wanted to angrily defend myself to her. Another part of me felt hurt and a little ashamed. I'd never imagined that my biggest acolyte would turn on me.

But, I guess she was a bigger fan of *Galaxy* than she was of me. No surprise there, and I'd obviously crossed a line I didn't know existed.

Since Bamber was gone, I had to sort through my own slush, which was more out-of-control than usual. Used to be that only industry people read Publishers Marketplace, but in recent years, writers had started subscribing, and many knew about the big deals. My deal with Justin was highlighted in the Publishers Lunch newsletter, and that meant even more writers hoped I would take them on.

Around five I got a text.

Hello, it's Philip Habersham. I pray I'm not disturbing you. May we talk?

I smiled. So damn formal.

Of course. Call me.

I mean in person. I'm here in New York at the White Horse Tavern.

In New York? Wow. Did I get the days wrong? I thought you were coming next week.

Change of plans. If you're too busy, I understand.

I'd planned to work until at least seven. Besides, it had only been a week since we saw each other last, and I'd been so swamped, I'd barely had time to miss him. But I couldn't tell him that. I simply texted: *OMW.*

Forgive me. What does OMW mean? Oh my word? If it does, I wouldn't blame you. I know this is a tremendous surprise and not an altogether convenient one.

OMW means on my way, and it's plenty convenient.

I arrived at the White Horse Tavern in less than twenty minutes. In a corner booth, I saw a familiar figure with a bowtie, sitting under a horse-head chandelier that hung from a pressed-tin ceiling. He was drinking a brown, fruit-festooned cocktail in a tall glass.

"Hi, Philip."

He gave me a puzzled look, almost as if he didn't recognize me, which wasn't surprising. At the beach, I mostly wore t-shirts and flip flops, but not in Manhattan.

"It's Claire."

"Of course. For a minute, I—"

"I look different, I know. This is my work persona."

He nodded, taking in my sleek, blown-out hair, my expertly-shaped brows, my pencil skirt.

"You look… formidable. And your freckles are missing."

"Makeup."

I found myself feeling a little embarrassed, as if he'd caught me playing dress up. In a way, he had. Also, I wasn't sure I wanted him to see me like this. It was as if I were giving away too much about my life in the city.

We hugged, and he said, "I apologize for dropping in on you this way."

"No apology necessary. I'm excited to see you. But why the change in plans?"

Philip continued to look at me in a wide-eyed and wary way, as if I was some kind of big-city harlot. "You're talking much faster than you did at the beach."

"Sorry. Still in work mode, I guess. A drink will help."

The waiter came by and asked Philip if he wanted another Pimm's Cup.

"A what?" I said.

"British cocktail," Philip said. "To get me in the mood for London."

I was starving so I ordered steak frites. Philip took way too long figuring out what he wanted, and I could see the waiter was getting impatient.

This is New York not Savannah, I thought. *Decide already.* Immediately, I felt awful about my impatience.

You really like this guy, I reminded myself. And yet somehow, he seemed different in Manhattan. A little out of synch.

"About those change in plans?" I began.

"Do you know why I chose this place to meet?" Philip said, ignoring my question.

I glanced around at the surroundings. "It's old and historical?"

"I take it you don't know the history of the White Horse Tavern?"

I shook my head.

"The poet Dylan Thomas drank here just before he died. His last words were 'I've had eighteen straight whiskies—I think that's a record!' He died the next day."

"It's shame that substance abuse used to be so common among writers," I said, wondering where he was going with this.

"He was a brilliant poet, and serving the muse cost him. I don't imagine it's easy being a writer. There's so much rejection, it rarely pays well, and it's such a solitary pursuit."

I smiled politely. Philip wasn't telling me anything I didn't know.

"In fact, it's a miracle that writers continue. Once when I asked my brother why he persisted when the rewards were so paltry, he said, 'At some point in a writer's evolution it becomes an act of generosity.' He quoted Simone de Beauvoir, saying 'You give your all, and yet you always feel as if it costs you nothing.'"

"A lovely sentiment," I said, although I had never met any writers like that.

"As you well know, I had issues with my brother," Philip continued. "But I admired his devotion to his poetry, which had nothing to do with money or fame. I think it was one of the qualities that attracted Elizabeth to him." Philip drummed his fingers against his chest as if in a state of deep reverie. "But I digress."

Yes, you do.

Geez. What was wrong with me? Why was I feeling so snappy and ill-at-ease?

"My point is, I don't think Justin will ever experience his father's evolved attitude to his creative work."

"Why is that?"

"He went for the easy money."

A stray lash was making my eye water, and I tried to blink it away. "Why do you say that? Did you read Justin's book? I told you not to, because it's not the final version. His editor will—"

"I didn't read Justin's book."

"So, why would you say—?"

"I read Wendy's book, and I read Dani's book and two more of your authors' novels."

I grabbed a napkin to dab at my leaky eye, and it came back black with mascara. "You read my clients' books?"

"Yes, and unless you've done a one-eighty in your business model, I imagine Justin's novel is on the same uninspiring level. Despite your comparison to *Galaxy*. My nephew showed me the deal announcement."

I'd gone too far with the *Galaxy* comparison. Bamber had made that clear. Likely, I'd gone too far with *The Secret History* comparison as well.

"Listen, Philip, Justin's novel sparkles. Is it perfect? No, but readers don't expect that of debuts." The leaky eye was making my nose run. I swiped it with the back of my hand.

"Do you need a handkerchief?"

I shook my head. "You don't know how publishing works. Hyperbole is a big part of it."

"It is, indeed. After I saw Justin's announcements, I paid for a subscription to Publishers Marketplace and looked up your deals. Every single book you sell is supposedly better than sliced bread, but not a single one has endured beyond a few weeks or months."

God. My nose was running like a sieve now, and my eye was still leaking from the lash. "Excuse me, but did you happen to notice how much editors paid for those books? Obviously, there's merit there."

"Is there? Or is it all smoke and mirrors?" Philip took a sip of his cocktail. "I must confess I'm disillusioned. I envisioned you as a champion for new literary voices, a person of the book, and that's not who you are at all. You might as well be selling hydraulics."

The waiter set a beer in front of me, and during that break in the conversation, I tried to gather my thoughts. I dabbed my eye and my nose with my napkin. Both, thank God, were drying up.

"It's very common for people to romanticize publishing," I said, feeling a bit more under control. "Especially someone like you who loves books so much, but it is a business. In fact, it's a corporate conglomeration."

"But aren't you worried that your business practices are damaging to the future of books? Eventually, people might get so frustrated with the quality of new novels that they'll give up on them for good."

I thought about Hazel/Faith in the Strand and how disenchanted she seemed about debut novels, and certainly the book club ladies had plenty of complaints. "It's not a perfect system, but I'm just one person. How am I supposed to change the way things work?"

"I agree it's daunting, but if everyone felt the way you do, nothing would ever change, would it? And don't misunderstand me, I know how difficult change is, especially when you're a wild success."

Did he really understand how heady my success felt? Yes, Philip sold rare books and put out a small magazine, but he wasn't regularly making seven-figure deals. He wasn't being promoted to partner in New York's most prestigious agency.

"I'm sorry I've disappointed you," I said.

"Believe it or not, I understand your choices," he said gently. "There was a time when lassoing the moon was everything to me. But when your life gets derailed, your definition of success changes drastically.

Now, instead of trying to master the world, I'm working on self-mastery. A more modest endeavor, but even more challenging."

I kept swallowing, having no idea how to respond. It was if this guy was from outer space, saying things no guy my age had ever imagined saying. Philip knew things about life, and part of me wanted to learn them as well, but was I ready for that?

Philip gently took my hand and suddenly, I didn't feel like I was in Manhattan anymore. I was on my mom's porch, longing for more of his kisses. How could I ever be impatient with this person I liked and admired so much? How could I have ever let him down?

"It seems as if we're on different pages," he said. "That's even clearer now that I'm here. Perhaps..." He took a deep breath. "Perhaps, it was a mistake to think a relationship between us could work."

Suddenly, the spell broke. I scooted away from him. "So, this is a break-up?"

His eyes looked sad and weary behind the lenses of his horn-rimmed glasses. "We've barely begun being a couple, but, yes, I'm afraid it is."

"And you flew to New York for this?"

"You seem surprised."

"I am. Most people break up by text these days, or they ghost."

"Ghost? I'm afraid I don't understand."

"Never mind. My point is no one gets on a plane to dump someone."

"Dump? What a terrible word. I just... well, I don't envision a future for us, and, of course, I had to say it face-to-face. Any other way is cowardly."

Both my eye and nose started leaking again, but this time I let them go. "You can prettify it with your Southern gentleman talk, but you're still dumping me."

I felt unexpectedly gutted but not surprised. He was so evolved. Why would he want to be with me?

"I would never dump the Claire I knew on Gull Island, the one who actually made me question my thoughts on solitude as the ideal companion. But since then, I've met a new Claire, someone who seems like a stranger to me. Perhaps you can clear up the confusion. Who is the real Claire?"

I hesitated, wanting to say, "The Gull Island Claire," but that would be a lie.

"Do you even know?" Philip said.

Of course, I knew. Maybe I just didn't want to admit it to him.

"I was on Gull Island for a couple of weeks," I said. "But this is where I live and work the rest of the time. So, obviously, this is who I am."

"Or is that just a fable you tell yourself over and over?"

Evoking my favorite *Galaxy* line again.

"Maybe it is a fable. But it's the only story I have." Damn! Would my eye and nose ever quit with the leaking?

"Claire? Are you crying?"

"No! I have a lash in my eye, and it's making my nose run."

"Do you want me to take a look?"

Yes, I wanted to say. Remove my lash. Comfort me. Make me feel better about myself. Erase the last few minutes of my life.

Instead, I brusquely said, "No. I'll go to the ladies' room. I don't need your help."

Philip stood. "Then I'll be on my way. I've moved up my London trip and have decided to stay abroad until I can sell off the remainder of my collection. That could take months. This truly is goodbye."

He took out a worn wallet and laid out a few bills.

"Let me get the check, please." I rummaged in my purse for my wallet.

Philip held up a hand. "You know my policy."

"Guess what? You're in New York now where women actually pay their tabs." I slapped my wallet on the table.

"If you insist." Philip picked up his bills, which surprised me. I'd expected more of a fight. Part of me wanted one. It would keep him here longer.

"Goodbye, Claire," he said.

I willed him to linger but no such luck. After he left, I took out a compact and looked at my face. One eye was red, and black tears stained my cheeks. *Such a mess*, I thought, angrily cleaning myself with the napkin.

The waiter approached. "Are you okay, miss?"

"Fine," I said, but I really wasn't.

You just let the best man you've ever met go. There was no doubt in my mind that was true. I might never meet another Philip.

But if I'd stopped him, then what? Was I supposed to give up my entire life so we could be together? What would I do on Gull Island every day? Comb the beach for shark teeth? Become a barista at Plain Jane Java?

Those thoughts were sobering, particularly when I compared them with my life in New York with million-dollar deals and the media dubbing me as a Pitch Queen.

My time with Philip on Gull Island was enchanting, and I loved every minute of it, but it wasn't real life. Of course, romance seemed effortless while I was idly watching coastal sunrises or strolling under live oaks, dripping in Spanish moss.

Now that I was back in Manhattan, it was obvious to me how different we were, and how I would continually disappoint him. And, when it came down to it, I didn't have time for him.

Women wanted to believe they could have it all, but that was a fairy tale. Even my own mother with her small literary agency had never married. And Bea was married to her writing life. Kippy was right. The book life demanded everything from you. A high price, but it gave so many thrills in return.

Cheap thrills.

"No," I whispered angrily to myself. "I love my work. I do. And there's value there... Maybe."

I picked at my meal, but I was no longer hungry, so I asked the waiter for a to-go container. "And the check," I said.

The waiter was young but with a weathered forehead and deep lines around his mouth; maybe the late nights of the food-and-beverage world were eroding him. He cast a sympathetic look in my direction as if he knew I'd been dumped. "The gentleman already took care of it."

No wonder Philip had given in so easily; he had no intention of letting me pay. Maybe it was sexist. Maybe it was archaic. But one thing I knew for sure, it was well-intentioned. The waiter was right about him. He was a gentleman, and I was going to miss him. Terribly.

Chapter Eighteen

The *Culture* article hit the stands, and it was a triumph. Both Kippy and I came off like literary superstars, and Justin praised me as if I was an all-powerful genie who could turn tap water into Perrier. The cover photo was extremely flattering, and after the issue came out, my inbox and phone overflowed with congratulations. Bea sent me a beautiful orchid.

I got love from everyone except Dani and Meredith. I texted Dani to check in and she said, *"Sorry. Sick with pregnancy. Mostly bedbound."*

She didn't say anything about her novel, which, despite being a Charmi pick, had run its course in impressive sales and recognition. I hoped Dani wasn't holding it against me, but that would be a pipe dream. In the end, clients always blamed me.

I should have been giddy about the magazine, but I could only focus on one thing: Morris was still number one in debuts. How long did it take for Publishers Marketplace to change the rankings? Was there some kind of oversight on their part?

Yes, it was a trivial matter. But it gnawed at me. I knew I was number one, but until it was publicized, it didn't feel real.

And also, why hadn't Meredith called? She religiously read *Culture* on her iPad, no matter where she was. I thought about her lack of contact all day long until I couldn't stand it anymore. I had to call.

When Meredith picked up, we chatted for several minutes about my dad and his recent eczema flare-up, but she still didn't mention the *Culture* article. I should have let it go, but I couldn't resist bringing it up. "Did you see this week's *Culture* cover story?"

The issue was sitting on the top of my desk; I couldn't pry my gaze from it.

Meredith didn't immediately reply. It was almost as if she didn't know how to answer such a straight-forward question or didn't want to. "I did see it. I've been so concerned about your dad's skin I forgot to mention it. So sweet of Kippy to include you."

"Include me? Did you even read it?"

"I didn't read it word for word, no. Nice picture of you, although you looked a little washed out. I know how much you city girls love black, but that color's not for everyone. It might also scare off the boys. Men like feminine colors."

"Did you show it to Dad?" I bit into what I thought was a chocolate Jelly Belly, but it was licorice. I spit it out into a tissue.

"Also, they like ruffles and florals. Think Diane Von Furstenberg."

"Meredith. I asked you if—"

"Or even Kate Spade. She's not just about handbags, you know."

"Meredith, did you show my dad the—"

"For God's sake, Claire. Your father doesn't care about New York gossip. You know that."

"Hello? It's not gossip. It's a story about me, his daughter." I leaned so far back in my chair I almost tipped over.

"Good lord. If you want me to show him the magazine I will."

Suddenly, I was irate. "Of course I want you to show him. It's a big deal to be on the cover of *Culture*."

"Excuse me, dear, but people who are truly big deals don't have to advertise it. And speaking of big deals, the commemorative edition of

Galaxy went up for preorder on Amazon, and its already number one in upcoming releases. We're hearing rumblings that Oprah might pick it for her club. She's picked older books before. Like *A Tale of Two Cities*."

Why in the world had I imagined that being on the cover of *Culture* would make Meredith suddenly care about my accomplishments? It had been the silliest of fantasies. No one, especially her, could see my little match burning under the glare of my father's inferno.

Obviously, I should have stopped right there, but I didn't. I said, "Meredith, without Kippy, there'd be no *Galaxy*. She made it happen. Literary agents matter. A lot." I swiveled around to gaze at the impressive collection of books I'd sold.

Meredith was silent for a couple of beats as if she didn't have a rebuttal. Highly unusual for her. Finally, she said, "Who's your favorite film star?"

"Why do you want to—?"

"Who is it?"

"Uh... I guess, Cate Blanchett."

"Who is her agent?"

I sighed.

"I know you're feeling puffed up, Claire, what with making million-dollar deals for your authors."

Ha! So, she'd looked at the article after all, but she just couldn't bear to give me the tiniest shred of praise.

"Let's not forget who matters most in any type of entertainment business. And, in case you don't recall, let me give you a hint: it isn't the agent."

Every ounce of pride I had rushed out of me like air from a leaky dirigible.

"By the way, do you want to talk to your father?"

"Sure," I said in a near whisper. That was a reversion to childhood. When I was a kid, Meredith was always saying to me, "Louder, please. It's almost like you're afraid to speak." She'd been right about that. Why speak when whatever I said was either ignored or ridiculed.

My father got on the line. "Claire? Claire? Are you there?"

"Yes, Dad."

"Did you know there are eight different types of eczema? I have the most common— atopic dermatitis—but there's another variety called nummular eczema that seems far more interesting. It leaves coin-shaped spots on the skin. The ancient Egyptians used bread meal and rotten cereal as a treatment, but Meredith, ever the practical soul, prefers a topical steroid."

"I'm sorry. I hope it gets better soon."

I heard Meredith talk in the background and a door shut, as if she'd left the room.

"Claire," my father said. His voice was so soft I could barely hear him.

"Yes?"

"Don't listen to Meredith."

"Excuse me?" My father rarely contradicted his wife.

"The fact is agents do matter. Maybe not to everyday people, but to the author, their literary agent is everything. I remember the early days when a call from Kippy felt like Christmas.

Writing is a solitary profession. Even to this day, when I hear Kippy's voice on the phone, my heart inevitably beats a little faster. She's my lifeline to the publishing world and, of course, the readers. Editors come and go, but the agent is always there for the writer. What would we writers do without our dear agents, cheering us on, and sticking up for us? But Claire…"

"Yes?"

"Please don't tell Meredith I said so. You know how touchy she can be."

We ended the call, and I picked up the magazine and stared at the glossy cover. They'd chosen a photo of me alone; Kippy was just a small inset.

I was the epitome of the fashionable, high-powered agent with gleaming chestnut hair and flawless make-up. Not a freckle in sight. My chin was held high, and my arms were crossed over my chest in a power pose.

Big block letters spelled out, "The Pitch Queen." A subtitle said, "Literary agent Claire Wyld spins books into bestsellers."

I'd been so pleased with the cover, but suddenly it looked odd to me. Kind of like when you constantly repeat a word until you drain it of its meaning.

I'd admired my cover so often that now I thought, *who is that person?* It was a weird, disconnected feeling as if I didn't recognize myself, as if the person on the cover was a stranger.

And maybe she was.

Chapter Nineteen

The next morning, I got a phone call from a reporter from *Mox*, the publication that dubbed me "Pitch Queen." I assumed I was going to be the subject of another praise piece, but no… It turned out the reporter was working on a rebuttal article.

According to her source, I was far from the dream agent in the *Culture* piece.

"In fact, you're portrayed as the opposite," she said. "There are a few things I want to confirm. I have a source who says when you're not lying to your clients, you're ghosting them. What's your response to that?"

"Who is this source?" I was walking back to work after lunch at La Devozione in the Chelsea Market. A power editor at St. Martin's, who used to blow me off when I called, had arranged the lunch and was now eager to work with me.

"The source wishes to remain anonymous."

I'd been caught by surprise and part of me wanted to say, "No comment" and hang up but I had to keep it together.

"I've had numerous clients over the years, and unfortunately some writers want to blame their agent if their careers aren't going well," I said. "It's extremely common in my line of work."

"Do you ignore clients after you sell their books?" the reporter asked.

Before speaking, I breathed in deeply through my nostrils and said, "Once a deal is made, authors have more contact with their editors than they do with me. But that's normal. And I'll certainly step in if there's a problem with the cover or royalties."

"How many of your clients are career authors as opposed to flashes in the pan?"

I was crossing the street and didn't notice the light had changed. A taxi blared its horn, spooking me. I shook a fist at him even though it was my fault.

"Obviously, I'd need to research that. Off the top of my head, I can't say."

That was a lie. I knew exactly how many career authors I had: one. That was Bea, and I had nothing to do with her longevity as an author.

"Do you read the books you acquire?" It started to rain, and I tried to open my umbrella, but it was stuck.

"What a question. Of course, I read the books I acquire. How else would I sell them?"

"All the way through?"

Bamber. She had to be the source. She'd acted weird about Justin's book and then, of course, she disappeared.

"Yes, all the way through," I said, struggling with the umbrella. I was getting wetter by the minute, and I still had five blocks to go. "Every single solitary word."

"Thank you. That's all the questions I had."

"When will this appear?"

"Hard to predict. I still have some loose ends to tie up."

"Stupid piece of crap," I whispered to the umbrella; it refused to open.

"What did you say?"

"Nothing. Sorry."

The reporter ended the call, and I stuffed the broken umbrella into an overflowing trash can and tried to run through the downpour in my Chloe patent leather pumps.

How bad was this going to be? Hard to say, but I felt as if I handled myself well. Regardless, I needed to keep Kippy in the loop.

I texted her, and she said she'd see me in her office as soon as I arrived. By the time I got there, I was soaked. My blouse was plastered to my body, water sloshed in my shoes, and my hair looked as if I had just gotten out of the shower. Before going to see Kippy, I dried off in the bathroom, but I was still a mess.

Kippy, on the other hand, looked beautiful and serene in a creamy twinset with pearls. Her thick blonde hair was loose, and soft waves framed her face. I felt like a wet mutt entering the den of a freshly-groomed poodle.

"Claire. What happened?" Kippy said with alarm.

"I'm the Wicked Witch of the West. Water makes me melt," I joked. Certainly, it washed away everything that made me look polished.

"The *Mox* reporter left a message on the office voice mail, but it's such a small, specialized media publication, I doubt I'll call back. Still, why don't you get me up to speed."

I relayed my conversation with the reporter, and Kippy said, "You're right. Her source is likely Bamber. We might have to get assistants to start signing non-disclosure agreements. Wait. Have you considered the source might be that mentally unstable ex-client of yours?"

"Wendy? Good point. Could be."

"Whoever the source is, I'm not at all concerned about that silly article. You know who works at these papers? Frustrated writers who feel they haven't gotten a fair shake and want to punish publishing people for not living up to their fantasies. They have outmoded ideas about publishing, thinking it's all Max Perkins, coaxing genius out of authors or lofty discussions over dry martinis at the Algonquin. Well, sometimes it's more unpleasant than that, and we both know it, but it's far from despicable." She plucked off a couple of drooping leaves from a white hydrangea arrangement on her desk. "You're not smothering kittens in their sleep or pulling the wings off butterflies."

"Low bar."

"Quit flogging yourself." Kippy's tone was uncharacteristically forceful. "You're giving the gift of flight to your authors, but once they're in the stratospheres, it's up to them to stay there. You can't spend your time following them around, holding a net under them in case they fall. You'll exhaust yourself."

"But too many authors fall."

Yesterday, out of curiosity, I scanned seven-figure deals from the last few years. Not just my deals but from all literary agents. There were only a few author names I recognized. Most had only enjoyed five minutes of literary fame and disappeared.

And yes, a million dollars was a lot of money, but it was a lot less after commission and taxes.

"Few can handle the rarefied oxygen at the summit. If you spelled all of this out to your potential clients beforehand, how many would turn down a lucrative publishing deal?" Kippy's fingers formed a zero.

She was voicing the justifications I constantly used in my head, and I nodded along, eager to dispel my recent doubts. Yet, a part of me wasn't convinced.

"For heaven's sake, pat yourself on the back," she said. "You're making things happen in this industry, and you're only twenty-five. I'm so ridiculously proud of you."

"Thank you." Unlike Meredith, at least someone admired my achievements.

"Visit your favorite boutique or shoe store and buy something wildly impractical and impulsive because you deserve it. By the way, that's a direct order."

"How could I possibly ignore that?"

She gave me a cool smile. "Actually, it's more of a suggestion. Now that you're a partner, it's inappropriate for me to tell you what to do anymore."

Kippy was right. I'd worked incredibly hard to progress in my career, and it was time to treat myself. In the past, I'd have called Dani to see if she was interested in a shopping trip. But considering how poorly she'd been feeling, I suspected she'd turn me down.

I missed being with her. Since she'd gotten pregnant, she hadn't been up for much of anything. Also, I wondered if our friendship would be the same.

I stood and was about to leave Kippy's office when I said, "Can I ask you a nosy question?" Her calling me "partner" emboldened me.

"You may ask," she said, surveying me with her thousand-mile gaze. "But the question is, will I answer?"

"I know you see a lot of your clients socially. Is there one in particular you'd consider to be a good friend?"

"And you want an honest answer?"

"Yes."

She folded her graceful hands on her lap. An emerald cocktail ring glittered on one of her fingers; it matched her eyes. "None of my clients are friends. Friendship is about give and take, and when it comes to my clients, everything revolves around them and their successes and concerns. One minute they see me as God, and the next they're asking me to fetch them an espresso."

"Seriously?" I said in disbelief. Kippy as an errand girl? It would be like asking the queen to clean up after her corgis.

She nodded. "And yet I wouldn't trade my life for anyone else's. Authors aren't always the most well-adjusted people, but they fascinate me. It almost feels as if they tap into a mysterious world the rest of us aren't privy to. Also, since I'm not at all creative, I can live vicariously through them. Any other questions?"

"No. That's all I wanted to know."

"Good." She smiled. "Because partner or not, one nosy question per fiscal year is all you're entitled to."

Chapter Twenty

The title of the *Mox* article was "Pitch Queen Breaks Spirits." I blanched when I saw it. The *Culture* article had dubbed me a dream agent, but this one was obviously going to snatch the halo from my head and stomp on it.

All sources in the piece were anonymous. It sounded as if they'd talked to several clients, and they weren't complimentary, mostly complaining about my inattentiveness and my habit of using an assistant as a buffer. I wasn't surprised at the complaints. The *Mox* reporter had hinted about what was coming.

But the most damning quote was this one: "Claire doesn't always read the novels she sells. When I signed with her, she told me how wonderful and accomplished my novel was, and I believed her. As time went on, I began to wonder if she was telling the truth."

Who could this be? Wendy?

"It was heartbreaking," the source continued. "I'd been reluctant to go out with the novel, but she assured me it was ready. It's so hard to be objective about your own material. You need a trusted advocate to be candid with you, but Claire only told me what I wanted to hear. Our relationship was completely inauthentic. That was confirmed when I asked her about specific events in the novel, and it became clear she'd failed to read it."

Too sophisticated and articulate to be Wendy. My heart twisted, knowing with certainty the identity of the source: It was Dani.

I reluctantly visited Dani's Goodreads page. The book was at 3.12 on a 5.00 scale, which meant it failed to resonate with readers. I skimmed the reviews, and there were many remarks about the book being dull in the middle. Dozens of comments complained about the novel's comparison to *The Secret History*.

Not even close.

That was a common sentiment.

Sometimes, a compelling pitch coupled with an irresistible author created enough glamour that people either didn't notice the novel's weaknesses or didn't care. Gary Fisketjon, who edited *The Secret History*, once told the *The New York Times*, "If the book's not that great... at least the publicity brings it some notice."

If you were lucky, readers who saw through the hype were reluctant to be outliers. They remained silent about the book, or if they dared to write a review, it usually started with an apology: "I know I'm in the minority here."

Or they'd doubt their own opinions and say, "There's so many five-star reviews here, it's probably just me."

But that didn't work with Dani's book. Even though she was a powerful editor—a status that should have offered some protection—it didn't. No one was afraid to point out the novel's weaknesses.

"I'm sorry, Dani," I whispered.

Rebecca burst into my office. "I just read *Mox*. Who were the turncoat clients? Wendy was one, I'll bet."

"I'm not sure," I said quietly. Beneath Rebecca's girly dresses and pinafores beat the heart of a honey badger, and I didn't want her to badmouth Dani. If anyone deserved badmouthing, it was me.

"I don't know who *Mox* talked to, but you got those authors hefty advances for their books. And how do they thank you? With a cowardly interview."

I might have agreed with her if it had been anyone but Dani. But I knew what this meant for my friend. She couldn't go back to editing. Not with such a colossal failure. And it would be challenging for her to ever get another book deal under her real name.

"Pick your chin off the floor," Rebecca said. "This article will blow over, and no one will remember it in a week. And you, my precious, will still be the toast of the literary world."

I gave her a weak smile. "Thanks for being my cheerleader."

"You're welcome." Rebecca plunked down her bowl of Jelly Bellies. "You're going to need these more than me. But trust me, that stupid article already feels like yesterday's news. Wendy or whoever else contributed thinks they set off a bomb, but it was more like an alarm clock."

"Maybe." I was beginning to think I deserved a bomb. "Regardless, this hasn't been a good day."

***

Rebecca was wrong. The article didn't blow over. Someone on Twitter had started #*Claireless*, and it was trending. Legions of ticked-off writers retweeted the *Mox* piece, and gripes about me and other literary agents filled the Twitter feed:

Took over a year to read my latest manuscript.
Submitted to three editors and gave up.
Hates every book idea I give her but is vague about the reasons.
Always acts like she's doing me a huge favor.

Fired me after my book didn't sell. On my birthday!

Cheated me out of royalties.

Never gives me a straight answer.

Pitched my book as a romance, and I write mysteries.

Total spaghetti agent. Threw my manuscript at every editor to see what might stick.

Evasive about submissions.

The list went on and on. So many complaints from so many writers, and they didn't sound like authors who needed excessive handholding. They sounded like normal, sane people who'd been misused and mishandled by those who were supposed to be their sherpas.

I was the villainess leading the pack. Writers claimed they'd never query me, and it looked as if everyone was trying their damnedest to cancel me.

However, a quick peek at my slush inbox proved otherwise. My queries had quadrupled since the article was published. After skimming a few letters, I saw why. Writers thought if they took my side, I might be interested in repping them. The desperation was alarming but also heartbreaking.

Furthermore, when I checked my inbox, I heard from three editors I'd never worked with before who wanted to schedule lunch dates. One wrote, "I hope you're not worried about that article. Just writers throwing fits."

How bizarre that the article seemed to be helping me instead of hurting me. I was reminded of a conversation I had at a party with a tipsy publishing executive. It was my first year as an agent, and he said to me, "In our business, editors and writers are punished for their failures, but agents are like cockroaches. Nothing kills them."

At the time, I thought he was a clueless boor. Besides, I was going to be the world's best agent. I was an idealist. But now I realized maybe he had a point. I felt like the world's worst agent and yet, no one in publishing was calling me on it.

Chapter Twenty-One

It took two days, but I finally got the nerve to text Dani: *Can we talk? I owe you an apology. I made mistakes.*

It took a couple days to get a reply.

Hey Claire. This is Bryan, Dani's husband. She's trying to eliminate all stress in her pregnancy and doesn't feel like chatting. If she changes her mind, she'll let you know. Thanks in advance for giving her space.

Dani wouldn't change her mind, I thought sadly. The friendship was over, and I knew it. It was upsetting enough to lose Philip's respect, but now Dani's as well?

At least I still had my career, which seemed bullet-proof. One of my favorite movies was *The Devil Wears Prada*. There's a scene when Nigel, an important player in the fashion world, says to Andie, an assistant, "Let me know when your whole life goes up in smoke. Means it's time for a promotion."

That seemed to be the price of being a wildly successful career woman working in an incredibly competitive field in the world's most exciting city. The book life was a demanding mistress but a thrilling one as well. I kept reminding myself of that. Yet, somehow, it was getting harder to believe my own fables.

The outrage over the *Mox* article finally died down, and, after a week, it was as if it had never been published. I was working even harder than usual while I tried to decide what my next big project would be.

My inbox was stuffed with possibilities, and yet I was indecisive about which one to pursue. That wasn't surprising. Now that I'd reached the height of my career, all eyes were on me, waiting to see what my next deal would be.

Also, there was still no sign of my number one status on Publishers Marketplace. Maybe they didn't want to honor someone like me. Not that I cared so much anymore.

A white-faced Rebecca came into my office. "Are you sitting down?"

"Yes." I pointed to the chair I was very obviously perched on. "What's wrong?"

Rebecca walked around in a circle like a puppy trying to find a spot to settle on the rug. "I'm just so freaked out. I couldn't believe when I heard the news."

"What news?"

"Prepare yourself. It was such a shock that... I don't know how to say this." Her hands fluttered around her face. Something had to be horribly wrong. Rebecca was not one to soft-soap. I shut my laptop and looked up at her, bracing for horrible news.

"Morris is dead."

"Dead? What? When?"

Rebecca rubbed her tattooed arms as if she were cold. "That's the creepy part. He died at the beginning of August in his sleep. In summer, he kept his apartment as cold as an icebox so none of his neighbors noticed the smell until a couple of days ago when the compressor failed."

I took several deep breaths before speaking. "How is that possible?"

"Morris worked for himself, so there were no coworkers to wonder why he hadn't showed up at the office. Apparently, a few clients had emailed and called, but he was often unresponsive for weeks, especially during the slow summer months, so none of them were alarmed."

"How do you know all this stuff?"

"I'm friends with his ex-assistant, and somehow, she got the scoop. Apparently, Morris had no friends, and his only family is an estranged son who lives in Seattle."

"I can't believe it." I felt I might faint.

Rebecca grasped at her Peter Pan collar. "Supposedly, this sort of thing happens all the time in Japan. Men dying and no one knowing for weeks, sometimes months. There are actually biohazard companies that specialize in dealing with the remains, which can be—"

"Stop!"

"You're right. Too grizzly. Poor Morris. He was a jerk, but no one deserves that. Are you okay? You're turning gray before my very eyes."

I was definitely not okay. I'd never liked Morris, but I'd admired his success. Certainly, I coveted his number one spot in debut dealmakers, and now.... What a terrible way to go. *Alone.* With not a soul noticing or caring.

Kippy stuck her head in my door. "I'm glad you're here. I just got off the phone with Gloria, and it turns out her daughter Sheri, who used to be a runway model, has written a novel about her experiences. Guess who she wants as her rep?"

Gloria was a beloved children's author and Newberry award winner.

"Me?" I said weakly. The news about Morris was still making its impact on my body, crawling up my spine and curdling my stomach.

"Exactly," Kippy said. "Gloria wanted to know if I'd put in a good word and naturally, I said I would. Sounds like the perfect project for you."

Beautiful author, nepo baby, glamorous premise based on real-life experience. I'd barely have to pitch it. The novel would sell itself.

"Sounds amazing," I said.

"It does, doesn't it?" Kippy said. "So why aren't you smiling?"

Suddenly, it all hit me at once: the estrangement from Philip, the loss of Dani as a friend, the *Mox* article, Morris's death. All I wanted to do was put my head down on my desk.

"Claire?" Kippy said with concern.

I opened my mouth. I needed to say, "I'm thrilled," but the words wouldn't form on my tongue. I looked at Kippy and back at Rebecca.

"I'm sorry. I can't do it."

Kippy frowned. "I don't understand."

"I can't do this anymore." This time my tone was emphatic. I meant it.

"Do what?"

"This." My gaze swept the room. "This job."

Kippy frowned. "Is this because of that silly article?"

The so-called silly article was part of it, but there was so much more. The disillusionment started on Gull Island, when I saw myself through non-publishing people's eyes. I kept ignoring it, but like an aching, infected appendix, it finally burst.

"Morris died," Rebecca said. "And she's in shock because his death was grizzly. Obviously, Claire doesn't mean to quit. Who quits when they're at the top of their career?"

"I do," I said. "It's so much more than Morris's death, and it's not that his death was grizzly, it's that, despite his success, no one cared enough to check on him. When you lead the book life, you die alone."

"Claire," Kippy said. "You're being dramatic."

I shook my head. "Consider this my resignation. In fact, I have to leave this office. I can't stay here one more second. Don't worry. I'll tie up all my loose ends, but right now I have to get out of here."

I fled the agency, sneaking glances behind me to see if anyone was following. I rounded the corner and leaned against the cinder block of the building, absorbing the news about Morris.

His death was far too close for comfort. Maybe I wouldn't decompose in a New York apartment, but I could easily end up so wrapped up in my career that my life would be seriously unbalanced.

Wasn't I already on that road? I'd lost the only true friend I had, and a guy I'd grown to really like. The only people in my life were co-workers. My clients certainly wouldn't mourn me.

Except for Bea. And yet you were embarrassed to have her as a client.

The *Mox* article had me pegged. I didn't care about my clients or the readers or the editors or anyone. All I cared about was being the number one dealmaker in debuts.

And here was the irony. The only reason I was going to achieve that meaningless honor was because Morris was dead.

The sun was high in the sky, emitting a mean exposing light. Like a bare bulb in an interrogation room.

"Claire? Is that you?"

A woman wearing bug-eyed sunglasses minced over in ridiculously high heels. I shot her a questioning look, and she whipped off her glasses to reveal eyelashes as long and thick as the legs of a wolf spider. Her long, gold-brown hair was tangled and ratty.

"It's me, Wendy. How dope is this to run into you? Been a minute, hasn't it?"

"Yes," I said with a shaky voice. "It has."

"I was in the neighborhood. Never expected to see you."

Wendy was an awful actress. It was obvious she'd been hanging around the office, hoping to run into me. Fine. It would give me an opportunity to make amends. Ever since our last conversation, I'd felt bad.

"Hi, Wendy," I said, trying to maintain my composure. "How are you?"

"Doing great. Aces, in fact. I'm just..." Tears sluiced down her cheeks. With all the mascara she was wearing, her face resembled a mud slide.

I fumbled in my purse for tissues I knew I didn't have. I offered her a torn napkin. "I'm sorry, Wendy. I upset you terribly."

She waved away the napkin. "You? Upset me? Just because you fired me? Just because you used me?"

I nodded, feeling past the point of defending myself.

"Remember when you used to be my biggest fan girl? 'Wendy, you're so funny. Wendy you're so sharp.' You were emailing me and calling me all the time and then, when the book came out, it all stopped."

"You're right. I didn't handle myself well."

"So, I wrote another book. And you didn't want to read it, and when you finally did, you hated it, and you didn't even give me any feedback. When I told you how I felt, you copped an attitude: 'How dare you upset the mighty and powerful agent? You're not allowed to complain. You're supposed to bow down to the Pitch Queen.'"

I felt my chest tighten, remembering the conversation.

"And then you put me on the side of the road like I was a worn-out ottoman. I wasn't of any use to you anymore. And why would you need me? I read the *Culture* article. And it turns out you have a shiny new client. Too bad your precious Justin doesn't know that one day you're going to toss him aside as well."

"You're right. I made mistakes with you, and I'm truly sorry."

Wendy got very still; her eyes darted as if she was being bombarded by a dozen thoughts. "You can make it up to me, you know?"

"How so?"

"Take me back."

"What?"

"You heard me."

"You'd want me to represent you after all this?"

"Why not? You're good at what you do. And besides, I have a great new idea. It's about a psychologist who sleeps with her clients. We can call it *Moodie Call.*"

I held up my hand. "I'm sorry, Wendy, but I'm not an agent anymore."

"What do you mean?"

"A few minutes ago, I quit."

Wendy looked momentarily confused as if she couldn't process my news. "You're lying," she said.

"I'm not. I swear."

"How are you going to make it up to me?" Her voice was pouty and a little girlish.

"Well, I could give you my opinion. Maybe look at what you have so far."

Wendy's cheeks flamed with color. "Who cares what you think? You're not a literary agent anymore."

"No, but I—"

"Which means you can't do anything for me." She wrinkled her nose in disgust. "Can't believe I'm even talking to you. You're a nobody."

I smoothed my pencil skirt. "I deserve that."

"I see you, Claire. I've always seen you. You're this bookish nerd who decided to be a literary agent so people would pay attention to you. And like all sad little wannabes, you got power mad. But now all that's gone. So, what are you going to do now?"

The sun above seemed to get even brighter. "I don't know."

"You're still Peter Wyld's daughter. There's that at least."

There was a tickle in my throat. "I should get going."

"Yeah. Get out of my sight."

"And again, I'm sorry."

"Cry me a river, Claire-less. You're not the cool one. I'm the cool one." She attempted to give me a shove but lost her footing. That made her cry again, and she stumbled away.

I should have been angry, but I wasn't. Even though Wendy was crazier than a rabid raccoon, I deserved her rancor.

When I first started out as a literary agent, I was in awe of authors. Like Kippy said, they seemed like magical creatures, and I wanted to be an advocate for them. But, over the years, so many writers had sublimated themselves to me that I acquired a skewed view of my role.

But now that I was no longer an agent, I was exactly how Wendy described me: a nobody. I had no power and thus, no longer mattered to her or any other writer. I also didn't matter to the publishing world. Which meant the power I used to have, as formidable as it once seemed, was just an illusion.

It had never really belonged to me at all. I'd only tried it on for a while.

Chapter Twenty-Two

New York overwhelmed my senses. Were the lumpy garbage bags always piled so high? Had they always stitched the summer air with such a powerful stench? Were sirens always so piercing and frequent?

When I returned to my studio apartment in West Chelsea, I saw my place with fresh eyes. Even in the middle of the day, it was gloomy. There were no overhead lights, and my only window overlooked a brick wall and a fire escape. My collection of lamps didn't offer much light, but they did reveal the disregard I had for my living conditions.

No pictures on the wall, no plants (how would they survive?) and lots of dusty, dark wood. The furniture I owned was strictly utilitarian. A double bed with no headboard, two mismatched chairs, and a desk that doubled as a dining table.

And why didn't I do anything to make it more pleasant? Because I always imagined my real life took place in the office, during lunch meetings or evening book parties. But now, everything about work life seemed fake: my so-called agent persona that could be washed away by a heavy rain, my pitches, and all the lies I'd told clients.

I was in my awful apartment for only five minutes when I decided I couldn't stay there. Grabbing a few clothes and possessions, I stuffed them into a bag, planning to check into the nearby Hotel Chelsea.

Once I arrived, I sat on the bed and took in my new environs. There was a purple sofa and animal print chairs. On the walls hung photos from the hotel's heyday.

I knew the Hotel Chelsea had a history with famous musicians, but an information booklet inside my room said it also hosted writers like Mark Twain, Arthur C. Clarke, Allen Ginsberg, Patti Smith, and Dylan Thomas, who stayed in the hotel before he died.

Hopefully not in this room, I thought. Talk about poetic justice.

All the same, the hotel was preferable to my apartment. If I died during the night, at least I wouldn't breathe my last breath in a dark, cheerless box, and the hotel maid would find me before I turned into jerky.

For the next few days, I was a zombie. I didn't "rage, rage against the dying light." Instead, I slept a lot, ordered Chinese from DoorDash, and slept some more. I also finally read Dani's novel, and just as everyone said, the middle was a mess. For hours afterward, I was lying in bed, rigid with regret.

I turned off my phone and stared at the television, barely comprehending what I was watching. When the maids came, I stayed in the bed, saying I didn't need anything but come back tomorrow just in case.

My dreams were surreal. Mark Twain made an appearance. He blew cigar smoke into my face saying, "An uneasy conscious is a hair in the mouth."

Patti Smith haunted me, looking like a wraith with her long, yarn-like white hair, saying, "Agents like you are the enemy of artistic kids like me."

Dylan Thomas tossed back whiskies and said in his Welsh accent, "I drink because of people like you."

Allen Ginsberg howled all night long.

On the fourth day, I woke up at four in the morning and couldn't find the remote. There didn't seem to be any way to use the TV without it.

My stomach growled, but it was too early for DoorDash. I pawed through my bag, looking for a protein bar. I didn't find a bar, but I found the Strand bag that contained Bea's novel.

Great. Maybe hearing Bea's voice in my head would be a comfort, and I'd fall back asleep. Better than Ginsberg's howl or Patti's sneering indictments.

I opened the novel to the first page and started reading, hoping to get drowsy. But by the time I'd read the first two pages, I found myself being pulled into a story almost against my will.

Gradually, while I plunged deeper and deeper into the world of Bea's characters, everything fell away: my empty stomach, Morris's death, and the ruins of my career. All I cared about was turning the pages.

Bea wasn't Instagram savvy, and her novel didn't have a white-hot concept or gimmicks or a littering of oh-so-clever phrases. Instead, it offered characters I cared deeply about, an immersive storytelling experience, and a sense of hopefulness that somehow life's difficulties could be overcome.

Four hours later, when I finally finished, I relished in the afterglow of a tale well-told, feeling so much better than when I started. It was as if the characters were still in the room, whispering into my ear, tugging me into their lives. How could I have forgotten the natural high a great book could give me?

I'd been reading so many debut manuscripts, I'd forgotten what it was like to be in the hands of an expert storyteller. Bea had cast a spell on me, making me temporarily forget my troubles, and for that, I was extremely grateful.

I picked up the book and paged through it again, feeling like a kid who scrapes his spoon over an empty ice cream bowl, hoping for a final taste. What I got was the acknowledgements.

"My late literary agent, Glenda, was what Emerson calls 'a beautiful enemy,' giving me medicine I initially resisted but desperately needed to swallow. Every writer should be lucky enough to have a Glenda in her life, a person who cares about writers but also makes us look at the soft spots and flaws that we would rather patch over or ignore.

She may be gone from this world, but her influence isn't. She didn't just give advice; she also empowered me to be my own beautiful enemy, and that is the most precious gift I have ever received."

I found myself tearing up. Bea always said my mom had a huge influence on her career, but to read her own words about it made an emotional impact.

"I wish I'd known you better, Mom."

Just one more thing for me to be ashamed of. Never once had I considered modeling my career after my mom's. Instead, Kippy inspired me. Why? Because I could see the way she bedazzled my father and even Meredith. But perhaps my mom had more to teach me than I might have imagined.

Suddenly, it felt selfish and childish to sit in a hotel room licking my self-inflicted injuries. It was time to go back to Gull Island and give my mom a proper memorial. And once and for all, I needed to write a eulogy that would do her life justice.

I turned on my phone to call Bea and was confronted with a couple of messages from colleagues, congratulating me on becoming the number one dealmaker in debuts. Finally, finally Publishers Marketplace posted it for all to see.

I'd wanted this for years, but now it felt like an empty, pointless honor. How many people had I run roughshod over to get it? I had no desire to visit the site and see it for myself. Instead, I called Bea and said, "I just read the most wonderful book."

"Hooray! I've been sniffing around for something new to read. What's the title and author?"

"Unfortunately, you've already read it." I got out of bed, stretching my stiff muscles. "It's your latest novel, and it was sensational. In fact, while I was reading it, I forgot that my life sucks. Who needs Prozac when you can read a Queen Bea novel instead? And that's not literary agent hype. That's the real me talking."

"Whoa, doggie. We need to put that comment on the cover of the book. But back to your so-called sucky life. Are you talking about the *Mox* article?"

"You read it?"

She laughed her hearty laugh. "*Mox* has the juiciest literary gossip so, you bet your bottom dollar I did."

"Do you hate me?" I glanced in the mirror. There was a tangle of Spanish moss on my head passing for hair, and pillow marks creased my pale face.

"Lordy. What a question. Of course not. You're family to me which means I want to snatch that reporter's hair until she's baldheaded."

"I just worried you might not want to be associated with someone whose nickname is Claire-less."

"Claire, hon', that article didn't tell me anything I didn't already know."

"So why don't you hate me?" I swiped my teeth with my tongue; a sour taste filled my mouth. "Everybody else does."

"Number one, that's not true, and number two, although I don't always approve, I understand why you do the things you do. Can't be easy living in the shadow of your father. You needed to find your own way to shine. And in that regard, you scored a home run."

"Not anymore," I said quietly.

"What happened?"

I related the events of the last few days, including my breakup with Philip. In typical Bea fashion, she seemed unconcerned that she didn't have an agent anymore. Instead, she wanted to know the dish on Philip.

"How dare you date someone on the island and not tell me?"

"It wasn't dating. Philip was helping me find a spot to scatter my mother's ashes, and we forged a friendship that was on the cusp of turning into something more."

"What's the full name of this Southern charmer who's turned your head?"

"Philip Habersham." I dabbed at the sleep matter in the corners of my eyes.

"'Scuse me? Are you talking about *the* Philip Habersham? Former CEO of Habersham Media Corp?"

"Media corp? I'd hardly call a quarterly magazine on rare books a media corp."

"Is he a young widow?"

"Yes but—"

"That's him! Resigned from his position after his brother and wife died, but before that, he was known as a media whiz kid. Brought the family's company back from the brink of bankruptcy at the age of twenty-three. Likely book dealing was just his hobby."

I picked up the Chinese cartons from last night and tossed them in the trash. "That can't be the same Philip. This Philip was living in a loft in his bookshop. Sleeping on a cot."

"Probably escaping his memories. There were rumors he turned into a recluse after the accident. But he doesn't need to sleep in a loft. He has a mansion on Gaston."

Was that the house Justin was looking after?

"And a palatial beach house not too far from Glenda's cottage. The gate is likely visible from the backyard."

"I saw that! It's the one with trespassing signs all over it."

"He also spearheaded Gull Island's re-invention as a book town. He also bought all the public art. You are perfect for each other."

The news was disorienting. I had to completely reframe my idea of Phlilip.

"As I said, it's over. Philip flew all the way to New York to break up with me."

"Awww. Sounds like you could use a hug. Wish I was there."

"That's the other reason I called." I picked up bits of stray clothing from the floor. "I need to get out of the city, so I'm coming back to Gull Island."

"Hallelujah. Can't wait to see ya. I'll warm up the blender for some mojitos. But I have bad news. I won't be able to pick you up from the airport."

I laughed, thinking she was joking, but she said, "Yesterday, I fell down my back steps and fractured my arm."

"Are you okay?" I dropped the pair of sweatpants I'd been holding.

"Except for a broken wing, I'm fine. But I can't use the computer. Or drive."

"Then I absolutely must come to Gull Island. Why didn't you call me earlier? I'm glad to help you."

"Busy girl like yourself, I didn't want to put you out. Right now, the book club members are pitching in."

I glanced at my mussed hotel bed with its twisted sheets. "Not busy anymore and I'm always at your disposal. I'll catch the first plane out in the morning."

***

After getting off the phone with Bea, I googled Philip and discovered she was right about him. He'd rescued the family's media company, which included twenty city magazines, ten newspapers, and a collection of specialty magazines, covering archery, fly fishing, horses, and yes, rare books.

Apparently, after Philip's grandfather died, his father mismanaged the company, causing heavy losses, and once he passed away, Philip's older brother John took over and continued the downward trend. When Philip finally manned the helm, he vowed to restore the company "so as to honor my grandfather's memory and vision."

Everyone doubted he could do it. Philp was incredibly young, had no experience in business, except for a joint degree in accounting and statistics, but he bucked expectations. There were scores of articles about his business savvy.

After he resigned, *The Savannah Morning News* interviewed him, and he said, "The death of my wife Elizabeth and brother John put my own career pursuits in perspective. I focused more on clicks than a quality product, and I can no longer support a flashy business model that only benefits stockholders."

Lord have mercy, as Bea would say.

So that's what Philip meant when he said we were alike. Both of us were youthful movers and shakers without much thought about the value of our daily career moves.

After the tragedy, Philip obviously saw the emptiness of his career. Was it any wonder that he didn't want to be involved with someone who was still entrenched and bedazzled with money and power at the expense of others? Someone who might never wake up?

I had a powerful urge to call him, but feared it was too late, and besides, I still felt undeserving of his friendship. He was so much farther along this road than I was.

Instead of calling Philip, I spent the rest of the afternoon telling clients I was no longer representing them, and they'd have to find a new literary agent.

Kippy only repped prominent literary authors, and she wouldn't be interested in any of my clients. Bea, with her sales record, could have her pick of most any agent she wanted, but the rest of my list might struggle.

Only a few of my clients earned back their bloated advances, and that was usually because of their preorder sales. It would be easiest for me to send a mass email to all my authors, apprising them of the situation. That's what the old me would do. But the new me decided to call each one of my clients, except Dani, who likely wouldn't talk to me.

I started with my most agreeable client, Alison. In the acknowledgements of her debut novel, the first paragraph read like a love letter to me, calling me the world's best fairy godmother.

She was the ideal client, never complaining or nagging me when I got behind in correspondences. Every time we spoke or emailed, she always made a point of saying, "Thank you for all you do. I'm so grateful to have you as an agent."

Now I'd have to deliver bad news to dear, sweet Alison. I sat at the desk in my hotel room and called her. The phone rang and rang. That was unusual. Typically, Alison picked up after one ring—almost as if she always kept her phone in her hand.

Finally, she answered, "Claire? Is everything okay?"

"I'm afraid I have bad news." I launched into my farewell speech, and a couple of sentences in, Alison interrupted me.

"Um, Claire. I haven't been your client for at least three months."

"What do you mean?"

"In June, I sent you an email about it."

"I must have overlooked it, or maybe it went to spam. But what happened? Are you quitting writing?"

"No. I just... I felt you'd lost interest in me."

"Oh."

"You've had my latest novel for a year. That seemed like a long time." A child babbled in the background.

"A year? Really? I had no idea I'd been sitting on it so long. I'm so sorry. You should have nudged me."

"I thought about it. But I was ashamed because my first novel didn't do well. I felt like I didn't deserve a second chance with you."

There was a time when I wouldn't have discouraged that line of thinking, but no more. "Alison. You absolutely deserve a second chance. Listen, do you want me to give you a few names of agents I respect? I could make some introductions."

"That's so generous of you, Claire, but not necessary. I have a new agent. Nora Young."

"Nora? Congrats. I hear she's one of the best in the business. I'm sure she'll find a great house for you."

"She already has. Simon and Schuster bought my second novel in a pre-empt."

"I don't remember reading about that."

"Nora doesn't post her deals on Publishers Marketplace. She says it can damage an author for everyone to know how much money they got for a book. If it's a huge amount and the novel fails, when people think of that writer, they think of how badly she bombed. And it's hard for anyone to recover from that stigma."

Like Wendy and Dani and too many others.

I sighed. "Smart lady." And clearly a much better agent than me.

"Nora really cares about her clients. Not that you didn't, of course."

Same old Alison. Generous and sweet no matter what.

"It's okay, Alison. I know I'm not like Nora. Not even close, and I'm sorry about that. On the other hand, I'm glad my neglect worked in your favor. Congratulations on your success. You're a class act, and you deserve every bit of it."

"Thank you, Claire. And best of luck whatever direction life takes you."

Where would life take me? At this point, I had absolutely no clue.

The child was babbling even louder, and Alison said, "Shush, Mia."

Mia. Suddenly, I remembered Alison telling me she had an autistic child. It was just after her book sold at auction.

"I'll be able to make a living as a writer," she'd said tearfully. "And stay home with my Mia."

Many of my colleagues warned their clients not to quit their day jobs, citing how difficult it was to make a living as a writer. And it was almost impossible unless you were a regular bestseller.

How could you forge a career if a publisher dropped you after one or two failed books? And if you were a fast writer, non-compete clauses made it challenging to sell more than one novel a year.

Since the average advance for novels were $15,000 to $30,000 gross, most writers' earnings were well below the poverty level. Editors and agents could make a living from books, but writers rarely did.

"I'll let you attend to Mia," I said to Alison. "And I'm so glad Nora sold your book for you. Can't wait to read it when it comes out."

The last client I contacted was Justin. It was a difficult conversation because I had to confess to him that his book's success would be subsisting on hype fumes alone. Word of mouth might be nil. The manuscript needed work.

"But won't my editor help make it better?" Justin asked.

"Unlikely. However, if you're willing, I'll help with revisions. You have several months before the final manuscript is due."

Justin was quiet for a few seconds. He finally said, "You compared my book to *Galaxy*."

I squeezed my eyes shut at the memory. "I was wrong to do that, and I'll always regret it. My father's book is beyond comparison."

Another long silence. "Gotta tell you. It's tempting to just take the money and run."

"I hear that."

"But in honor of my dad, who loved the written word almost as much as he loved me, I'll do a rewrite."

"Wise move. I'll send you a revision letter asap."

When I finished contacting clients, I had one last thorny task for the day. I wrote a letter to *Mox* owning up to the article's accusations. I also wrote this:

I'd like to apologize to a dear friend who agreed to be my client and trusted me with ten years of her creative work. I'll always regret that I didn't do everything possible to ensure it was given the best chance with readers.

I cried when I wrote the letter, finally understanding how wrong my actions had been. As an agent, I'd served no one. Not the editors who overpaid for my books. Not the clients who exchanged their futures as creators for a big payout. Not the readers who bought half-baked books based on hype.

For years, I'd been on a treadmill of chasing, catching, and abandoning writers, and it had all added up to nothing.

Chapter Twenty-Three

When I left Hotel Chelsea for the airport, I imagined Patti Smith and the other writers, hanging from the wrought iron balconies of the iconic Queen Anne building, celebrating my departure by tossing cigarette butts and flipping birds.

A few hours later, I arrived in Savannah and took an Uber to Rest Ashore, Bea's cottage. When I went inside, I discovered my friend was truly helpless and would be for at least six weeks. The book club ladies had stocked her freezer with casseroles, and they were bustling around Bea's cottage like ants on a sugar cookie.

I wasn't particularly domestic, but there was one thing I could help Bea with: entering her novel-in-progress into the computer. When I volunteered for the job, she seemed extremely grateful.

The next morning, I grabbed two coffees and some pastries from Plain Jane Java and showed up at Bea's door at eight a.m. for a day of writing.

"A bear claw," Bea said, gratefully. "Just the thing to scratch my itch for sweetness."

We went into her sunny office, which had floor-to-ceiling windows and an ocean view. Sailboats negotiated waves in the distance, and white clouds scooted across the horizon.

Little Gull Island looked tantalizingly close; I could make out the tops of wax myrtle trees and a fringe of sea oats. Naturally, Philip came to mind.

"So, this is where the magic happens," I said in awe. I felt like I'd entered a sacred space.

"A little magic, a profusion of procrastination, and a whole lot of Cheez-It munching," Bea said. She handed me her laptop. "If you can type notes for me, that'll be a big help."

I opened the laptop. The screen saver was a photo of Bea and an elderly woman wearing pearls and a polka-dot dress.

"Who's that?" I asked.

"Zelda," Bea said with a smile. "I met her at a signing for my first beach book, and she wanted a picture with me. A year ago, her daughter, Barbara, wrote me. Zelda had gotten so frail she'd moved into her daughter's home. One night, Zelda was up later than usual because she was reading my latest book in bed. 'I always read a Queen Bea book in one sitting,' Zelda told her daughter. The next morning, Barbara checked on her mom and found that she'd died in her sleep."

"Oh my," I said.

"Barbara said her mom had a peaceful smile on her face, and my novel was beside her. Zelda's bookmark was on the last page."

I whistled softly.

"Barbara sent me a copy of the photo of the two of us, and it's been my screensaver ever since. A poignant reminder of why I sit in this room for hours alone each day."

I felt a thickness in my throat for sweet Zelda.

"Time for work." Bea clapped her hands as if to dispel the sentimentality in the room. "You'll have it easy today because I'm in the 'what if' phase of writing, which is the beginning of my process."

"What if?"

"Meaning, I'm throwing out ideas. Like what if I write about a jaded literary agent who visits the beach, meets an antiquarian bookseller, and falls in love? But circumstances drive them apart."

"Not circumstances," I said. "Just the literary agent being short-sighted."

"But who has now seen the error of her ways," Bea said. "So how do I get them back together? Maybe a hurricane? It's the right time of year. They decide to ride out the storm and run into each other just before the surge. They commandeer a mattress, and as the waters rise higher, the differences between them seem petty. They share a kiss, assuming it'll be their last, but then—"

"The waters recede, and all is well? Too bad Philip is in London."

Bea chewed on the end of her pen. "Not to mention that the twist is too predictable, and I've already done a hurricane. And besides, it's a cheat. *Deus ex machina*, as we say in the trade. In other words, we can't have the weather getting them back together. It needs to come from them. They need to dig down deep and realize that they're better together than apart. Although one of them has to make the first move."

"Is this advice disguised as a novel plot point?"

Bea laughed. "Not at all. I'm just explaining how love stories work. But, come to think of it, maybe the main character shouldn't be a literary agent. Too inside baseball, as your mother might say. That's always a danger with novelists. They're tempted to write about their own working lives, wrongly assuming readers will find it interesting."

"Maybe you should ask Zelda," I said in a teasing voice.

"Grand idea. What do you think, old girl? Are literary agents interesting to you?" Bea cupped her ear, as if listening. "Zelda says no. Make her an interior designer. That's a job readers can relate to. Type this: 'My main character is Sadie, and she's an interior designer who specializes in high-end beach houses, but ironically is too busy to ever get to the beach herself. Her outer world is gorgeous, but internally, it's a different story.'"

I spent the next hour immersed in Bea's imagination, recording whatever she said. The words flowed out of Bea almost effortlessly, and even though I was a decent typist, I had trouble keeping up.

Her eyes were closed, as if she were having a waking dream that was almost seamless. At some point, she said, "And then Sadie... And then..." Her eyes opened and she said, "I have no flipping idea what Sadie does next."

"Writer's block?" I said gently.

Bea grasped her throat and nodded.

"Is there anything I can do?" I'd heard of writer's block and how debilitating it could be, but I'd never witnessed an episode in real life.

"I have some mental laxatives in my bathroom medicine cabinet," she said in a hoarse voice. "For emergencies like this. Will you fetch them?"

I stood. "Of course. Right away. What does the bottle look like?"

Bea threw back her head and let out one of her appealing, full-throated laughs.

"What?"

"I'm pulling your leg."

"How was I supposed to know that?"

"Mental laxatives?"

"Why not? It seems like they have a drug for everything these days."

"Not that I know of. Whenever I get stuck, I just take a walk on the beach, watch some crabs scuttle around, and the answer comes. Works like a charm."

"Sounds easy enough."

"It is. And it doesn't just work for writing. Solitary walks can help you iron out most any problem. Like figuring out what you should do for the rest of your life, which I suspect will be long and lovely."

"Fingers crossed."

Philip had also talked about the importance of solitude, but the idea of being alone with myself and my flaws wasn't appealing. Unless I was sleeping or vegging in front of the TV.

"Anyway, I'm ready to knock off. Let's sit on the porch and have a glass of pinot grigio."

I prepared happy hour refreshments for us on Bea's porch. We sat in a pair of rattan chairs surrounded by a collection of impatiens planted in galvanized metal pots. The scent of tea olives tinged the air—far more pleasant than the stench of piled up garbage—and I was even warming up to the wind chimes.

"I've gotten so attached to porches," I said. "In New York, I didn't have any outdoor space."

Bea sipped from her sweating wine glass. "Your mom loved her porch. When it wasn't too hot, she'd even work outside."

"That reminds me. A while ago, you mentioned a letter my mom wrote to you."

"Yes! I found it and put it aside for you. It's in the top drawer of my office. Why don't you get it?"

I retrieved the letter and brought it out to the porch. "You laminated it?"

"You betcha. I consulted it so many times over the years, I feared it was gonna get raggedy. Anyway, she wrote me this letter because I needed a wake-up call."

"What happened?"

Bea waved a paper funeral fan in front of her flushed face. "You know I used to write mysteries before I switched to beach books."

"Yes. Under a pen name."

"The first mystery was a smash hit, and I thought I was the new Agatha Christie. Expectations were high as corn in July for my next novel. But you can probably guess what happened."

"Sophomore slump," I said knowingly.

"Exactly. My second novel tanked, and I blamed everyone for it. Cover designer, publicity, marketing, and your mother. The only person I didn't blame was me. When your first novel is a hit, everyone tells you how brilliant and talented you are, so how could it be my fault?"

Sounded familiar. How many times had I given an author exaggerated praise? It was a common habit among publishing people, treating writers as if they couldn't function without a steady diet of gold stars.

"I kept writing mysteries, and each one did a little worse than the last, and my advances got punier and punier. The only reason my publisher kept me on was because that first novel continued to sell well, which attracted readers to the rest of the novels in the series. I was always complaining to your mom, and she kept saying, 'Time to leave your comfort zone. You're blindly playing the same slot machine, hoping for another jackpot, and it's not working,' but I ignored her. Finally, circumstances forced my hand. My publisher dropped me. That's when your mom sent me a wake-up letter. Why don't you read it aloud?"

"I'd love to," I said.

Dear Bea,

You asked me how you could improve your career trajectory, and I'm going to give you advice, but it's likely not the advice you expected. In fact, after this letter, you may not want to work with me at all. But I'll take that chance.

You've been given a gift for words, and there are expectations for that gift, none of which have anything to do with your own enrichment. A gift has only one purpose; to be passed on to others. It's an act of generosity, and it is in that spirit that you need to write your next book.

Don't know what to write next? Let curiosity instead of panic guide you. Be attentive to the spark of inspiration. Expect it. It's going to lead you in a direction that may puzzle you. Bewilderment is a good sign. Don't be afraid of it or try to chase it away with hackneyed ideas. Follow the sparks where they lead. Trust that they know more than you do.

If you've faithfully followed the sparks and let them lead instead of your ego, you will have eventually written a book that matters, although you might not know what precisely it's saying until the very end. Enjoy the mysterious unfolding, the act of discovery. Let go of your need to have all the answers at once.

When you're finally done, other people might say, "This is not what we expected from you." Which is ridiculous. What do they know about you and your sparks? Not one darn thing.

Get your book out, knowing that once you release it, it's no longer your business. Trying to control the uncontrollable erodes your power. Do what you can control. Write another book. And another one. Just keep following those sparks. Curiously, the less you care about your personal glory, the more you tend to get it.

Love, Glenda

Bea smiled after I finished. "And that's how I ended up writing beach books. Instead of worrying about outcomes, I followed the sparks. Not that it was easy. Without a dead body hanging over the narrative, I was floundering. I must have gone through ten rewrites, but finally, it was ready. Your mother sent out the novel, and because of my past sales, most editors put it on the back burner. She kept nudging them, never once giving up. It took a while, but eventually, the novel found a home for a modest advance. When it came out, sales were slow but after a few months, it made the list."

"A true word-of-mouth bestseller. So very rare."

Bea raised her glass of wine. "That's the power of storytelling. Publishing is a tough business. It doesn't nurture talent, and it's frequently short-sighted. Every year it seems to get a little more broken. It's easy to forget whom I'm doing this for."

"The reader," I said, picturing Zelda's sweet, wrinkled face.

"An obvious lesson but one that took me an armadillo's age to learn. Yet, once I quit focusing on myself and made it my goal to serve and honor the reader, my writing career completely changed."

Our discussion reminded me of what Philip said to me before he broke up with me: "At some point in an author's evolution, writing becomes an act of generosity."

I hadn't experienced that attitude in my clients because they were all newbies. It was obviously the mark of more mature writers.

"How did my mom get so wise?" And how, as her daughter, had I been so dumb to miss her wisdom until now?

Bea shrugged. "Maybe she was born that way. In storytelling, there's an archetypal character called the traveling angel. They come into the story, and their whole purpose is to coax greatness out of others. Mary Poppins is a traveling angel as is John Keating in *Dead Poet's Society*. I think your mother was also one."

I looked down at the letter in my hand. "I wonder if she's written others like this?"

"I'd imagine so. Why would it just be me? But you'd have to ask her clients."

Excitement stirred in my belly. "I will. If there are more letters, I'd love to read them."

"So would I. I've never met anyone who understood writers the way Glenda did."

I nodded, wishing I knew how to draw out the magic in writers. Maybe my career would have gone in a completely different direction.

Chapter Twenty-Four

After helping Bea during the day, at night, I read Justin's manuscript and made extensive notes on how to improve his episodic narrative. Since Bea was so gifted at storytelling, I asked her advice on several plot points.

I also emailed my mom's clients, asking them if she'd ever written them a letter with advice. Most answered in the affirmative, and the letters started trickling in.

Each one of my mom's missives was a gem. Over the years, she'd addressed all types of writerly woes like rejection, writers' block, frustration, hopelessness, and more.

A week later, I had about twelve letters. Some of her clients remembered getting letters from her but couldn't find them on their computers. That frustrated me. I hated that some of my mother's words could be lost forever.

Bea had asked me to forward the letters to her on her computer, but I decided instead to compile them into a bound booklet she could keep. One afternoon, after we'd finished working, I gave it to her.

"This is wonderful." As Bea turned the pages, her eyes got misty. "Thank you. I can't wait to read through them all."

"I just wish there were more. Some have been lost."

"Have you gone through your mom's computer yet? Glenda was so organized. My guess is she kept a file of any letters."

"I haven't done a deep dive. She has so many documents."

"Try looking under 'empowerment.' I can't tell you how many times she said to me, 'A writer who strengthens her personal power is much better able to weather the ups and downs of publishing.'"

That night, I took Bea's advice. After searching my mom's computer, I found a file called "Dearest Writer."

There were dozens of letters to an unknown writer, filled with advice. I spent the next couple of hours reading them and nodding along. Once I finished, I was glowing from within, and wished every writer in the world could read the letters.

***

When I wasn't helping Bea, I went through my slush pile, sending writers a notice that I'd left the business and wishing them luck. Sometimes I'd stop to read a few and, for the most part, the letters couldn't conceal the writer's desperation.

Pick me. Please. I'll do anything.

I was tempted to write back, quoting from one of my mom's letters: *Pick yourself first. When you know your own worth, others can't help but recognize it. Instead of being the beggar at the table, you'll sit at the head.*

It was a shame that these writers didn't have someone like my mother in their lives. Someone to remind them of their own worth and power as a creator. That night, I woke up at three a.m. with an idea that should have been obvious to me as soon as I'd found the file of letters.

There are more than enough letters for a book. I can share my mom's wisdom with the world.

But, as a former literary agent my second thought was, *is it salable?* I'd never repped non-fiction before so I had no idea. Mulling it over, one side of me said, "It's brilliant." But my literary agent side wanted to send out a terse rejection letter.

In the morning, I asked Bea what she thought, and she hooted.

"Is that a hoot of delight or ridicule?" I asked nervously.

"Delight, silly girl. And I'd be happy to write the foreword."

Bea's contribution would help with the pitch. No doubt about it. Could this really happen? *Of course it can*, I thought. *Just put on your Pitch Queen hat. Finally, it'll be good for something worthwhile.*

Chapter Twenty-Five

My days on Gull Island took on a distinct shape. I spent mornings with Bea, working on her next book.

When she didn't need me, I worked on my mom's letters, curating, editing, and rearranging. Sometime during the process, it occurred to me I'd finally found the perfect tribute to my mother. So much more meaningful than selecting the ideal place for her ashes or writing a moving eulogy.

Now and then, after reading one of her letters, I'd burst into tears. *Nothing wrong with that*, as Philip would have said. I was finally, truly grieving, a process I'd resisted for far too long.

Six weeks after Bea's fall, her cast came off, and she no longer needed my help. A few days later, she sent me the foreword she'd promised. I cried when I read it. It was such a moving tribute to my mom as an agent but also as a dear friend.

A week later, my mom's book was done. I was excited but also a little sad. It had been satisfying to put the letters together in book form, constantly hearing her voice in my head, and I'd miss working on it.

But my job was far from over. Now the letters needed to be published. Which meant I had to look for my own literary agent.

Yikes.

Chapter Twenty-Six

After sending out my first letter to an agent, I expected a wait but, I got a response in an hour. My heart leaped in anticipation—very often, agents pounced on intriguing projects—but it wasn't a letter expressing interest. It was my first rejection.

"Good to hear from you, Claire, but this is a pass for me. An epistolary writing advice book from an unknown person? Too touchy feely and not very practical. Sorry."

I found myself bristling at her response. I wanted to say, "It's not meant to work for you! It's for writers. And there are millions of practical books for them, but this is the stuff they really need to hear from an amazing woman who knew what she was doing."

Was karma cackling with glee? If so, I deserved the lashes of her whip, but the writers who would benefit from my mother's advice didn't. That's who I needed to think of during this process of submission, which was likely going to be humbling.

A week into my hunt for literary representation, another agent I knew finally called me, and I assumed my search was over. After some pleasantries, she said, "You know what would really make this project shine? If your father were to write a foreword along with Queen Bea."

As if I, former Pitch Queen, didn't know that.

"This project is about my mother and her gift to writers. Not about Peter Wyld."

"Then it's a pass for me," she said. "But should anything change—"

"Not happening," I said.

More and more rejections trickled in. I was tired of getting turned down. If rejection was a meal at a restaurant, not only would I send it back, I'd write a one-star Yelp review. But my mother had addressed rejection in her letters, and this piece of advice resonated:

Action is the best antidote to rejection. If you wallow and lament, you're giving rejection more power than it deserves. When you persist in your goals, rejection becomes like a pothole or a construction slowdown. Annoying, yes, but certainly not a reason to abandon the journey.

Excellent advice. Since the project didn't seem to be resonating with agents, what was my next course of action? I had no idea.

One morning after the Thanksgiving holidays, I was walking along the shore, going against the wind. A metaphor for my current situation. Still, I continued to trudge along, deep in thought until I'd gone at least a mile.

As soon as I turned around to head back, a fogginess in my brain lifted. It was obvious what I needed to do: self-publish. In fact, self-publishing should have been my first choice, but I couldn't immediately see that. I was a former literary agent; traditional publishing was all I knew.

But, if I self-published, I could set the price, making it as accessible to as many writers as possible, and that was the goal.

Chapter Twenty-Seven

During the month of December, I hustled, getting ready for my projected release date, January ninth, which was also my mom's birthday.

A week before my pub day, Rebecca called me. "Are you calling your book your baby yet?" she teased. We used to roll our eyes at authors who did that. To us, books weren't babies, they were units.

"Not just baby," I said. "But precious doll baby."

"Oh no! She's crossed over to the enemy camp."

I'd hoped to have my book launch at Irene's Bookstore, but she'd finally retired, and the store was up for sale. Sadly, a souvenir shop was slated to take its place.

Lacking a bookstore, I decided to launch the book and host a celebration of life party at my mom's cottage with Bea and the book club.

I provided copies for everyone at the party. The book club members shared memories of Glenda, and many of her former clients tuned into the ceremony via Zoom, sharing their own memories. Tissues emerged from purses, and fat tears slid down weathered cheeks.

I still didn't know what to do with my mother's ashes, so I stored them on a bookshelf in a swirly blown-glass vase I'd found on Etsy. Maybe one day I'd find the perfect place for them, or maybe they'd just stay there indefinitely. Now that I'd given my mom a proper send-off with *Dearest Writer*, the question of where her ashes should be scattered didn't seem as important anymore.

That night, I finally gathered the courage to go up to the attic and go through my mom's purse. I'd been eyeing it for months, but every time I thought, *not yet*. A woman's purse was so personal, and I didn't know how I'd feel about sorting through her things, knowing she'd never touch them again.

Inside was her wallet, ChapStick, tissues, lipstick, a lint-covered Hershey's Kiss, and a book. I knew my mom never went anywhere without a book. Even while she was struggling to breathe, she didn't forget to tuck one into her bag just before she left for the emergency room.

The novel my mother had been reading was *Where the Crawdads Sing* by Delia Owens and a crocheted bookmark held her place at the beginning of the last chapter.

As usual, my mom had underlined passages she liked. This one caught my eye: "Lots of times, love doesn't work out. Yet even when it fails, it connects you to others and, in the end, that is all you have, the connections."

It almost seemed like a special message from her to me. I fingered her bookmark.

My mom's never going to finish the book. She will never know how it ended.

It was real. My mother was gone, and the world was a lesser place because of it. I cried so hard and ugly that if Philip had been there, I would have needed more than one of his lovely handkerchiefs.

Chapter Twenty-Eight

Two days after the release of *Dearest Writer*, I got a call from my father and right away, I knew something was wrong. Meredith always made the calls.

"There's been an unfortunate occurrence." He sounded like he was in the bottom of a well. "We got back home from Mallorca two days ago." He cleared his throat. "And last night, Meredith had a stroke."

"Is she okay?"

"She has some weakness on her left side. But she's not herself anymore."

"How so?"

"Perhaps you'd like to come by and see for yourself?"

"I'm in Georgia," I said. "But I'll get the first plane out."

I caught a morning flight into Newark and was at my dad's house in Short Hills, New Jersey by noon. It'd been over a year since I'd been to my childhood home.

It was a classic English manor on a pristine two-acre lot with geometrically sculpted boxwood hedges and an Olympic pool. The grounds and house were so sprawling that only aerial photos could properly capture them.

To my surprise, my dad answered the door. He was wearing his old NYU sweatshirt, which I knew Meredith hated. Also, his wispy gray hair was uncombed, and he was unshaven, two more unacceptable crimes in Meredith's eyes.

I gave my dad a hug; he smelled like grilled cheese sandwiches. In fact, the whole house smelled like that.

"Where's Calypso?" I asked. Calypso was head housekeeper, and she was the person who usually answered the door.

"I gave her time off. Come on in. Meredith is in the kitchen, and we just finished our lunch. Would you like a grilled cheese sandwich?"

"The chef made that for your lunch?" Didn't seem probable, but maybe grilled cheese, like artisanal toast, was having a moment.

"I made the grilled cheese," my dad said proudly.

"What?" My father was helpless in the kitchen. He could start a fire making a peanut butter sandwich. "And Meredith ate this grilled cheese?"

"I told you she wasn't herself."

I followed my father into the kitchen. My dad or Meredith rarely used it even though it was spacious and airy with white marble counters, yards of gleaming brass, and Southern exposure.

Meredith was sitting at the breakfast nook in front of a bay window which overlooked the gardens.

She looked almost as unkempt as my father. Her signature backed combed mane now hung lankly around her face. She wore a striped top and plaid pants, almost as if she was trying to clash. And someone, my father maybe, had filled out her eyebrows with a pencil, but they were a squiggly mess.

Thank God, I'd arrived. My father clearly had no idea how to care for Meredith.

Meredith didn't notice me coming in because she was hunched over a piece of paper. As I got closer, I saw a charcoal pencil in her hand.

She glanced up at me and gave me an unexpected beatific smile. "Claire! I'm so happy to see you. Look at this." She held up an incredibly accomplished portrait of my father.

"Did you do this?"

"Yes. Do you like it?"

"Very much."

"Thank you. I worked hard on it." She looked me up and down. "You're so pretty, Claire. I like your necklace."

It was a cheap rope necklace I'd bought at one of the beach stores, and normally, Meredith didn't approve of costume jewelry, but clearly nothing was normal anymore.

"Claire and I are retiring to the library for a bit," my dad said. "You have your kazoo if you need me."

"I do." Meredith blew into the kazoo, as if to test it.

"We won't be long."

Meredith had gone back to her drawing and didn't appear to be listening.

I followed my father to the wood-paneled library. A couple of shelves displayed foreign editions of *Galaxy*, along with his writing awards.

"So, now you see," he said.

I did. The woman in the other room was nothing like the Meredith I knew. "Is her condition permanent?"

Wrong question to ask because my dad had read reams of material and shared a barrage of stroke statistics with me. It seemed to comfort him to have done so much research.

But at the end of his soliloquy, he said, "The more I read, the less I know. However, I did come across an article in *The New York Times* that sometimes a stroke can make a person compulsive about making art. It softens emotional roadblocks."

"I'd never heard of such a thing."

"Since the stroke, all Meredith wants to do is draw. It's been a challenge for me. She used to take care of most everything."

"I had no idea she could draw so well."

"She's always been a bit of a doodler. Especially when she's on the phone."

I nodded, remembering her doodles. Lots of geometric designs. "But the sketch I saw was on another level."

"She's obsessed, but I can't complain. She took such good care of me all these years, it's only fair that I return the favor. Also, I've never seen her happier."

"Me either," I said.

"That's why it's time to change our lives. I want to sell the house and buy another, much smaller one that doesn't require a staff. I've already phoned a realtor."

"All by yourself?" It was so out of character of my dad to handle even the simplest tasks.

"Google Assistant has become my biggest friend. I went to ShopRite for the first time in years, and I bought some cherries, but couldn't get the produce bag to open. So, I asked Google Assistant, and she said I needed to dampen my finger. Worked like a charm!" He looked delighted, as if he'd discovered a solution to global warming.

"I'm glad you're learning new things, Dad."

"I enjoy grocery shopping. It's relaxing to glide about the store with your cart, listening to piped-in, less jarring versions of the Beatles or the Rolling Stones. I bought whatever fancied me, including several different kinds of popsicles. Would you care for one?"

"Maybe later," I said.

"I have Push-ups, Nutty Buddies, and fudgesicles. Such an abundance of riches."

It wasn't just the popsicles that made my father seem so relaxed. He reminded me of Kevin from *Home Alone,* finally able to exercise some agency over his life. He could wear what he wanted, eat the foods he preferred, and most of all, stay in one place for a while. Meredith had been relentless in her determination to see every nook and cranny of the globe.

***

I stayed a week with my dad. Part of the time, I was teaching him some basic life skills, like how to pay bills online and how to operate basic appliances.

Most of the time was spent in his study reading together. I was flying through Bea's novels. Dad was reading books on New Jersey, reflecting on his new reality of staying put. As was his habit, he'd share tidbits.

"The first drive-in movie theater opened in Camden, New Jersey in 1933," he said one afternoon. "The idea came about because the inventor's mother was rotund and couldn't fit into indoor movie theater seats."

During my stay, I learned more about New Jersey than I cared to, but it was lovely spending time with my father without Meredith constantly inserting herself.

My stepmother couldn't have been sweeter to me, something I'd craved from her all my life. Oddly, I found myself slightly nostalgic for the old Meredith who would have asked me why Kippy had fired me and had I ever considered dental hygienist school because I'd meet some nice men that way. "You can tell a lot about men by their teeth," she'd likely say.

I had always resented those kinds of comments, but now they seemed like a clumsy form of love. At least, she'd paid attention to me.

The new Meredith had little interest in my life. She was too absorbed in her drawings.

But, one afternoon, she handed me a piece of paper, saying, "This is for you."

To my suprise, it was a drawing of me, and it was beyond flattering. I looked incandescent; every feature lovingly rendered with exquisitive detail.

"It's astonishing," I said, not being able to keep my eyes off it.

"Glad you like it."

There wasn't a drop of fakery in that drawing. It was as if there was a direct connection between the pencil and Meredith's heart. As it turned out, she had been paying attention to me, just in a different way than before.

The portrait continued to draw me in. I wish I could see myself that way, I thought.

An hour before I was due to go back to Georgia, Meredith was taking a nap, and my father and I were sitting in the kitchen, drinking strawberry milkshakes that he'd made himself. He'd forgotten to put the lid on the blender and made a horrendous mess, which I cleaned up.

My dad was remarking on how much he missed milkshakes and why only children seemed to drink them anymore. Suddenly, he abruptly changed subjects and said, "I need to ask you a personal question."

"Okay," I said. That was a first.

"Should I write another book?" he said. "Meredith was always against it, but she doesn't care anymore. I received an advance version of the commemorative edition of *Galaxy*, and she barely glanced at it."

I paused before speaking, imagining millions of readers, thousands of booksellers, and everyone at his publishing house shouting, "Yes, yes write another book!"

But I played it cool and said, "Is that what you want?"

He sighed, "So much easier to read books than to write them. Yet it has crossed my mind. Meredith is so happily engaged in her art that it reminded me of how much I used to enjoy writing. Although, I don't know that I could write anything that would measure up to *Galaxy*. Not without your mother's guidance."

I nodded, not wanting to say the wrong thing for fear he'd drop this serious discussion and return to the banal.

My dad slurped the remains of his milkshake, which left a pink moustache on his upper lip. "I cried when I heard Glenda died."

"You did?"

News to me. He'd sent me a generic $2.99 sympathy card when my mom died, one Meredith had obviously selected and prompted him to sign.

"Meredith didn't speak to me for days. Glenda was Meredith's Achilles' heel. She couldn't contain her jealousy. Even when Glenda was gone." My dad glanced toward the open door as if worried his wife might be eavesdropping. "And I never told Meredith this, but I think she suspected it. I was sick with love for Glenda. Not that she returned my feelings."

"Not at all?"

"Glenda also doubted my love for her. Claimed it was transference. She said, 'You think I'm the muse, but I'm not. It's inside of you.' She told me I was getting too dependent on her, and it wouldn't be healthy to see me after the book was done."

My father took off his glasses and wiped the lenses on his t-shirt. "Your conception was happenstance. After I finished the book, and we drank champagne, we were both so giddy, we found ourselves in bed. I thought it was the beginning of something, but it was the end. She quit working for Kippy, and I didn't hear from her again until shortly before your birth. By that time, I'd already married Meredith. A bit on the rebound I fear."

I nodded, familiar with that part of the story except the rebound part. My mom was only nineteen, and her family were extremely strict Baptists and not at all supportive. That's why she allowed my dad full custody.

"I was smitten with her, but Glenda wrote me a letter explaining herself. Said it was nothing personal. She simply preferred women over men."

My father shared the news so matter-of-factly, if I'd sneezed, I could have missed it.

"Glenda also told me she didn't want anyone to know her preferences," my dad continued. "Again, her family would shun her."

It took me a minute to gather my thoughts and speak. "Mom was gay?"

My dad nodded.

"Did you tell Meredith?"

"I'd never do that, but she found out anyway. Meredith was snooping and came across Glenda's letter in my things, which was unfortunate because she used it against your mother. She told Glenda that if there was ever any hint of a relationship with a woman, she'd not allow any visitation with you whatsoever."

"And you approved of this?"

My dad shook his head. "You know Meredith. You can try to fight her, but you'll never win."

That explained why Meredith was always worried about my disinterest in dating guys. Clearly, she was concerned I'd inherited my mother's sexual preferences. My brain practically blew a fuse as I reframed the idea of my mother with this new information.

"That's why Mom never had any relationships," I said softly. I'd always assumed the demands of the book life kept her from ever marrying.

"On the contrary, I strongly suspect she had a lover in Georgia. She moved there right after her mother died."

And then, suddenly, it hit me.

Bea.

Who also never had any relationships. Who was closer to my mom than anyone? I assumed that Bea, like my mom, was wedded to her work, but had I been wrong?

"Thanks for telling me, Dad."

"Honestly, I wasn't sure if Glenda confided in you or not. I hope you're not upset."

Why hadn't she told me? Or why hadn't Bea?

But I should have guessed. Bea's boisterous personality would contrast beautifully with my mom's bookish reserve. My mom once said, "If there's anyone who can make me howl with laughter, it's Bea." And it was also clear that my mother's quiet wisdom had bedazzled Bea.

"Back to my original question," my dad said, skimming over the family secret he'd casually lobbed in my lap. "I want your professional opinion. Should I write another book?"

I'd almost forgotten about his earlier inquiry. My dad was full of surprises today.

"You're the only one who can answer that question," I said.

"Sounds like something Glenda would say."

I smiled. "Best compliment you could ever give me."

I would have loved to have stayed longer, but I had a plane to catch. I ordered an Uber, and once it was a few blocks away, I gave my father a copy of my mom's book, simply saying, "Lots of good writing advice in there."

He studied the cover, and his eyes widened. "Glenda?"

I nodded.

My dad hugged it to his chest. "So glad she left a part of herself behind. I'm sure I'll be inspired."

On the way to the airport, I thought about Meredith's art locked away, which included the most valuable piece in her collection—my father's legacy. But perhaps now that Meredith was obsessed with her own art, it was time for him to risk it.

Meanwhile, my own future legacy was a complete unknown.

Chapter Twenty-Nine

I returned to Gull Island and as expected, Bea picked me up at the airport. It was mid-January, so the top of her convertible was up, and she greeted me wearing a coat with a fur hood and snowflake patterned mittens.

I chatted about my visit with my dad and Meredith, and as soon as we crossed the now familiar bridge and entered the city limits, I took a minute to bask in being back at the beach.

Even in the gray of winter, Gull Island seemed like summer with its soaring palmetto trees, sunny skies, and colorful cottages.

I'd been waiting for the right time to ask Bea about my mom, but suddenly the question leaped out of my mouth. "Why didn't you tell me about your relationship with my mom?"

Bea's mittens tightened around the steering wheel. "Lord have mercy. How did you find out?"

"My father told me my mom was gay, and I put two and two together. Why didn't I hear it from you?"

"I was looking for the right opportunity to tell you, and it never seemed to pop up. I also had to grapple with my own grief. It's been a bear. She'd always planned for both of us to tell you when you visited Gull Island."

I turned up the heat on my side of the car. "Do all the book club ladies know?"

"No. Your mother didn't want to come out to just anyone. Not with that Baptist upbringing of hers. So, she bought the loneliest cottage on the island so we could be together without people gossiping." Bea stole a sideways look at me. "You mad? Disgusted? Outraged?"

"Of course not!" In fact, if she wasn't driving, I'd have thrown my arms around her. "I'm thrilled she had you. I thought it was the island that made her happy but, all along, it was you."

"That's a relief. It's been preying on me ever since she passed."

"You're one of the best people I know, and my mom was lucky to have you in her life. And you've solved a problem for me."

She lifted her white-framed sunglasses. "What's that, hon'?"

"You were the one she was closest to. Her ashes belong with you."

"What? No. You're her daughter. Doesn't seem right."

"It's perfect. There was a reason I've yet to scatter them, and now I know why."

Bea didn't speak; she was staring straight ahead and blinking away tears. Quickly, I dug out a travel package of Kleenex from my purse and handed her one. Philip would have been proud. Thanks to him, I was now always prepared for tears, mine or anyone else's.

***

A week after returning to Gull Island, I had become as big a reader as Philip. My mother had hundreds of books on her shelves, and I was tearing through them, savoring the passages she'd underlined. Reading became a full-time job for me, but without pay.

I'd done well as a literary agent and had a cushion of money, but it wouldn't last the rest of my life. I hadn't earned a penny since September, and here it was late January. At some point, I'd have to figure out a different career plan.

In addition to reading, I made it a habit to bundle up and take a long, solitary beach walk daily. At first, I hated it. My regrets about the last several years of my life were loud and condemning. But Philip had been right. The more I allowed the unpleasant thoughts, the less power they had over me.

One Wednesday afternoon in early February, the temperature rose to the mid-sixties, and I decided to participate in Bring a Book to the Beach Day. I almost got sunburned because the book I brought was so engaging.

When I finished, the back cover revealed an endorsement from Bea. The author, Laura Bright, had three other books, and I spent the next couple of days devouring them as well. The last one saw publication in 2016, and there were no more after that. What happened to the author?

I googled her on my phone; she still had a website, but it hadn't been updated in a while. During our next happy hour on Bea's porch, I asked her if she knew what happened to Laura.

Bea frowned. "I saw her a few months ago at a book festival, and we had coffee. Her last book didn't perform to expectations, so her option wasn't renewed. She hasn't written any more books because she lost heart."

"But she's so good."

Bea topped off my glass with peach sangria she'd made in celebration of the warmer temps. "I agree. That's why I endorsed her book, but publishers aren't patient with authors who can't move units. You know that better than anyone."

"There are ways to get around poor sales." I thumped Laura's book, which I held in my hand. "This author can write circles around the debut authors I used to sign."

"Well, publishers love the new and shiny," Bea said. "But, in truth, it's the authors who have been around a while that end up selling the most books. Jodi Picoult, for instance, had ten books under her belt before she broke out with *My Sister's Keeper*. Imagine if her editor or agent had given up on her?"

"I wasn't aware of that."

"And what about Dan Brown? His first three books sold less than ten thousand copies. Most people would say his chances of getting published again were slim, but he had an editor who advocated for *The Da Vinci Code*. Those are two stories just off the top of my head, but I'm sure there are many, many more."

I felt that familiar twinge of inspiration in my midsection. "I wonder how many writers are out there who have lost heart like Laura? Who were maybe one, two, or three books from a huge hit? Who deserve a true advocate? One who is willing to play the long game?"

Bea smiled. "Is this going where I think it's going?"

A yellow butterfly alighted on a pot of purple pansies, and I took that as a sign. "It's perfect. Instead of discovering debut authors, I can coax seasoned authors to reinvent themselves. Beginning with Laura."

"I imagine she'll be thrilled to hear from you," Bea said.

"Thank you. I just hope I can make it work."

***

The next morning, I emailed Laura Bright and arranged for a phone call. I told her about my new business plan. To my delight she said, "I finished a novel almost a year ago."

"Wonderful. Can I read it?"

"Of course. But, fair warning, my latest agent dumped me, so I had to query again. It's been sent to fifty agents. Thirty never replied, and a few of those were referrals."

"Ignored you? With your experience? Not even a courtesy rejection?"

"It's rough out there. Ten rejected it after reading the query letter. Five rejected it after reading the first ten pages, and five have had the full manuscript for months. I'm worried there's something wrong with it."

"Nonsense. I've read all your novels, and you're the real deal. If there's something wrong, it can be fixed."

"Okay. I'd love to see it find a home."

Laura sent the novel to me, and I immediately started reading. The first twenty-five pages didn't suck me in but, after that, the story was wonderfully involving like all her other novels.

The next day I called and said, "I read it, and I'm offering representation. Lop off the first two chapters because they're mostly throat clearing. Start with a more engaging scene, and you're done."

"That's all?"

"Yes, ma'am. Take as long as you like, but if you accept my offer, I'll start planting the seeds for a sale right away."

Laura started crying. I used to cringe away from authors' tears, but not this time. These were good tears.

"I honestly thought my writing life was over with," Laura said. "Everyone kept acting like it was."

I'd just read an amazing book from an accomplished author who knew her craft, and it was a travesty that, for one second, she'd imagined she no longer had anything to offer.

"No one decides your career is over except for you," I said trying to keep my pique under control. "The people who tell you otherwise don't know what they're talking about." I was parroting my mother's words in one of her letters.

After we hung up, I started thinking about my pitch for Laura's novel. Her concept was intriguing, and I'd certainly talk it up, but I would also be focusing a lot on Laura herself and my connection to the material. The warmth and humor that shined through all her novels. The places in the novel that moved me.

Should an editor mention previous lackluster sales, I'd say, "Did you know Jojo Moyes wrote eight novels before breaking out with *Me Before You?* Or that no one would touch George Martin for ten years after one of his books flopped until a forward-thinking editor gave him another chance. Those are just a couple examples among many. Laura Bright's poised to breakout. Wouldn't you like to be the publisher who was responsible for that?"

My pitches were going to be quite different than they used to be. Now I'd emphasize the expertise and background of the author, and I'd need to do thorough reads to tease out the emotional and thematic strengths of a novel.

I recalled the *Life of Pi*, about a boy and a Bengal tiger marooned on a lifeboat. No possibility of a simplistic pitch like *Tiger King* meets *Huck Finn*. Yet someone came up with a winner: "*Life of Pi* will make you believe in God."

It was far more intriguing than the usual mash-up. And there was something to be said for teasing out the true originality of a book instead of making it seem derivative.

A week later, Laura provided me with an engaging beginning to her novel, and I sent it out. Two weeks later, we had a deal. Was it a sexy seven-figure deal? Not even close. But I wouldn't be surprised if one day Laura would command that kind of money.

After I brokered the deal and called Laura with the news, she said, "It's true. You really are the Pitch Queen."

"No. You're the true queen. And don't you ever forget that."

***

After Laura's deal was posted, I was sitting outside Plain Jane Java, having an afternoon pick-me-up when I got a call.

"Hi. This is Quince Washington. Do you remember me?"

I was tempted to laugh hysterically. "Of course I do. What's going on with your novel?" Since I'd had my moment of reckoning, I hadn't visited Publishers Marketplace even once.

"Nothing. Initially, I thought Morris was ignoring me. You hear about literary agents doing that to clients. But then he died, and I've been in a funk, not knowing what to do. Finally, I called Prestige, and Rebecca said you started your own agency."

"I have. It's called Dearest Writer." The name would always remind me of who I was working for.

"I don't suppose you'd be interested in repping me. Especially after I chose Morris over you."

I topped off my coffee with some fake creamer because real half-and-half was too much of a frill at Plain Jane Java. "Initially, it upset me, but I've gotten over it."

"Does that mean you'd consider it?" Her voice surged with hope.

"Fair warning. I've changed my business model since then. If you're interested in doing revisions, we could talk."

Quince had written what's known as a stylish thriller, which is code for a thriller that doesn't really thrill. The stylish part referred to the author's marketability and tendency to throw in some elevated prose.

"But back in August you said my book was ready to go as-is."

"And I stand by that. It's very salable. But not by me. I no longer rep books that will just excite editors; they must also be a satisfying reading experience. One that my book club would like."

"Seriously?" I could imagine her perfect Roman nose wrinkling.

"As serious as the National Book Awards ceremony." I took a bite of the bear claw which, thankfully, made up for the bad creamer.

"Not to be a snob, but I really don't care what book club people think."

"You should care. They're the ones who read the most books and, by the way, they're extremely discerning. Also, I no longer make deals that aren't in a writer's best interest."

"What do you mean?"

"Big, flashy deals often kill a career if the author doesn't earn back her advance."

She sighed. "Thanks, Claire, but I think I'll take my chances and go with another agent. One who will send it out right away."

"You'll have no problem finding one."

"Exactly. Goodbye, Claire."

I hung up feeling a little sad. I, better than most anyone, knew what Quince's literary future would hold. But I could only help authors who were willing to help themselves.

Chapter Thirty

I decided to stay on Gull Island. Why not? I could easily do my job remotely, and I'd grown to appreciate its leisurely pace. Sometimes, when I craved a little action, I made the drive to Savannah and strolled the squares or visited the Plant River district to eat fresh seafood and watch the colorful container ships glide toward ports unknown.

I cleared out my mom's attic room and put out her personal items like photos, vases, piggy banks, throw pillows, a mirror with a mosaic frame, and fairy lights. According to Bea, she'd strung lights everywhere. One day I might put my own stamp on the cottage, but for now, I found it a comfort being around her things.

One day, I was picking up around the cottage, and saw a woman with curly hair, freckles, and glasses. My heart hitched at the sight of this dear, beautiful person.

"Mom?" I said.

Was it possible that painting over the haint blue ceiling had worked?

It took me a moment to realize I was looking at my own reflection, and, for the first time in a very long while, I smiled, enjoying who I saw in the glass.

I talked to my dad regularly. He sold the big house in Short Hills, and now he and Meredith lived in a bungalow a few miles away from their old estate. He spent the days writing, and she continued to be preoccupied with her drawings. During one of our conversations, he said, "We've both never been happier." He asked me if I'd read his book when it was finished, and I said I'd be honored.

Occasionally, I'd peek behind the bamboo in my mother's yard to gaze at the gate that led to Philip's beach property, hoping perhaps to see Philip himself, but there was never any sign of activity.

One day, a "For Sale" sign appeared in front of the gate. Did that mean he was never going to come back to the beach?

In mid-March, I got a postcard in the mail announcing the grand opening of a new bookstore. Gull Island had been without a bookstore ever since Irene had retired.

The new bookstore was serving champagne and hummingbird cake, which was an insanely delicious Southern confection with cream cheese, pineapple, pecans, and bananas. They asked for an RSVP, and I texted the number on the postcard saying I'd attend.

Two days later, I arrived for the grand opening, but when I went inside, there was nobody there. Had I gotten the day or time wrong?

The new owners had created a cozy environment, scattering plenty of comfy leather chairs throughout, and the arrangement of the shelving created several inviting nooks.

An old-fashioned claw tub held a collection of discounted books. A sign said, "So cheap you won't mind getting them wet."

I smiled, thinking how much I loved tub reading. Steps leading to the children's area were painted to look like the spines of books with titles like *Peter Pan* and *Charlotte's Web*.

I glanced at a display of books with shelf talkers, all of which described the titles from an emotional perspective.

"A hopeful book if you're smarting from the loss of a love," or "if you're feeling disgusted with world events, this novel will make you believe in human goodness again." Also, there was an unusually large section devoted to bird watching.

If that wasn't enough of a giveaway, a small table boasted a big bowl chocolate-covered pecans.

"Philip," I called out. After a moment, the man himself stole out from behind a bookshelf. I was so tickled I could barely take a breath.

Finally, I managed to say, "Am I early? Where are all the people?"

"They're coming later. Your invitation had a different time than everyone else's."

Color flared in Philip's cheeks. I forgot how easily he blushed and how charming I found it. He was wearing a linen jacket, but this one looked new. His bowtie was patterned with pictures of books.

"Well, that's uh—"

"Presumptuous?"

"Not at all. Congratulations on this wonderful bookstore."

"Remember when I told you I needed a new calling?" Philip said. "There were rumors that a souvenir shop wanted to come into this store. Can you imagine that? Shark teeth and Day-Glo t-shirts supplanting books? In a beach town known for reading? I couldn't sit still for that. So, I immediately left London and closed on the store and its inventory."

"It makes me want to sit down and read. After buying a book, of course."

He smiled. "I tried to incorporate some elements I've seen in other bookstores. The tub idea comes from a store in Venice. Might be handy in a hurricane. And there's a cat, wandering around here somewhere. E. Shaver's in Savannah has several, but my allergies only allow for one." He sneezed.

I smiled. "Or maybe none."

"A little sneeze never hurt anyone." Philip gazed around his store with wonder, as if he couldn't believe it was his. "Books have given me so much insight and solace, I want to pass those gifts to others."

"The perfect vocation for you," I said, pointing at the display with the shelf talkers.

"Isn't it?" Philip adjusted a shelf talker that was slightly crooked. "I haven't been this excited since I don't know when. And you know, so many readers dream of being writers, so I have the perfect book to recommend."

He made his way over to the cash register, and I followed.

There was a huge display of copies of *Dearest Writer*. Big enough to build a lean-to shack. "I've been told you didn't do a book signing in a store, so this is a surprise book-signing."

"Wow," I said, feeling overwhelmed. I'd never seen so many of my mom's books in one place.

"I know how much you wanted to give your mother a proper send-off, and I can't imagine a more moving tribute than *Dearest Writer*." He nervously adjusted his bowtie. "Champagne?"

"Yes, please."

He filled flutes for both of us. After we clinked glasses. I said, "Where are you living here?"

"I've rented a beach cottage, two blocks away. I sold the places I shared with Elizabeth. They were just oversized shrines. Justin tells me you've decided to settle here?"

I nodded. "Suits my new way of living."

"He also told me how much you've helped him with his novel."

"*Your Place or Mine* is now a much better story. And the promotion materials won't include comparisons to *Galaxy*, but it's not needed. Justin's novel has its own unique strengths."

Philip touched my shoulder. "Thank you for shepherding him and teasing out his gifts."

"Justin deserves almost all the credit. He really pushed himself."

"But it helps immensely to have someone supportive in your creative life. Every time I talk to him, he says, 'Claire always has my back.'"

"He said that?"

I felt dizzy with gratitude. That simple statement from a client made me feel more validated than any seven-figure deal ever did.

Philip nodded. "And he meant it… I'm sorry I was so hard on you the last time I saw you."

"Don't apologize. It's what I needed to hear. Too bad I wasn't ready to listen."

"To be truthful, I never expected you to. By most anyone's definition, you were a major success story. Who would walk away from a high-powered life like yours?"

"You did. I heard about your media whiz kid days."

"Not my finest hour. If a section wasn't getting enough eyeballs, I killed it, and here's the deplorable crime I committed. The one I never wanted to tell you."

"What?" I said, wild with curiosity.

"I killed book coverage."

I gasped. "You didn't?"

"I told you I had an awful secret in my past. My brother was horrified; it was one of many rifts between us, but to me, numbers trumped everything. Later, when I came to love books for their content instead of their resale value, I deeply regretted my decision. But before the tragedy, the only voice I listened to was my own ambition."

I thought about how hard I used to drive myself, working until my exhausted body finally forced me to crawl under the covers for an entire day. How I was always too busy and jacked up to ever consider widening my lens to see the effects of my lifestyle.

"I know all about the voice of ambition," I said.

"But you quit listening. What happened?"

"A combination of things, but honestly, while I struggled to define my mom's legacy, it helped me clarify what I wanted mine to be. I'm still an agent, but a very different kind."

Philip pushed a strand of white hair behind his ear; it was almost shoulder-length now. "And you're happy with your new work?"

I nodded. "I started my career searching for a magical story like my dad's, and when I couldn't find it, I manufactured it with a killer pitch. Now my job is to draw out the magic from writers. It takes longer, it's not as lucrative, yet it's so much more meaningful."

Tears slipped down my cheeks. I reached for my tissues in my purse, but Philip was quicker with his handkerchief.

"Thank you. Also, I came to another realization.

"What's that?"

Did I dare say it?

"My new career, meaningful as it is, well..."

"Yes?"

"It isn't enough. I want to have someone in my life who understands where I've been and where I'm going."

"I'm listening."

I took a deep shaky breath. "And since you're going to be here on Gull Island, I was wondering if you and I could—"

"The answer is yes."

I laughed. "You're an easy sell considering you don't know what my question is."

"I don't need to. Because for any question you, Claire Wyld, might ask me, the answer is always yes."

I dipped my head, feeling uncharacteristically shy. "Would you like to pick up where we left off the last time I was here?"

Philip gave me a tender look. He opened his mouth to speak and then closed it. "I have no words…"

I took a step in his direction. "Honestly, do we need any?"

"No, we don't." He pulled me into an embrace and ran his fingers through my curls. "I've missed these."

Our first kisses had been unexpectedly passionate, but when he kissed me this time, it felt complex. It was like aged wine with any number of nuances, one you wanted to keep tasting to see what else you might discover. Licorice, cherry, maybe even notes of tobacco.

"Oopsy daze. Sorry to intrude."

It was Bea and the book club members, who were all wearing bright spring attire and following her like colorful ducklings.

I introduced a flaming-cheeked and hair-tousled Philip to the ladies, who were making approving noises about the store.

"But what's the name of this bookstore?" Vera said. "It didn't say on the invite. And there's no sign outside yet."

"When I sent out the invitations, I hadn't decided," Philip said. "Everything I thought of was too cutesy or beachy."

"And what's wrong with cutesy?" I said. I was getting used to all the kitschy names on Gull Island. Yesterday, I went to the plainly named Coastal Drugstore, and I thought, *you people aren't trying hard enough*.

"Certainly, I'm open to suggestions," Philip said.

"Pleasure Bound, The Scholar Ship, Wit and Wisdom," I said.

"Possibly, possibly," Philip said.

"The Happy Booker, A Novel Idea, Shelf Indulgence," I continued.

"I have a thought," Philip said.

"Let's hear it."

"On the Same Page."

It took me a second to reply. "It's beyond cheesy. But then again, I never turn down cheese."

"It's settled then," Philip said. "Now who would like some champagne?"

In Manhattan, when I attended book events, it would always feel as if there was a constant electric current running underneath my skin. I was so thrilled to be a part of the publishing scene, I could scarcely sit still. Here on Gull Island, I was still part of the publishing world, but quieter, more satisfying triumphs had replaced the thrills.

"Toast, toast," Bea led the chant, and everyone else joined in. Philip raised a glass and said, "To Claire and her mother's wonderful book, *Dearest Writer*."

I lifted my glass and said, "To On the Same Page and a new direction for Philip Habersham." I paused for a moment and said, "And to leading the best life which, for me, is and will always be, the book life."

I can't tell you how much I wanted to add, *Here's to the newest chapter.*

But, as much as I loved cheese, there was more than enough at this event. In addition to pimento cheese, there was brie, gouda, and one of my favorites, Humboldt Fog. So instead, I said to Philip, "Where is that hummingbird cake you promised?"

"I almost forgot." Philip disappeared into the backroom to get it.

As soon as he left, Bea sidled up to me. "Gotta say, I love me a happily-ever-after."

"And you do them so well."

"Wish I'd written this one."

I gave her a suspicious look. "Are you sure you didn't? I almost feel like you've been plotting this since our last lunch in the city."

Bea laughed, a robust sound I'd never tire of. "If that's true," she said. "I'll never tell."

"Imagine that you did plot this story, what would be the last line?"

Bea closed her eyes, as if preparing for a dramatic recitation: "So we beat on, boats against the current, borne back ceaselessly into the past."

I shook my head. "Perfect for *The Great Gatsby*, but not this tale."

"Putting me on the spot, are you?" Bea glanced upward, thinking for a few moments. "How about this? It was a long, complicated journey, but not only did Claire find herself, she realized she'd never been lost."

"Because...?"

"Because she had books in her life. And when you have books in your life, they eventually lead you back to yourself."

"An excellent last line," I said. "And so very true."

If you enjoyed *The Pitch Queen*, you will likely also enjoy *Love Literary Style*, about a snobbish literary writer who falls in love with a self-published romance novelist.

If you are a writer, consider joining my email list called "Pitch Your Novel" and receive a free 119-page book called *How to Structure and Pitch Your Novel*.

THANKS!

Thanks to Tiffany Yates Martin who has read three of my last manuscripts and one of them twice! There's no repaying you, but I'll be happy to spend years trying. Your advice is always wise, kind and invaluable.

Thanks to Pamela Kelley. Your generosity to me and other authors is astounding. When, out of the blue, you asked to read the manuscript, I felt so honored. But a day later, when you gave me your endorsement, I was over the moon. I've been watching your amazing career for a long while, and I'm so delighted we've connected.

On another note, thanks for telling me about Laura Horah or, as I like to call her "Eagle-Eye."

Laura, it was wonderful that you fit me into your schedule for the final spit-and-polish. It is so hard to find every error in a manuscript but I feel like you did. You're a treasure!

Thanks to the wonderful Ayden Rails for the first proofing round. You're always such a joy to work with.

Immense gratitude to critique group members Tracey Buchanan and Susan Reinhardt for early reads. How amazing to have such talented writers give me such helpful feedback.

Thanks so much to Katherine Caldwell, Annette Nauraine and Julia Bartgis for also reading early drafts and to WFWA for connecting us. What a supportive organization.

Thanks to my husband, David. You ar so patient with all the time I spend writing and "maven-ing" as you call it, and to my son, Brandon. You always have my back and are so encouraging.

Thanks to Harriet for always being so, so supportive. I can't tell you how much that means to me.

ABOUT THE AUTHOR

Karin Gillespie has an MFA in Creative Writing and lives in Savannah with her husband David, her son, Brandon and her dog, Rosie. She's been writing novels for over twenty years. She's also been a book columnist, humor columnist and non-fiction writer. She's written about the writer's life for the New York Times and pens a Substack about creativity called The Creative Genius in You.

AFTERWORD

I love satire and that's why I wrote this novel. Not because I have a poor opinion of literary agents.

I've had five literary agents and while that make seem excessive, my career spans over 20 years. Changing agents is rather common.

While I'm no longer with any of these agents, I'm grateful to each one them, and they were nothing like Claire. All added value to my writing journey in their own unique ways.

As Peter, one of my characters, says, "Agents do matter. Maybe not to the everyday person, but to the author, their literary agent is everything."

Made in United States
Orlando, FL
14 June 2024